TIMELESS

Dana Lyons

Black Lyon Publishing, LLC

TIMELESS
Copyright © 2017 by Dana Lyons

Our books may be ordered through your local
bookstore or by visiting the publisher:

BlackLyonPublishing.com

Black Lyon Publishing, LLC
PO Box 567
Baker City, OR 97814

This is a work of fiction. All of the characters, names,
events, organizations and conversations in this
novel are either the products of the author's vivid
imagination or are used in a fictitious way for the
purposes of this story.

ISBN-13: 978-1-934912-78-2
Library of Congress Control Number: 2017914795

Published and printed in
the United States of America.

Black Lyon Romantic Adventure

For
my
daughter

CHAPTER ONE

The Song of Spirit: Before there was the sun and the moon and the stars ~ there was love.

The Shaolin Academy of Arts, outside Bimthang, Nepal, Near the Chinese Border

"You must prepare for turbulence," Master Chan said.

James Royce McNeill looked at Master Chan, his spiritual and martial arts mentor, and saw far more in the deep brown eyes than the simple words indicated.

This is not a weather alert.

His heart thudded painfully through an adrenaline punch. A sweeping pitch, as though he were in free fall, invaded his equilibrium, making him feel off-kilter. He queried softly, "You have seen this?"

The only response was the slow descent of Chan's eyelids.

Royce licked his lips. He looked down at the tea setting used only on certain occasions, a clear indication his mentor had special words for him.

"For this defining event," Chan said. "You are her salvation, just as she is yours. You will both experience challenges created to refine your common soul. To accomplish this, Royce, you may have need ... to be in two places ... at once."

Royce's mind was crowded with questions, but he remained silent, giving Chan room to elaborate. Perhaps his warning would continue with words of enlightenment for the path he apparently had seen opening before Royce.

"Beware of darkening clouds," Chan said. "The winds of karma are coming across dimensions for this special event, coming for you and for Alex. Use your non-physical resources to save her ... and survive." He set his teacup down, watching.

Royce leaned forward, straining to hear every word and nuance as Chan continued.

"You will leave here ... and enter the dimension of no time," Chan went on. "There, your heart and mind are free to work in other realms."

The old man's usually placid eyes bore a light of excitement. Abruptly he reached out and grasped Royce's wrist.

"Salvation is a circle beginning with the past. Find Jamie McNeill. He is the key if she is going to save all." Chan released Royce and sat back, his message delivered. He picked up his teacup and sipped.

Royce felt his mouth fall open, yet he was speechless. He was overrun with questions, the first being: Who is Jamie McNeil?

Beyond the mystery of this and his many questions, his heart rang with fear. Instinctively his concern was for Alex. He resisted the urge to jump up and ... do what?

Call.

"The phones, are they working?" he asked, feeling

the urgency of the warning.

Chan's disappointment was a frown. He shook his head in the negative and shrugged. "Chinese wiring."

Of course, Royce thought, which meant there was no Internet, since the academy's excuse for Internet came over the same wires. He felt an expanding bubble of surreal frustration envelope him.

You can see the future and receive visions of alternate dimensions from here, but you can't make a freakin' phone call.

He scrubbed his face.

The satellite phone. Run. Call her now!

Chan was watching closely. With a stiff effort, Royce gained his composure. He exhaled deeply and recalled Chan's words. "Use my non-physical resources," he repeated with chagrin.

The frown on Chan's face dissolved into a quick bob of approval. "Yes," he encouraged.

Still, frustration squeaked its way through Royce's chest. Chan's message was disturbing enough to leave Royce acutely feeling the circling karmic wind that bore his name. Dread of the unknown tumbled across his neck as though a rat skipped across his bare shoulders.

"I leave in the morning," he announced, hoping his near departure would inspire Chan to share more. Seeing the bare bones of encouragement in Chan's face, Royce continued. "I'll fly straight to Kathmandu before catching a commercial flight tomorrow night back to California." Feeling the karmic wind press more insistently, he added, "Perhaps we can discuss this more before I leave?"

"Sleep well this night, my son," Chan responded. "In the morning, we will see you off on your journey."

This response left a gap of uncertainty Royce found troubling. But as Master Chan smiled with encouragement, Royce felt hope. He allowed a tentative smile to break free. Whatever challenges were poised ahead, he and his ever-resourceful wife would survive together.

Certainly Chan would say something if they didn't. Wouldn't he?

•

Royce went straight to his small room, desperate to reach Alex in spite of Chan's encouragement. With his mind awash in messages of warning about an alternate dimension, he saw the satellite phone and his eyes watered with joy. He grabbed the phone and turned it on with a small prayer.

Come on, come on, last night there was service.

The little orange light came on and the display screen flickered, tentatively delivering its message.

Acquiring Satellite ... Acquiring Satellite ... Acquiring.

Abruptly the phone beeped and the screen changed to *No Service.*

"No," he whispered softly. "No, not now."

Concern swamped his heart, making his chest feel crowded. He looked at the sat-phone with dismay. "Come on," he begged, but the device refused to help. "Turkey," he cursed as he plugged the device into the battery charger, giving the phone a threatening scowl. "There, you're plugged in, should you decide to be a little more cooperative later."

He left his room and descended to the dining room where he collected his tray and moved to a table by himself, feeling too distracted to converse. His mind was busy with Chan's words.

Turbulence; lives and dimensions brought together; being in two places at once; a dimension without time. Save Alex.

"But who's Jamie McNeil?" he asked the chaos in his thoughts. "What's his part in all this?" Feeling Chan's eyes on him, he glanced across the hall. Again his mentor's words echoed.

You must use your non-physical resources to survive.

Along with Royce's extensive financial wealth, he also possessed what he liked to call, "My 'other' toolbox."

Buddhist deep meditation, or Samadhi was but one tool. There was also Silva Mind Control for guiding the physical world; Monroe Institute techniques capable of eclipsing time and space; and Heart Math vibration methods for manifesting.

The timeless dimension where my heart and mind are free to save her.

Royce finished his meal and returned to his room immediately, his chaotic thoughts driving him. With no other course available at the moment, he settled in to meditate.

He lowered the wick on his lamp, dimming the wild shadows cast by the shrinking flame. He sat slowly, folding his long legs to sit cross-legged on a mat on the bare floor. Once his legs were adjusted into a full lotus position, he began the deep breathing process. After several minutes, he started the countdown taking him to a deeper level of consciousness.

Three, two, one.

A sea of energy surrounded his mind, attracted by his desire. His heart provided the vibration. Using this energy, he formed in his mind a blue picture frame. Inside this frame he inserted a simple question.

Who is Jamie McNeill?

Next to the first frame, he built another, this one in white, and left the contents blank.

Expectation for an answer made his stomach pitch with hope. He focused on his breathing as his mind rested in the calm space between his exhalation and the next inhalation. In the moment beyond the release of a breath, an image appeared in the white frame and seared into his mind like a flash of green lightning.

"How can that be?" he exclaimed.

•

In spite of his best efforts, Royce woke the next morning bleary eyed after a fitful night tossing and turning. He couldn't get the image in the white frame out of his thoughts. What he saw was as exciting and unsettling as Chan's warning.

Immediately he reached for the satellite phone.

"Please," he implored under his breath. The power came up and surprisingly, the screen immediately announced, *Service Available.*

He dialed quickly. What Chan said about being in two places at one time played hauntingly against the image from the white frame, constructing a vision, a possibility he was trying to wrap his head around.

"Absolutely impossible," he blurted.

Adrenaline made his heart run chaotic. As impossible as his vision was, it somehow suddenly seemed less so. He brought his attention back to the phone as the call went straight to messaging.

"Alex, go to Santa Barbara. In that huge desk from Europe is an old record book of the family history. Look in the book for a Jamie. Look for Jamie McNeill. I'm coming home, and I love you." Breathless, he powered down the phone and put it away, allowing himself a deep exhale of relief.

Alex is unstoppable.

"If anyone can find this Jamie, she will."

He packed and carried his bag of belongings, softly walking through the winding halls of the academy and out to the exterior gate. In the early morning mist of the high elevation sunrise, his Sherpa airplane, a bush plane specially designed for short takeoff and landings, sat waiting.

"There's my big girl," he said affectionately.

The airplane's massive engine and fat tires allowed him to take off in little more than a hundred feet, perfect for the wild terrain of the Himalayan Mountains.

After placing his bag in the cockpit, he slowly walked around the plane, doing his pre-flight inspection. As he finished, he gave one tire a solid nudge with his right boot, grateful for the dependability he could expect from modern technology. "All is in order with you, big girl. I wish I could say the same for myself," he offered in half-complaint as he reached down to remove the tire chock.

A movement of bright orange and red robes at the gate caught his eye. Royce's heart fired with stuttering hope at the sight of Chan. "Yes," he blurted under his breath, the single word thrumming with anxiety. "Please, you have to tell me more," he implored the gods. He walked to the gate, a fixed smile on his face.

Chan reached for Royce's hand. "You will remember all I have told you," he said.

"Yes, of course ... but there are many—"

"Questions, I know." He held on to Royce's hand and

forearm, as if to keep Royce secure for one last moment before the Karmic winds came calling. "Today, the last day of August, this is your birthday, am I correct?"

Royce nodded slowly. "Yes, today is my birthday."

Chan went silent, seeming to ruminate deeply upon this fact. "That would be appropriate," he stated at last. He gave a nod of confirmation, as if just learning a key answer. Royce waited for his mentor to share with him this understanding.

"What your heart desires, your mind can achieve," Chan said. "For success, you must stay strong. This journey you begin is your life's greatest challenge, but a challenge you are prepared to meet. Remember, the past, or the future for that matter, is merely another day in the present ... somewhere."

Royce felt his mouth sag open.

That's not exactly what I wanted to hear. Where are the answers?

He swallowed and gathered his thoughts. If he had only one question to ask Chan, it would be—

Chan spoke, seeming to know Royce's mind. "This journey will not be easy, and much depends on Alex. Protect her. Only she can call you to return."

Royce drew a chest full of cold air and fought for words. Feeling he wasted his time on questions, he stated, "There is nothing I won't do to keep her safe." Chan released his arm and Royce felt the opportunity to learn more fading with the mist. He backed up a step and bowed his head with respect. With nothing more to say, he returned to the Sherpa.

Once settled inside, he completed his engine run-up, magneto check and adjusted the flaps to takeoff position. He scanned the visual field and, seeing nothing to disturb his take off, said, "Nothing coming in, nothing going out … but me."

He glanced back to the gate where Chan stood waving. Before taking off into a cloudless sky, Royce clearly saw his mentor's lips form his parting words.

"Beware the darkening clouds!"

Royce extracted his oxygen mask and put it on, plugging in to the oxygen delivery system. From this altitude, and with a rate of climb at two thousand feet per minute, he would need the oxygen within seconds. He took one more glance at the sky and saw not a cloud in sight. Still, the warning "Beware the darkening clouds" gave his backside pause to pucker.

With nothing else to stop him, he throttled up, feeling the powerful 850 HP Honeywell engine vibrate with enough energy to literally toss him from the planet. Having about one hundred feet for his take off, he was thankful for every horse she had to give him.

He released the brake. A wave of air from the thirteen-foot propeller helped pull the rear wheel up, and in half a breath, he was in the air.

"Not a cloud in the sky," he said with confidence. "At one-hundred fifty-four miles per hour, Kathmandu is only thirty-five minutes flight time."

Hang on Alex, I'm coming.

The big bush plane steadily climbed to reach the twenty-four thousand feet necessary to cross Manislu peak, the highest obstacle between him and Kathmandu. "Cross Manislu," he said, "and it's downhill all the way."

Barely five minutes into the flight he could see the clear sky beyond Manislu opening up all the way to Kathmandu. He flew over the last of Manislu's great peaks and descended to eighteen thousand feet. "I'm on my way to Kathmandu," he sang.

His singing was cut off as the Sherpa shuddered violently and dropped, throwing Royce forward against his seat belt. "Damn," he cried, pushing the Sherpa's nose forward to gain air speed and level the wings. Feeling like his lungs were lodged in his throat, he was grateful for the oxygen. The Sherpa flew stable again and his controls all showed green.

"Whew, clear air turbulence," he muttered. The word 'turbulence' was out of his mouth before he realized what he said. "No! No turbulence," he blurted. "All is well. Still skies ahead and behind ..."

He glanced behind him to the right and left just to visually verify.

"Oh, holy shit," he choked out.

That little bump was not clear air turbulence.

Behind him, and moving his direction, was a dark wall of cloud. The menacing presence snaked its way down over the face of Manislu. Lightning streaked, tearing ugly gashes of green in the deep grey depths.

"Incoming," he growled. The fast moving mass seemed set to overtake him. "Come on, baby, get me out of here," he begged the Sherpa.

He slammed the throttle forward and the Sherpa bucked with thrust, jumping to its maximum one hundred eighty-eight miles per hour. Royce leaned forward, straining to keep an eye on the cloud while trying to outrun it.

Not gonna' make it, he thought.

As the dark mass closed in around him, all light from the rear was blotted out. Darkness filled the high visibility cockpit as though a giant specter moved in to swallow the plane. A sudden flash of light obliterated the darkness inside the plane followed closely by a boom that rocked the air with ear-splitting volume. Royce looked starboard and saw a streak of lightning strike the Sherpa's wing with the kiss of death.

"Uh oh," he grunted as the display panel glowed red across the board. A wailing sound like the howl of a train in a tornado made him cringe for he knew what was coming next. He gripped the Sherpa's yoke just as a violent down draft swatted the mighty bush plane out of the air. The ground was rushing up at him with sickening speed.

"Not gonna' make it," he shouted.

To Kathmandu.

•

Los Angeles, California,
11,000 Miles Due East of Kathmandu

Alexandra Martine McNeill sat on her balcony overlooking the Pacific. A glass of iced tea sweated on the table beside her, and a woven bamboo screen gave her shade as she enjoyed the late summer sunset.

"He's leaving Bimthang today," she spoke on her cell phone. "In fact, he should be in the air and on his way to Kathmandu right about now. I really missed him this trip. Yeah, that's what I get for staying home. I'll pick him up at LAX just before 2:00 AM tomorrow night."

She covered her eyes and cast her gaze into the sunset, as if able to see him coming to her from around the curvature of the earth. "In the morning I have a demonstration at the dojo, but I'm free the rest of the day. After I pick him up at LAX, we'll drive straight to the ranch, probably in time to wake you up way before the crack of dawn."

Alex chuckled, imagining her sister's face at such a prospect. "You'll need to get up extra early so you can make those cinnamon rolls," she coaxed. She held the phone from her ear as Fallon's complaints escalated. Alex added, "Of course I love you, and we'll see you tomorrow night."

She set her phone down and let her eyes drift back to the setting sun. She stared intently, for the moment of phenomena was at hand. The sun dipped into the horizon followed by the imaginary hiss that comes from impossible heat hitting infinite water. In the same instant a bright flash of green erupted.

"Ah," she sighed with satisfaction. One had to be very fast and committed to catch the flash of green. She sat back and drew a shawl over her shoulder, luxuriating in the soft twilight. She wished her husband were home for this sunset. They had shared the green flash all around the world.

"Tomorrow," she whispered. "He'll be home tomorrow."

Her eyelids drifted down. Around her shoulders, the cashmere shawl warmed her body, and her breathing slowed as she drifted into light sleep.

Beyond her, out into the Pacific, the sun continued on its path, bringing light to darkened places, and leaving shadows in its wake, shadows that slowly moved over Alex's sleeping form.

Her eyes moved back and forth beneath her eyelids; she moaned and her feet twitched and jerked. Suddenly, her hand shot out, reaching to grasp the unknown as she shrieked. She bolted upright, her back rigid, her hands extended like claws. Tears filled her eyes.

"Mrs. Mac, Mrs. Mac, Que paso? Que paso?" Maria, the housekeeper came running.

Alex shuddered and hugged her shoulders. "I was falling," she whimpered. To her own ears, her response sounded thin and frightened. She went on, unable to silence her distress. "I was falling ... falling like nothing in time or space would ever stop me." She looked up and saw the stark concern on Maria's face. "I've never felt so un-tethered."

She shook again and felt hot tears gathering behind her eyelids. She didn't know what was more surreal, the sensation of falling, or that she was so upset. She was not a woman prone to tears and fits.

Maria rubbed Alex's shoulders, seeking to chase away the chills. But Alex knew more than consolation was necessary for her to forget the sensation of falling.

"Were you dreaming?" Maria asked.

"No, no dream I can remember," Alex answered. "But there was just this sense of falling." She looked at her watch, a furrow of concern creasing her brow. "What time is it in Nepal?" She did the math. "Almost noon, he should have landed in Kathmandu by now."

She picked up her cell phone and dialed Royce's cell number. "It's going straight to voicemail," she said as a small wiggle of alarm shook her nerves. "Royce, call me. Love you, bye," she said. Unsatisfied, her fingers drummed on her thigh.

"Bring me the satellite phone, will you?" she asked in a soft voice. She would not let worry intrude into her mind until she knew more.

Maria returned with the phone.

Alex turned it on. While she waited for messages to

come on, she said in a half-hearted attempt to sound unconcerned, "I'm sure he's just running a little late."

With a smile Maria agreed. "I am sure that is what happened."

There was a message. Alex covered her free ear and turned her full attention to the phone. She breathed a sigh of relief when she heard her husband's voice.

"Alex, go to Santa Barbara. In that huge desk from Europe is an old record book of the family history. Look in the book for a Jamie. Look for Jamie McNeill. I'm coming home, and I love you."

Alex pulled back and looked at the phone as if she had heard something uttered in Martian. "Who's Jamie?" she said with a frown. She replayed the message, at once relieved, but at the same time mystified by Royce's instructions, and the strain she detected in his voice when he said, "I'm coming home."

Something's not right.

"Buenos noches, Mrs. Mac ... You will be all right, si?"

"Yes, Maria. Gracias," Alex answered.

After Maria left, Alex remained on the deck, drawn to the open ocean. "Where are you?" she whispered, feeling a strange ache spread through her chest. She called the airport in Kathmandu. Royce had not arrived.

By 10:00 PM, she was nearing a panic. After calling the airline, she knew he had not checked in with them either. His flight had left thirty minutes ago without him onboard. Her calls to the academy in Bimthang all ended with, *The Number you have dialed is unavailable.*

"Phooey," she complained with frustration. "No phone in Bimthang means no Internet in Bimthang. Double phooey."

Everywhere she turned, her husband was out of touch.

"I'm overreacting," she announced. She stood with her hands on her hips and stared out the windows at the dark Pacific.

Having no way to contact him, it was only reasonable she wait twenty-four hours. She kept her gaze on the horizon through the windows and spoke in a robotic tone. "You have until noon tomorrow to call me." Her voice rode the thin line between determination and desperation. Her unease was growing. She shook herself, and saw her reflection staring back.

"You look tired," she stated. "And you have an early demonstration at the dojo. Be sharp or get your Sensei butt kicked." She went upstairs and washed before crawling into the large bed that seemed even larger now that it was half-empty.

"Don't worry until you have something to worry about," she admonished. She rolled over and pulled her knees up, making a small warm spot in the cool sheets. The warmth spread out and she stretched her legs down into the bed. Remembering Royce's instructions, she blurted into the silence, "So who is Jamie?"

A snort of reluctance followed, and she wiped the slate of her mind clear. "Try to remember you're a warrior, not a ninny who falls prey to vapors and whimpering," she muttered, and closed her eyes, commanding her heart and mind be still.

But her heart trembled with an unknown fear, and her mind kept asking ...

Who is Jamie?

•

The Following Morning, Los Angeles, The New Shaolin Academy

In the hushed silence of the crowded room, Alex stood blindfolded on the dojo floor, ready to demonstrate her skills. Beneath the blindfold, she kept her eyes closed, not needing to see.

Go within. Find the power to see—within.

She smiled, knowing the small facial gesture would not go unnoticed, working subtly to unnerve those who watched. They would soon learn they did not have an advantage over a blindfolded woman.

A deep inhalation and she could smell them, their fear and their anticipation. She drew upon everything she had learned from Royce and from Master Chan to assess their forces. In her mind she saw their colorful bioelectric field imprints, much like a thermal scan.

Only four?

Not enough, she thought.

They should have brought more.

Externally, her smile expanded while she brought her internal focus deeper into her mind. Her hearing was acute, picking up the shuffling feet of one off to her right. Another stood straight ahead. She heard the brush of his sleeve as he brought an arm up in movement to silence the restless one.

Predictable. They were both young. She noted two more—one on her left and another behind her. Those two were cautious, holding back. Their auras were a map of their thoughts, giving her their plan of attack. Alex exhaled and rolled lightly onto the balls of her feet.

The attacker on her right moved forward. She aggressively lunged at him and brought her right foot up in a roundhouse kick to the stomach. That one fell to the mat floor.

The other young one came at her, stupidly crying, "Aiiee." Honing in on that cry, they collided in a flurry of fast hands and a volley of grunts. Alex blocked his multiple hand attacks before stepping back to deliver a perfect shitoe strike to the nerve plexus in her assailant's neck, designed to temporarily stun him, not kill him. His grunt of strain turned to a gasp. He fell on weakened knees.

Alex quickly whipped around to face the two remaining. She paused, still as a totem figure. They rushed her as one. She dove and swept the feet out from under one, hearing his *oomph* as the unexpected impact with the floor knocked the wind from his lungs.

One still to go.

From the floor she quickly rolled onto her feet. He was coming in fast. When he was almost on her, she stepped out of his way and, as he passed, kicked him in the back. Next came the sound of a body tumbling to the floor.

Applause filled the dojo. Alex removed her blindfold and gave a bow of respect to the gathered crowd. Her four defeated challengers came forward, rubbing their various affected body parts.

"Nice job, Sensei."

"Well done."

"Impressive, as usual."

She bowed again, giving them her respect before retreating to the corner where her bags lay on a bench. She fished out her cell phone and turned it on. "No messages," she whispered.

She recalled the first time she saw her husband demonstrate this very technique. "It's all about focus," she said softly under her breath.

Because anything is possible with masterful focus.

In spite of her fearless convictions, she shivered, wishing her husband were here. She had no more information about his whereabouts today than she did last night. All she had was his last message about Jamie.

Royce, where are you?

•

Royce was in the Sherpa, still falling long after the expected ground impact should have happened. Mist whipped by the cockpit. His instrument panel was out, and the controls were a dead stick. The Sherpa's extended dive fanned his disorientation; he wanted to stop falling, but not if it meant hitting the ground.

What the hell is happening? I must be dreaming.

He heard a faint whistle, a sound not part of the falling plane, and cocked his head to one side. The sound grew louder, like the approach of a train, sounding and feeling as though it would run through his center.

Not dreaming. Impact finally coming!

Bracing himself for the inevitable crash, he pushed back in his seat. The whistle filled the cockpit, painfully shrieking. He pulled his shoulders up and pressed his fingers to his ears, but the piercing vibration went beyond sound and was seared into his very bones. He closed his eyes.

And still he kept falling.

Light reached into the inside of his tightly scrunched eyelids, effectively obliterating the darkness. He opened his eyes to a cockpit no longer dark, but brightly illuminated. The piercing vibration and the brilliance of the light peaked and merged into a searing point.

Engulfed in the light and vibration, Royce felt his body go rigid, legs first, now arms and chest. His heart and back were wrapped with tendrils of stabbing energy, reaching for his head ...

He opened his mouth to scream.

CHAPTER TWO

"There are two ways to live your life. One is as though nothing is a miracle. The other is as though everything is a miracle." —Albert Einstein

Royce floated in the darkness of unconsciousness, a sweet thread of vibration surrounding him like the distant chime of bells. His heart quickened its pace, for within this comforting vibration was his wife's voice.

"Where are you?" she asked.

I don't know—

The despair in her words was palpable, and the vibration changed, clanging harshly in disharmony. She was slipping away, even as his heart cried, "I am with you always."

Darkness swallowed him again as his mind rose to another level. His memory stirred, bringing confusion to dart painfully through his rising consciousness. He remembered … falling, the wind ripping through his hair and watering his eyes, tugging at his cheeks. There was nothing holding him to any orientation. His heart labored with terror as the scream erupted from his throat. "Aaaahhhh!"

He opened his eyes.

He was in a bed in a small room. He looked down

and saw his feet poking up under the covers; he wiggled his toes.

Good, he thought. *No broken legs.*

Beside the bed, a young man wearing dark robes sat in a chair.

"What happened?" and, "Where am I?" were on the tip of Royce's tongue, but the young man jumped up and slipped out the door. In the silence of the small room, Alex's question, "Where are you?" echoed in Royce's mind, sparking a flare of concern. He could still hear her voice …

"Where am I?" he repeated. "Did I crash?" He ran his hands across his chest and felt no injuries; he didn't remember crashing. Confusion bloomed and he struggled to sit up. Not recognizing where he was, he mumbled, "Whether I crashed or not, where am I?"

He was occupying a simple wooden bed with what looked like a handmade mattress and rough sheets and a woolen blanket. The room was stone and seemed chilly. One small window let in soft light. On the floor by his bed were his shoes, and his clothes were folded and stacked on a side table against the wall.

Rising alarm thudded against his ribs. Even though there was no one present to speak to, he croaked again through dry lips, "Where am I?" A clay pitcher and mug at his bedside caught his eye and he reached to pour. Water filled the mug. He drank.

"Good, you are awake."

Royce licked his lips and eyed the man standing in the doorway. His clothing made Royce think he must have crashed on the far side of Manitu.

Never seen blue robes in Tibet, though.

He was a good six feet tall, dressed in a floor length

robe. While his hair was dark and his face smooth, Royce saw eyes that knew and understood much beyond what his appearance portrayed.

"Please, call me Andros," the man said.

"I'm Royce." Feeling his heart ramp up, he asked, "Where am I?"

Andros blinked slowly, drawing Royce's attention in a hypnotic way. "You are feeling well, yes?" Andros asked. "For some, the transition can be ... harsh." He came and sat in the chair by the bed leaning forward with his arms on his legs, his expressive eyes were serious. "As for your question?" He paused and looked at Master Chan's talisman around Royce's neck. His gaze moved up carefully to snare Royce's full attention. "I think you know the answer," he said.

As though a trap door opened beneath him, Royce clutched the edge of the bed to keep from entering free fall again. Chan's voice echoed in Royce's memory.

The timeless dimension?

How? Why?

Royce looked up sharply, still feeling as though he was falling, only this time emotionally instead of physically.

"You must not worry," Andros reproached softly. He placed a hand on Royce's shoulder before nodding to the small open window. "We have a beautiful afternoon. Won't you dress and come out into the garden?"

He stood and smiled, the warmth in the gesture reminding Royce of Master Chan. "Please, join me when you are ready." In a whisper of robe, he was gone.

Royce rose from the bed. When his bare feet touched the floor, he was shocked to feel the floor was warm, for his eyes told him the stone should be cold. Mumbling, "Not in Kansas any more," he dressed in his clean clothes and put on his shoes. As he stepped through the door he felt his mouth drop open in surprise.

Definitely not in Kansas.

"I know this place," he said with curious surprise. Immediately, he frowned, not sure how the scene was familiar.

Andros stood in a green wonderland straight out of a French painting. Tall trees surrounded a pond with a tinkling fountain. At the water's edge were two wrought iron chairs. Andros gestured Royce toward one of the chairs.

The haunting familiarity of the scene tugged at Royce's mind. "I know this place," he repeated as he sat in the chair. His butt clenched tight in expectation of cold hard metal, so he was surprised to feel the chair warm and comfortable. The inconsistent physical stimuli made him feel vulnerable. He braced for what might come next.

"You are experiencing a confusing of your senses," Andros said quietly. "That is normal when you come here. Do not be concerned."

Royce found Andros' suggestion an impossible task. He worked to take control of his breathing, to slow his heart and gain some equilibrium. Wildly, he thought to take off his shoes so his feet could touch the warm earth for grounding, but he wasn't sure the earth was beneath his chair. He looked up slowly, and finally remembered. "Ooh … I know where we are. This is Monet's Garden."

The pond where they sat was from a series of paintings by the French Impressionist Monet. They sat across from Monet's famous bridge, sheltered by towering willow trees.

"France, the Monet estate and gardens, this is where I asked Alex to marry me," he said.

"Ah," Andros murmured, nodding. "So you are here on her behalf." He gestured toward the pond.

The water moved gently, drawing Royce's eye. Light and dark shifted and moved across the surface of the pond until a scene slowly coalesced. A smile came to Royce's lips, for he could see his Alex reflected in the water, and he knew—

She is on her way to Santa Barbara ... to La Casa.

"Good," he whispered. He added with conviction, "She will find Jamie."

•

US 101 to Santa Barbara, California

Alex eased the Porsche into the left-hand lane and shifted gears, letting the car do what it did best. Her GPS was set for Santa Barbara and La Casa de la Paz, where she would find Jamie.

She called her sister, leaving a message. "I need to see the old family record book, the one from Europe. Pull that out for me, please. I'll explain when I get there about one o'clock. Have lunch ready, okay? Love you, too. Bye."

She ended the call and peered up at the clear sky as though she might see Royce in his airplane, which was purely wishful thinking. "Why am I looking for Jamie," she asked the sky. "When you are the one missing?"

La Casa is where she and Royce spent some of their best times together, where they had been closely connected. She grinned and laughed out loud, needing to feel as though Royce were in the car next to her, his long legs scrunched up in the compressed front seat. "Remember the day we first met? You nearly ran me down in the library, then you tried to steal my book, and ended up with ..."

She was at the UC Santa Barbara campus, researching a paper. She had a book in her hand and came around the end of a book stack just as a tall man came from the other side. They crashed into each other, scattering their books across the floor. She bent down to pick up his book at the same time he reached out to pick up hers. Without looking, they cracked heads with a resounding "oowww" in stereo.

Alex rubbed her head, looking down to see the book she held. "That's the book I'm after," she blurted out. She looked up to see this tall man staring down at her with the silliest grin across his handsome face.

"I was just going to say the same," he said with a smile.

Their eyes met and a heat fired in her heart and spread through her limbs to the floor, anchoring her as her soul sang in remembrance.

I know you—

As though in response to her thoughts, he thrust his hand out to her and said, "My name is Royce ... do I know you?"

•

Monet's Garden

Royce couldn't help but smile with the memory of that fateful day he and Alex met. His life had been complete ever since.

Until now, he thought. Added to his unease, he recognized that while these surroundings were pleasant enough, he still didn't know ...

Why am I here?

As the scene played out across the pond's surface, Andros nodded with understanding. "You and Alex have known each other a long time, haven't you?"

Royce understood he and Alex were two parts of one whole. "Yes," he answered. He held many memories of this incredible woman, his wife, his one true soul mate. "She's a fixer, my Alex," he added with a bittersweet smile. "Is she why I am here?"

Andros again spoke as though he didn't hear Royce's question. He offered, "You may speak to her, from here. Within the pond, you may view any moment your heart desires."

So many sweet memories of their time at La Casa provided a vast array of special moments in Royce's heart. "She will ride out to the coast," he mused. "I can see her there, under the trees ..."

He nodded, so deep in the experience, the sun warmed his face and a breeze from the Pacific blew up over the cliffs, filling his nose with salty air. His heart recalled being under those trees with her, where he once swore he would never leave her side.

•

Santa Barbara, California

Alex saw the entrance to La Casa come into view and pulled away from her memory of her and Royce's first encounter. "Come back to me," she stated, issuing a decree. "Whatever the problem, I'll fix it and bring you home."

She phoned her sister as she swung the Porsche through the big gates on the main road. "Hey," she said, grinning. "You got anything to eat? I'm famished."

"Oh, hey yourself, and you do remember I don't talk food to people on cell phones," Fallon quipped back smartly. "If you want to know what we're eating around here, you gotta show the whites of your eyes."

"Well, get ready, Sis, 'cause I'm coming down the road," Alex said, shifting gears. Her grin broke into a full smile. Her little sister was without fault and as wise as Solomon. She and her sister were so opposite in looks and disposition that Alex teased Fallon when they were little, claiming they weren't really related.

Coming around the last turn, and seeing the hacienda spread out before her made her heart pound bittersweet. She parked in the rear courtyard. For just a moment she sat in the car, basking in the utter quiet and stillness. The drive up from the city was worth this one instant of calm. She felt the knots in her stomach ease and she relaxed, knowing she would find answers here.

She turned her face to the ocean breeze and sniffed lightly. Beneath the salty smell was a mix of sweet notes filtering in from Fallon's flower garden—and then there was the smell of fresh baked bread, making her mouth water.

Suddenly, her ears picked up the telltale sounds of shuffling feet and she glanced into the rearview mirror. Gathered behind her car was a small crowd squirming with expectation. She looked back over her shoulder.

There they are, the people I love most, gathered together, waiting for me. How fortunate I am to have them in my life.

With a sigh of relief she got out to greet them as they

all rushed forward.

Her brother-in-law Jake grabbed her first and gave her a backbreaking hug. When he stepped away his blue eyes sparkled as he greeted her, "Good to see you, little girl."

Breathless from the squeeze, she answered with a squeak. "It's so good to be here."

From Fallon's arms, Alex took the littlest one, Katelyn. "Look at you, how big you're getting, you little gobbler." Alex pretended to pinch Katy's pudgy little thigh and was rewarded with a giggle as her niece settled into her arms.

The raucous crowd turned to enter the house. With one arm full of baby and the other arm full of sister, Alex let a rush of joy emerge, momentarily banishing her concerns.

The house and acreage of La Casa de la Paz were part of a Spanish land grant Royce's family held. The current holding was a hundred acres running in a narrow strip extending from the cliffs overlooking the Pacific at one end, across the rolling hills to sweep up to the sprawling house with its landscaped grounds.

"God, how I love it here," she moaned softly.

The house had three two-story wings wrapped around a courtyard. The cobblestone patio was abundant with flowering plants, iceberg roses, dwarf Japanese magnolias, and bougainvillea. It was cool and lush with a water garden and a fountain, both of which sang in testimony to the name, La Casa de la Paz.

They entered the house through glass doors into the dining room. Fallon took her daughter from Alex, saying, "Sis, go on up and unpack and wash up. When you come down, I'll feed you since I can see the whites of your eyes." She winked.

Alex laughed. "I won't be long." She went up the stairs with her single bag, trying not to think about the big bed upstairs. She sighed deeply for what couldn't be avoided and strengthened her step.

"Warrior, remember," she snapped.

She unpacked her bag and set out her toiletries. After a quick rinse of her face, she was ready for her sister's lunch.

"On the patio," Fallon called out when Alex came downstairs.

Lunch was chicken salad over arugula with Fallon's basil vinaigrette dressing. The meal was adults only as the kids were off with housekeeper Rosita to see a new foal down at the stables. Jake, Fallon, and Alex waved at the procession as they scampered off to the barn, raising a cloud of dust.

"What's the latest on Royce?" Fallon asked, wasting no time.

Alex took a quick drink, feeling her throat tighten. "I have no news. It's like he disappeared. I've been unable to reach Bimthang, and until someone there answers the phone and tells me where Royce is, they are my next stop. First, though, I had to come here."

"So what is this business about the old family records?" Fallon prodded.

"Well, the only message I have from Royce. He said to look in the old family records, in a book from the big desk from Europe. He says I'm to find a Jamie. Jamie McNeill."

Jake coughed, drawing all eyes. "How does finding a name written in an old book help when all those people are long dead. It's not like you can find this Jamie alive."

Silence settled around the table. Water trickled through the fountain and birds flitted from tree to tree; all sounded like they came from far off in the distance.

Finally Alex cleared her throat and picked up her glass of tea. "That's certainly part of the mystery," she said, trying to sound nonchalant. "I don't understand anything, but for now it's all I have to go on."

Fallon allowed no rest before adding, "And why are you looking for this Jamie person when it's Royce who's missing?"

Alex didn't bother to cringe at her sister's astute appraisal because it echoed her own thoughts. "Exactly," Alex agreed, but she shrugged. "I'm looking for Jamie because Royce asked me to. Royce and Jamie are connected … somehow." She emptied her glass and wiped her mouth. "Let's see what's in the records."

They gathered their dirty dishes and returned them to the kitchen.

"I'll go wash up," Alex said.

"We'll meet you in the library," Fallon called out.

Alex went to her room and washed her face and hands. She paused to examine her reflection, understanding her life had wandered onto shifting sands. "What's happening?" she asked. She looked long into her green eyes and saw only determination.

I will not falter …

She swung away from the mirror. "No time," she grumbled, and headed downstairs with long strides.

The library was in the east wing, a large room with clay tile floors and bookshelves groaning under the weight of countless volumes.

"Here," Fallon called out.

Before entering the room, Alex braced herself.

The portrait!

"Who is she?" she asked Royce the first time she saw the painting.

"Can't say," he told her. "The great desk and this portrait came together; they are family heirlooms from Ireland. She looks a little like you, do you think?" he teased.

The woman in the painting was Alex's twin, only younger and with darker, mahogany-colored hair. Something about the young woman filled Alex with unease whenever she looked at the painting. She avoided the portrait and instead fixed her eyes on the massive desk so large and heavy it was put together in sections made of hard oak. The desk was a masterpiece of workmanship, each drawer and hinge still moved perfectly.

"No fair peeking before me," Alex declared as she approached.

Fallon stepped aside, exposing the book on the desk. "I was waiting; I gave up competing with you when I was six." She smiled at her sister and pulled out the chair. "Do you want to do this alone?"

Alex reached for her sister's fingers and gave a warm tug. "No, please stay." After gazing at the slim leather bound book for a moment, Alex grunted with surprise. "Huh. I expected something bigger."

Only eight inches wide by twelve inches long, the book was bound with ox-blood colored leather and had the family crest pressed into the front cover. The corners were worn, but the binding was still solid. "Amazing," she said, lifting the book and looking at the back. She set it down and wiped her suddenly sweaty hands on her pants.

Why am I here? What is happening in my life? Where is my husband? Why is this obscure little volume impor-

tant?

Her heart was suddenly banging away with adrenaline, making her mouth dry. A clammy dampness spread across her chest and her shoulders felt like something heavy had landed on her. She jerked her shoulders and hissed under her breath. "Get off me."

"You okay, Sis?" came Fallon's concerned voice.

"No problem," Alex said. Tightening her lips with determination, she carefully opened the book's front cover. "Ooh," she gasped with surprise. The front page was hand inscribed in a strange language. "Not what I expected."

"That must be Gaelic," Fallon said.

The pages were parchment, and as Alex turned through them, she saw they were all filled with handwritten entries obviously done by a multitude of people with questionable writing ability. She turned more pages; near the back the Gaelic became English.

"Ah," she said. The handwriting changed and was now clean and precise, obviously from the same hand. "A woman," Alex mused. "Don't you think?"

She looked close, reading. "Marriages, deaths, births … it all seems pretty straight forward." She placed her finger on the page, following the names. "Here's a Jamie," she began, but came across another similar entry down the page. "Uh oh," she grumbled. "More than one Jamie here."

As she traced across more pages, she marveled at the history traveling beneath her fingers. "A lot of deaths, it seems. And here is one entry titled 'The Abandonment'—oh, it's a list of those who left in the flight of the earls.

"Here." Her finger came to a stop.

"James Roy. Born August—"

Her breath came to a halt, as though time had stopped. She looked up at Fallon, needing to make sure the sanest person she knew was still at her side.

Fallon squeezed Alex's shoulder and nodded. "Go on."

"Born August 31, 1580," Alex continued. "This must be the one, similar name and same birthday … but why?"

She read the next two entries. "Married to Fiona Flaherty in 1600. Oh," she said. "The bride died soon after the birth of … a son, Connor."

"What is that?" Fallon asked, pointing to a smear in the fine writing of the next entry.

"Can't say, the writing is washed out." She peered close. "It looks like something M married James Roy."

The rest of that page was torn out. She looked at the next page but there was nothing more about James Roy. "Well, I guess we'll never know what happened."

"Now what?" Fallon asked.

Alex rubbed her face, eyes strained from reading the ornamental cursive writing. "I don't know. I need some fresh air. I don't know what to think."

"Sounds to me like you need a ride on that rascally ol' Mister Blue," Fallon offered. "He'll clear your head out." She rose and added, "I think Jake was going down to saddle up some horses. He figured you'd want to ride."

They stood and Alex rose with her back to the portrait. "Some fresh air sounds really good. I'll change and be ready in ten."

After putting on jeans and a cotton shirt, Alex was eager to get out and ride Mister Blue, a tall blue roan gelding they adopted from a horse rescue farm. When Blue came to La Casa he was physically healthy, but his spirit needed healing. That's what happens at La Casa, the spirit is rejuvenated. She stopped and smiled, glad to be here; the memories were good at La Casa. She grabbed a straw cowboy hat and sprinted out the door.

At the barn, Jake waited, horses ready. Mister Blue looked especially fit and fiery and he gave an enthusiastic head toss when he saw her. With a quick pat and a check of the cinch, she mounted. The two riders took the path through the trees.

They rode in comfortable silence. Alex felt the sun and the cool ocean breeze as they rode down the familiar path she and Royce had ridden a hundred times. If she closed her eyes, she could see him beside her on his favorite horse. They would ride to the cliffs at the ocean end of the property and picnic in the shade of the trees. They were new in love then, and a day didn't pass that he didn't proclaim he would never leave her side. Alex shook her head, hearing their voices echo among the trees.

At the turn-around point at the cliff's edge, Blue ambled into the shade trees out of habit, and Jake's horse followed. Alex sat with her face lifted toward the breeze, the sun, and the ocean. Inhaling the ocean breeze, her anxiety eased.

With her eyes closed, she heard Jake's horse shifting next to her, and Blue responded. Finally both horses settled down, and the wind sighed up over the cliff edge bringing her the sounds from far below.

Ocean sounds, distant traffic, and …

What is that?

A soft effervescent sound seemed to float below the

wind, like a chime. Alex focused on the sound because it struck a chord and generated a sensation of familiarity.

This reminds me of the temple bells in Nepal.

Because the sound was pleasant, she allowed her mind to reach out. She felt the vibration coming toward her … closer, closer, closer, until suddenly she was engulfed in a sweet sensation of warmth. Instantly, she understood Royce was with her. His voice came as a whisper that reverberated oddly. She was not surprised, and yet—

Strange. He sounds like he's speaking under water.

Rippling goose flesh ran over Alex's arms and she forced herself not to shiver. Keeping her eyes closed, she made her mind relax, openly receptive, encouraging, beckoning.

Again she heard his voice, stronger, yet seeming to come from within her. She had to ask, "Where are you?"

"With you, my love, always with you, as I promised."

Tears squirted hot and burning under Alex's eyelids, but she grasped at the voice and the sensation of her husband's nearness. "Where are you?" she cried out. Instead of Royce answering, she heard Jake calling, sounding as if he were a dimension away.

"Alex?"

Jake's voice was pulling her back from wherever she had been with Royce and she didn't want to return.

"Alex?" Jake called. "Tell me you're all right," he said. "You're scaring an old man."

She ignored Jake and reached out again with her mind, trying to reclaim her connection with Royce, but the effervescent chime of bells was gone. The sweetness vanished and a wave of sadness entered the void. More tears, these of pain, rushed into her eyes. She angrily blinked them away.

"Did you hear?" she asked. She still held her face up-turned to the breeze, not wanting to move or open her eyes. "It was Royce. He spoke to me. I heard him."

Jake spoke, his voice solemn. "Well, I didn't hear anything, but that doesn't mean you didn't. I think we'd better go back."

He used his horse to herd Blue around until both animals set their noses back toward the barn.

Even as the horses made their way down the hill, Alex chewed her lower lip and twisted around in her saddle to stare at the trees.

Come back, Royce.
Come back.

CHAPTER THREE

Confirmed by Ben Rich, Former Director,
Lockheed Skunk Works:
All points in time and space are connected.

The Library, La Casa de la Paz

Alex paced back and forth, her mind and body a maelstrom of agitated activity. *Royce was with me, I'm certain,* she thought.

And his presence is another clue.

"What if you imagined this? What makes you think Royce was really there? Honey, you are under a lot of stress," Fallon said, shaking her head.

"I know how this sounds," Alex answered. "But what I experienced was *not* the product of stress, or an overactive imagination."

She came to a stop and looked beyond her sister, out the windows facing the ocean. Her voice was soft as she said, "I heard his voice, inside." She placed a hand over her heart, feeling the warm memory of Royce's words and voice.

"Somehow, we had contact. I don't know how, but this means we can reach each other," she said, her eyes filled with the memory.

I'll find you my love ... Just help me.

"Royce and I", she continued in a rush, "have been taught many techniques over the years, and what I experienced was similar to some of the things we've done before. Silva, and other mind-expanding practices like meditation, taught us techniques where our mind exists outside the body. Royce's mind reached out to me. I have no doubt."

Fallon glanced at her husband.

Jake's expression said, "Anything is possible." He looked at Alex, and said, "Something definitely happened. I'm inclined to give Alex the benefit of the doubt and say she knows what she's talking about. Maybe Royce was there, somehow, on some level."

"All right," Fallon said. "I won't waste my breath with you about all this since you know more about it than I do." She gave a reluctant nod, her face creased with concern. "Dinner won't be ready for a while, so you can go upstairs, maybe take a nap. You look as though you could use one." She hugged her sister before walking to the kitchen, shaking her head as she went.

"I'm okay Sis, really," Alex called out, watching her sister disappear through the door. She knew how bizarre her story sounded. But the truth was, she understood alternate levels of consciousness, and she intended to make this connection happen again.

This is the only path to Royce I have.

Alex shot a quick look at Jake. He gave her a look of encouragement, his eyes big, his mouth sealed tight. Finally he muttered, "I got horses to tend," before grabbing his hat and slinking out the door.

Seeing she was alone, Alex muttered. "Guess I'll

have to figure this out by myself." She sat abruptly on the edge of an overstuffed chair and rubbed her face. "Right after I take that nap."

In her bathroom she started a tub of hot water and dumped in a healthy splash of bath oil. Quickly she stripped and eased into the hot water, exhaling with a gasp as the heat claimed her weary body. As her muscles responded, the knots of tension in her mind worked loose as well.

"Ooohh," she sighed as she let go mentally and physically.

She stretched out with a sense of relief, allowing the water to lull her into a deep state of mind.

She was floating, a sense of peace surrounded her. She held no fear, no anxiety, and no concerns, only blessed peace and hope. Intuitively her heart and mind told her everything would be fine. Her heart's desire would be her reward, with all her goals fulfilled.

"How?" she begged. "When? What must I do? Please just tell me. Anything, I will do anything, go anywhere, just please bring my husband back to me."

"Time," came a whisper. "Time holds all the answers."

When nothing else followed, and sensing the message was complete, Alex quieted her questions. With a heart overflowing with good faith she understood that powers beyond her mere human comprehension had been called forth to help her.

Her prayers had finally been answered.

She slept until the cool water woke her. Feeling refreshed mentally and physically, she changed for dinner. From the kitchen she could smell a masterpiece in progress. Her stomach rumbled with joy as she came down the stairs.

Dinner came in delightful waves. First they had fresh spinach salad with hot bacon dressing, followed by a locally produced chardonnay with broiled rock lobster tail, fresh veggies from the market, and hot home-baked bread. Conversation was lean as the hungry family tucked into the meal.

When her plate was empty, Alex begged, "Please, no more." She held her stomach and groaned.

The entire family trickled out to the patio to enjoy the sunset. As Jake handed out glasses of port, Alex watched the children play, wondering for the thousandth time why she and Royce never had children.

He will come home, or I'll die searching for him.

No other option existed. No matter the problem, she would fix it. Nothing could stand against her undivided strength and determination. She was a trained warrior, and even though she had not actually gone onto a battlefield, she knew she could if she had to.

"You're looking pretty deep there, Sis." Fallon came to sit by Alex.

"Dinner was great," Alex responded. "How do you guys keep from getting fat?" She gave an appreciative pat on her belly.

"Well, when we don't have company," Fallon said drily, "we only get rice cakes and lettuce."

"Ha! I'd like to see that," Alex exclaimed. "I love you. Thank you for being so understanding. I don't know what I'd do without you."

Alex leaned forward in her seat. "I think I may be on to something about Royce's whereabouts. I know you think this is all funny woo-woo stuff you don't understand. But I believe there is definitely something going on here."

She sat back, integrity in her spine, conviction in her tone. "I guarantee, whatever is going on, I intend to sort it out."

•

Monet's Garden

The scene of Alex and her sister cleared from the pond's surface when Andros waved his hand.

Royce rubbed his face, desperate to clear his mind just like the pond's surface. Events were speeding along too fast; he couldn't keep up.

He didn't understand how he was here, or for that matter, where was "here?" He thought if he'd had more time to wrap his head around the concept of a timeless dimension, but the incongruity of this logic stirred a mad-man's chuckle to rattle in his chest. Running apace with this insanity was the image he saw in the white picture-frame in his mind when he asked, "Who is Jamie?"

"Obviously, family is important to Alex," Andros said.

Royce worked to garner his thoughts. There was a puzzle here, and he felt the solution close, yet just beyond his grasp. Andros' words pierced Royce's swirling thoughts, causing him to look up, startled. "Family?"

Of course, he thought.

Mamma Bear.

"Her parents died in a car crash when she was just fourteen and Fallon was ten. They lived with their maternal grandparents, but ... Alex really stepped into the role of responsibility. I call her Mamma Bear."

He stopped to give Andros a look of warning. "You

best not place yourself between her and anyone one she designates as 'cub.'"

"You feel the same toward her?" Andros probed.

Alex was everything to Royce. Were he made to choose between her and all his material wealth, there would be no contest—he would sacrifice everything for her. A clue to the puzzle danced through his mind like a vapor, maddeningly insubstantial. He responded, suddenly feeling the question and his answer were of critical importance. "Yes, I feel the same about her."

Andros tilted his head in approval. "Watch," he said. He waved his hand and the pond rippled.

•

After dinner Alex brushed her teeth and crawled into the big bed. She was on emotional high-alert, but she was also physically drained.

"Royce, Royce, tell me where you are," she whispered. She had intended to do a meditation, but her exhausted body had other plans. Darkness came as oblivion claimed her mind. Deeply, she drifted until a vision came in from her subconscious.

What she saw confused her, but this was a dream, so she relaxed and went along. She wasn't a part of the dream, but an observer.

A man rode a horse through green woodland. The man looked like Royce. Another rider came, a woman, but Alex could not see her face, only the back of her black riding habit.

Who were these people in her dream? she wondered. Why were they dressed in historic clothing?

Who is this man that looks like Royce?

The riders stopped to dismount, laughing.

"They are in love," Alex whispered.

The woman, her face still hidden from view, reached for her companion and pulled him in for a kiss.

"Who is he?" she asked.

"He is James Roy," her heart whispered in response. "Save him, and you save all."

Alex turned back to the dream, but the scene softly evaporated. She was left alone, in her dreams, in her life, in her journey; but she was not afraid.

She slipped deeper into unconsciousness to ponder the problem delivered by her mind, a single thought burning brightly.

Who is this man who looks so much like my husband?

•

Alex woke before sunrise. With the dream fresh in her mind she said, "Jamie, you are in my sights." Confidently she added, "Which means time is all that's standing between me and the solution to this problem."

She swung her feet to the floor and reached for her cell phone. Seeing she had no messages, she chewed her lip and reached for the satellite phone.

No messages there, either. She muttered, "Nuts to you, too." She powered off the satellite phone and reached again for her cell, dialing the Academy in Bimthang. She grimaced at the mechanical message: *The number you have dialed is unavailable.*

"Fine," she said. She tossed the phone on the bed and stood with her hands on her hips, remembering the summer she was ten and none of her friends wanted to help her build a lemonade stand. She stood alone, dejected, her hands on her hips as they were now. At her feet were a pile of mismatched wood scraps and a handful of nails. She stared at the hammer, uncertain where to start, when her father came and stood beside her.

He looked to ponder the situation. "You know what they say, don't you?"

Alex had no idea, but she nodded in agreement.

"Business," he said, "is what you do with friends and partners. But here in Texas, we have 'bidness'. Bidness is when you have serious stuff you have to do yourself." He walked off without another word.

Alex built the lemonade stand, working relentlessly all the long day. When she finished, the stand had a hand-painted sign, *Lemonade twenty-five cents,* and a shelf for the ice chest and a shelf to set the cups on for customers. Never would she forget how accomplished she felt, how really cool the stand was, and how proud her father's eyes were when he looked at her.

"It's just as well no one is helping me. Now I can take care of things the Texas way."

After showering, she dressed and pulled her hair back into a ponytail, needing no distractions. "Outta my way," she warned the world reflected in the mirror. "Got bidness to do."

She went directly to the library. "Jamie," she said as she walked straight to the old desk. She pulled up a chair and sat before the wooden behemoth. Admiring the smooth texture of the polished surface, she whispered, "You are amazing. I bet you were the love of someone's life."

A row of square drawers lined the top of the desk. She opened each and looked in, poking around, but not seeing what she searched for. A deeply recessed area was filled with old accounting books for a manor named Greyhaven and receipts for various farm animals, but she pushed them aside.

"I know I saw you here, come on out," she purred. She opened the top drawer on the left and rummaged around with determination. "Come to me, I need you," she intoned. She moved on to a bottom drawer on the left that slid out silently on oiled rollers.

"There you are."

She lifted out a large photo album and put it on top of the desk. A string wrapped around the album on all four sides and tied with a bow in the center top. When she released the bow, a gasp of air escaped the album like a sigh as a surge of loose photos poured out.

She slipped her hand under the outpour and let her fingers measure the crisp feel of each page until she came to the last one. Her thumb held the pages up as her fingers searched underneath for the soft feel of leather.

"Ah, just as I remember." Carefully she lifted the album contents just enough to withdraw the piece of leather tucked in the back. She set the leather aside and re-stuffed the album with the escaped photos, some old small black-and-whites with *Kodak* printed in the white margin. Before turning her attention to the leather piece, she replaced the retied album in the drawer.

She unfolded the leather, still soft and supple, out across the desktop. "The family tree, circa 1600," she said with satisfaction. She ran her hand across the leather, pressing it flat and smoothing out the folds.

The writing was cursive, yet readable, looking like the same handwriting she saw in the book they looked at yesterday evening. "Someone likes to keep things well documented," she hummed.

The library door opened and Alex suddenly smelled coffee. "Morning, Sis. What's got you up at the crack of dawn?"

Fallon set a cup of coffee for Alex on a side table and relaxed into an over-stuffed chair, throwing her legs over the arm.

The coffee drew Alex's attention. "Oh, do I need that." She picked up the cup and inhaled deeply before sipping and taking a seat across from her sister. "I had a dream last night." Alex felt her voice quiver with excitement. "What I saw gave me another idea." She set her cup down and went to the big desk. "Look." She ran her finger over the name James Roy at the top of the tree.

Fallon asked, "What's so important about this dream; what does it have to do with Royce's disappearance?"

Skipping her sister's logical question, Alex answered with breathless excitement. She blurted her thoughts out in a hurry before her sister could stop her with a thousand questions. "I saw another man who looked like Royce. The man was James Roy. I must find this man and save him, and by doing so I will save all."

The facial expression Alex got from Fallon was exactly what she expected—her sister's eyebrows shot up, her jaw dropped, and her mouth popped open.

Alex ignored her sister and continued. "See Fallon, he's here, at the top. The family roots are in Northern Ireland. Jamie is real. When I see the name now, something makes me feel as though I know this man."

Fallon's lips were clamped together in a hard line of disbelief. "Alex, of course you feel like you know him," she said. "His name is almost the same as Royce's and, as you say from your dream, he looks a lot like Royce. This doesn't explain the relevance, because Jamie is long dead. How are you supposed to save him?"

Alex sat back with a deflating huff. "I don't know how I'm supposed to save him." She ran her finger along the genealogy tree to James Roy's name. "How do I save you?" she asked. "And from what?"

•

Monet's Garden

Royce felt his trepidation rise, felt his heart ramp up with adrenaline. Somehow the answers were right in front of him, and he needed to see them, but his mind was still clogged with incomprehension about 'how' and 'why' he was here, wherever 'here' might be. Andros studied him like a sensei watching a student run kata; Royce's palms grew sweaty with fear.

"She is a strong woman," Andros remarked.

Royce smiled, thinking—

You have no idea.

•

La Casa, Santa Barbara, California

"Yes, can I speak with Master Chan?" Alex asked. At last she would discover Royce's whereabouts. She fanned her face, excitement bringing a roar into her head like she had her ear stuck to a giant seashell.

Come to the phone, quick, before the connection—

The line crackled and she held her breath so long she gasped in relief when Chan's voice erupted suddenly from the phone.

"Yes, Alex, good morning. How can I help you?"

He spoke as though nothing was wrong. She held a hope, momentarily, that this was true. But her dreams and her heart told her that wasn't possible. She gathered her voice and asked, "Sensei, where is Royce?"

"He is not here," Chan answered.

Alex resisted the urge to shout and forced herself to breath slower. "Royce is missing. His plane never made it to Kathmandu. Do you know what happened to him?"

"You have not ... heard from him at all?" he queried softly.

"When he was still there, he left a cryptic phone message about finding Jamie."

"Have you had any other ... communication?"

Chan's inflection told her he wasn't talking about a phone call. Suddenly all of Alex's alarms went off. In spite of her heart banging against her ribs, she answered slowly. "He ... I felt his mind, out by the cliffs at La Casa."

"This is a place you and he know well, together, am I right?" Chan probed.

This line of questioning made Alex's knees weak. She eased down into a chair. "Yes, we have many good memories from here."

"And what message did he have for you?"

"I asked 'where are you' and he said, 'With you, my love, always with you, as I promised.'"

Silence came long enough to make Alex think the connection had dropped. She looked at her phone and saw the call was still open. Suddenly Chan answered, bringing chills to her shoulders.

"You must come, Alex. Come to Bimthang."

•

Alex set the small carry-on bag by the door. Behind her, Fallon tapped her foot in agitation.

"I don't like this Alex," Fallon complained.

"I know you don't," Alex responded. "But it's what I'm doing, so try to calm down." She looked up at Jake. He stared out over her head letting her know Fallon was wearing the family pants today.

Alex snorted.

I got bidness to tend to.

She took her sister's hand. "Honey, I'm just going to Bimthang. Why are you so upset?"

Fallon's mouth crumpled into a wrinkle of fear. "It's not where you're going, it's your attitude. You scare me sometimes. I'm afraid you're going to do something … reckless."

"What you call reckless, I call determined," Alex soothed. "I have to go find Royce. The Academy is the last place he was seen." She looked off briefly, remembering the line of questioning from Chan, and fought to keep the unease from her expression. She brought her gaze back to her sister's tear-stained face and settled the argument. "If it were you missing, I'd do the same."

Fallon sniffed and dashed her free hand across her eyes. "Call me from the airport, every airport. Call me from Bimthang before you get to the Academy. Call me—"

"I will let you know everything, now stop worrying."

Fallon implored further, pulling on Alex's hand.

"You won't do anything wild or really crazy, will you?"

Alex knew 'wild and really crazy' had already moved into her universe. She managed a wry grin and lied to her sister.

"I promise."

•

The Shaolin Academy of Arts, Outside Bimthang, Nepal, Near the Chinese Border

"Sensei," Alex said with a deep bow.

Master Chan met her at the gate with his smiling face. His demeanor was encouraging, giving her tired heart and mind a brief respite. She had traveled in a first class whirlwind. With the time change, she felt like she landed in Kathmandu before she left LAX. She was emotionally and physically exhausted.

Master Chan bowed in return before taking her in his arms for a grandfatherly hug. "You are tired, child. You must rest, then we will talk."

Alex nodded, knowing when to concede, at least for the moment. She was too tired to pursue anything but sleep. "Yes, Sensei."

"Come to me after the evening meal. I will be in my quarters," he instructed. He gave her a departing bow; she responded in kind before he turned and left.

Alex picked up her bags and made her way through the maze of hallways and quick turns. As major financial supporters of the academy, she and Royce were allocated their own small room. She slipped in the door and dropped her bags.

"Oh," she moaned, and rubbed her face, scrubbing

at the fatigue. She quickly unpacked and put away her small collection of clothes and basic toiletries she had purchased in Kathmandu.

She sat forlornly on her mat, across from Royce's, and while she had sworn not to do this, she couldn't stand the separation. She crawled across the brief floor space separating the mats and melted into Royce's bedding. Sniffing lightly she inhaled his scent, knowing he had been here recently.

I miss you.

Her chin wobbled and her eyes watered, but she pushed the sob away. "I will not cry for you. I will find you." She gathered up the top bedding. The blanket felt warm, as if he had just left this bed. She pulled the rough wool to her face. His scent, so familiar, came with an ache, for her arms were empty.

"I will find you," she whispered again, even as her eyelids drifted down. In response to her spoken words, another thought emerged.

Find Royce ... or Jamie?

•

Monet's Garden

"I see what you mean," Andros said. "She is like the ant with a large basket. She will not stop until—"

"Until bidness is done, as she calls it," Royce completed. "Not until bidness is done."

•

Alex climbed the stairs to Chan's quarters with slow deliberate steps. Inside, her heart quaked, for she knew the next time she passed over these stairs, her life would be altered in some fashion. She felt this as if it were part of her being. She wanted to face this challenge with grace, representing her husband and Master Chan with honor.

And strength ... please, let me be strong.

She reached his door and rapped lightly.

"Come in," called Chan.

She entered. Seeing him prepare tea with his special occasion utensils, her stomach tensed with silent dread, knowing this was a truly momentous occasion.

"Come, child, sit with me. We have much to discuss," he invited. He waved his hand for her to sit across the low table from him on a large pillow.

She sat, crossing her legs. The pillow beneath her was smooth and flat, comfortably protecting her seat from the hard stone floor.

Chan smiled and poured the tea, carefully measuring his movements and the beverage to perfection. Alex waited while he set the stage for his presentation. When all was to his satisfaction, he passed her the small cup.

She took the tea with a small bow of her head and inhaled, drawing in the scent of fresh green leaves. While one part of her wanted to jump up and scream, "Let's get on with it, will you?" Another wiser aspect knew what she was about to hear could not be rushed, and could not be avoided.

"You are very special, you and Royce," Chan said. "I have long known you are both old souls."

He said this matter-of-factly. This was yesterday's news.

"Your lives are entwined, your karma interconnected. I see much greatness for you—and challenge. There is, unfortunately, also great opportunity for ... turbulence."

Alex heard Chan choosing his words and sensed something coming she didn't want to hear. She forced her muscles to relax lest she jump up and run. She gazed at Chan, resisting the urge to gulp.

"Royce did leave here in his plane."

Alex's heart leaped into her lungs.

"With my warnings." Chan finished the sentence with a pointed look. "Warnings about turbulence. I also told him to find Jamie."

Now how, Alex thought, *would he know anything about Jamie?* With difficulty, she pulled her attention back to what Chan was saying, trying to keep up.

"My thoughts on this unique event? You are part of an extraordinary culmination of karma and destiny. Master Royce, I believe, is in the timeless dimension, awaiting your participation in events from the past."

Alex felt the expression on her face freeze.

Okay. Ha ha for the candid camera.

She quickly cast her eyes around the room.

If this is one of Royce's jokes, I'll—

But Chan's expression was quite serious; there was no joke here. Her mouth went dry and her hand trembled; she suddenly knew how Dorothy felt when spinning through the winds of a tornado.

Turbulence.

She didn't know how to respond. She felt her shoulders droop, just as her hand relaxed its grip on the cup.

Chan took the cup from her drooping hand. "Do not be afraid, my child. I think all will be well in good time."

He continued, speaking softly as if to calm a distressed animal. "While an event of this magnitude is unusual, such is possible with a great power like love. Human DNA is proven to influence photons, and eclipse time. You know there are many dimensions beyond our senses."

Alex stuttered through the briefest query she could muster. "How? Why?"

Chan refilled her cup and passed it to her, pressing it firmly into her hand. "How, I can help you with. Why is a question known only by the heart."

"But, won't my actions affect the future?" Alex protested. "This future?"

Chan shook his head slowly. "Quite the contrary. Your actions will preserve the future. Without your actions, this future doesn't exist."

Alex sipped her tea, drawing sanity from the simple action. A sea of questions wanted to jump loose. "Save him, Jamie, and I save all," she whispered. "But what does that mean? Why is he important?"

Something inside whispered ... you know!

She resisted, uncertain.

I don't know—I don't want to know.

She backed away from the thought and drew her focus to Chan's words. "How? You say you can help me with the how?"

"You have found Jamie, am I correct?"

"Yes. He lived in Northern Ireland in the early 1600s. His name is James Roy, born August—"

"The thirty-first," Chan finished. He rubbed his hands together as though a great clue had been revealed.

"I have preparations to make for your journey. Until I call you again, meditate deeply on what is important to you, for you will certainly be challenged beyond your expectations. Think long, child, on what your boundaries are."

Alex rose in stunned silence, knowing her unspoken questions would eat her alive until she had answers. In the face of such mental chaos, the peace of meditation was her only solitude. "Yes, Sensei," she said. She bowed, eyes down, before slipping soundlessly from the room.

●

After Alex left, Chan felt the excitement building in his bones. To mentor such an extraordinary event was a great honor. He moved to a lacquered chest and opened a drawer.

The timeless dimension was very ancient myth, long predating the arrival of the Buddha. Since Chan's first vision of these events in Royce's life, he had been researching the timeless dimension. With all the many ancient texts available to him, his search had led him to one unique document.

He lifted the precious papyrus sheets from the drawer. The brief stack of pages was bound with small, perfect gold rings. Across the top of the first page, *The Place of No Time* was scribbled in a spidery weave of Chinese characters.

"Turbulence, indeed," Chan muttered as his finger traced the writing, passing through the columns of characters and finally stopping on the last page where an instrument was diagramed.

"It must be made of gold," he mused aloud. "Now, who do I know capable of such precision?"

There were few names to choose from, as such skill was a lost art. And this must be someone he could trust.

He really had only one option. He would have to leave tonight.

His gaze drifted out the window, a frown troubling his brow. "I must pray for them," he said.

Even I would tremble in the face of such a journey.

And what, he could only wonder, *does all this bode for the man named Jamie?*

CHAPTER FOUR

The Beatles: All You Need is Love

Montrose Court, Ireland, 1612

James Roy McNeill, Earl of Greyhaven, leaned against the mantle piece and suppressed his laughter as he eyeballed his host's latest attire.

Dear Lord in Heaven, somebody save me—please.

Jamie's neighbor, Sir Edward Burke, master of Montrose Court, strutted about his parlor, absurd and garish in yellow with black stripes.

What could Sir Edward have been thinking, Jamie wondered, when his tailor suggested those colors? Being out in the provinces as Greyhaven was, one was willing to forgive much in the name of entertainment, but this was unbearable.

Ha! The fool looks like a great bee.

He swirled the last drops of Sir Eddie's sickly sweet port in his crystal glass and brought his attention back to his neighbor's whining chatter, hearing another offer to purchase Greyhaven Manor.

"And so, my dear Earl, I repeat my offer to purchase your estate," said Sir Edward as he walked to the sideboard to refill his glass of port. "Refill, Milord?"

Jamie joined Sir Edward, but set his glass down on the sideboard. "Thank you Sir Edward, but I must go. The duties of the lord of the manor and such, as you well know. Perhaps another day, but for now I must take my leave."

After being closeted with the man for over an hour, Jamie needed fresh air. Between Sir Eddie's costume, his perfume and the port, Jamie had a headache.

Before allowing him to escape, however, Sir Edward pressed on, "So, what say you about my offer, Milord? I am land poor but very liquid with cash assets. You, on the other hand are rich in land, but not so in cash. I offer you a good price."

Jamie had no interest or intention of selling his estate to Sir Edward for any amount of money, but for some perverse reason he enjoyed stringing the man along. Perhaps he did this because the property now called Montrose Court had once been Greyhaven land.

He swept from the parlor, making for the front door. "I shall mull it over," he tossed over his shoulder. "However, right now I thank you for your hospitality. Until next time."

His long legged strides took him through the manor and out into to the courtyard where his horse, Pharaoh, waited. He mounted with the strength and agility born of long hours in the saddle and turned for the gate. With a cordial wave, he sent his adieu to Sir Edward as he departed.

Sir Edward, his mouth twisted with disdain, watched the Earl ride through the courtyard gates.

"Damn you Irish," he grumbled. "You are too proud, by far." He smiled, envisioning his dreams. "One day we will strip your precious pride from your backs."

Because of his secret yearnings, the acquisition of Montrose Court was especially convenient. Before coming to establish Montrose Court, he became aware of a certain potential, that all of Ireland was in chaos. Men were gone. Their women and children, abandoned, were now vulnerable. Such was the perfect cover for he and Raol to … satisfy their desires.

The once-Greyhaven land he possessed, now called Montrose Court, fell into his hands because he was in the right place at the right time. He was chatting with one of the King's advisors when the Lady Kathleen, Jamie's mother, burst through the doors and threw herself upon the King's feet. The vision of the Lady on her knees, her breasts heaving, stirred Sir Edward's desires, until this image took root and grew into something he could not deny.

Kathleen begged King James for the family land for her son Jamie's inheritance.

The King roared. "That brigand, your uncle, has plagued me for years. Just because he has fled Scotland does not mean he shall not be punished."

Sir Edward stepped closer to see the fracas for he had grown hard at the mention of punishment. He hoped fervently he would be allowed to watch said punishment.

"My Lord," Kathleen pleaded, "those who have earned the punishment you speak of are gone. Would you flay the innocent?"

"Humph," King James rumbled. "I fear there are none innocent in Ireland."

With the mention of innocents, Sir Edward's desire swelled even harder. *Yes*, he thought—punish them.

"The Greyhaven estate is vast," proclaimed the King.

"You could loose a quarter and feel little pain." He looked up at the courtiers gathered for this spectacle, scanning the crowd. His eyes came to rest on Sir Edward. "You, Burke, care you to move to Ireland?"

Sir Edward stepped out from the crowd. He looked down at the pleading Lady. "Well, my liege, there does appear to be something Irish worth having." He leered up at the king, hoping to have made the right impression with his innuendo.

Instead of bringing forth the approval of laughter, King James stared coldly back at Burke ... a long, deep examination, long enough to make the crowd shift with an anxious inhalation.

"Bring me a map," James said softly.

The crowd's exhalation came flooded with hesitant whispers, then silence. Documents were brought forth, and the rustle of heavy paper split the room's stillness like a saber.

James peered at the map, humming, poking a finger from here to there, squinting at the details and mumbling to the records keeper. At last he announced his decree. "Greyhaven will give to the Crown a section of Greyhaven land, about one-quarter the total, in payment for aggression waged by the Earl of Tyronne against this royal office. Your son, his name is Jamie, is it not?" he called to Kathleen.

She had risen to face the King. "Aye," she whispered.

"Jamie will retain Greyhaven lands excepting for this designated portion, which I am awarding to Sir Edward. Sir Edward will erect a manse, and the property will be called Montrose Court."

Excited whispers raced around the room. Kathleen bowed her head and went to one knee. "Yes, my

Lord."

She rose and turned to leave, sweeping her skirts out of the way when she passed by Sir Edward.

She is far too regal, Edward thought. He snatched her arm before she could pass. "We will be neighbors, Lady."

Kathleen drew back, seeming to tower over Sir Edward. Her chin came up with indignation, as though she had caught the odor of something unspeakable. Without a word she jerked her arm from his hand and marched out, her back stiff and her head held high.

A snicker raced around the room. Sir Edward went rigid, feeling the hot stares of the other courtiers boring into his back. He glared at Kathleen's retreating form with a mix of hatred and desire.

You will pay dearly for your actions.

Drawing upon a great deal of self-control, he fixed a smile on his face and turned away from the lady. He approached the king and his records man to finalize his ownership of the new land title, feeling every eye upon him. Once all was in order, he spun on his heel and walked out. He traversed the halls and corridors and twists and turns of the royal palace, his mind going over the many ways he would make the lady suffer.

"The pleasure will be all mine, I assure you," he muttered as he opened the door to his room.

A man stepped out from the shadows.

"Raol ... did you see?" Edward asked.

The Spaniard had been with Edward for years. He sat in the chair by the fireplace. "Your fortunes are on the rise this day. But that woman." He sucked through his teeth in distaste and looked at Edward, his dark eyes glittering like a snake. "She humiliated you."

Edward felt anew the hot stares of those disapproving courtiers. The pressure in his head increased at the memory of the Lady Kathleen's rebuff.

She will beg me to end her life—as they all do.

Suddenly he smiled broadly. "We will have our pick of the Irish countryside, my friend. Women enough for the two of us." He rubbed his hands together with anticipation. "We can build the dungeons of Montrose Court to our specifications."

Raol rose and stepped toward Edward, eyes alive with the promise foretold.

"We will need a staff," Edward announced.

"I know the perfect family," Raol responded. "Homeless French Huguenots; they speak no English, but understand enough to do their work."

"Excellent," Edward said. "They will have no one to talk to about what they might see." He held his hand out. Raol took the offering with a clasp of comradeship.

"To Montrose Court," Edward said.

"To Montrose Court, and to the Lady Kathleen," Raol added.

"She will be the first to feel our ... hospitality," Edward predicted.

Raol grinned. "We start with the woman who shunned you. And the rest of Ireland will follow."

•

Jamie took his time after leaving Montrose Court, letting Pharaoh pick his own pace. The early spring day was warm with a fresh breeze and the land was beautiful, promising a good growing season to come.

"Aye, I love this land," he said, stopping to view the

lush fields. "But being the lord of these lands," he added, "is boring as hell, an undeniable fact."

He shook his head, wondering at the perversity of his nature. "I am a grown man, how did I get so hard to please." He sighed with the old argument. "Live with your boredom," he chided, "and be glad ye' are safe from wild and foolish passions."

Boredom was safe, and that was how he intended to keep his life. "There has been enough madness in this family," he declared to the breeze. "We can not afford any more.

"First, my own da gets himself killed in a hunting accident, leaving me fatherless. Do ye see any wisdom in such a move?" he queried. He snorted with disdain. "Next comes wild man Rory's political passions costing us a portion of our lands and the title Earl of Tyronne." He stopped Pharaoh and leaned down to ask the animal, "Can you believe the bloody bastards?"

A soft whicker of understanding came, and Jamie stroked the horse's neck. "I may could forgive them all, were it not for that vermin, Burke. Aye, for having to suffer his presence, I have no forgiveness in my heart."

A breeze came soft and warm, momentarily clearing the regret from his heart. "Well, the insanity—'tis all behind us now. We keep the peace and hope the King of England forgets all about Greyhaven. No madness, no passion, just safe and quiet, that is the way my life shall stay," he said with a grim nod.

Pharaoh threw his head back and snorted, seeming to contest Jamie's words.

"Nay, Pharaoh, 'tis how it must be," he said as he spurred the big stallion on toward Greyhaven. "Aye, boredom will get me long before passion does," he muttered.

Cresting a hill, he spotted his steward and friend, Robbie Maguire, riding with Connor, Jamie's son.

Now there is a mystery.

Connor's mother passed away the year Connor was born. Unlike the McNeills, Fiona Flaherty had not been plagued by passion of any kind. "And yer son," Jamie said, "seems to bear the same mark."

Jamie did not know how to talk to Connor and the more he tried, the more he felt a failure. Now Connor watched Jamie, always maintaining a safe distance and a pensive expression. Jamie shrugged; he could only assume his own son was afraid of him.

We are a mess. Thank the heavens we have Robbie Maguire.

"Ho there, Maguire," Jamie called out, riding up to where they halted. As he came to a stop, he noticed Connor maneuvering his pony to Maguire's other side.

Probably in preparation to flee the ogre, his sire.

Jamie grimaced.

"A busy day with the traps I see," he said pointing. He gazed longingly at the brace of fat rabbits slung over the pommel of Maguire's saddle. There would be Mary's wonderful rabbit stew for their evening meal.

Maguire smiled his easy Irish grin. "Aye, here is something fine for Cook Mary's pot tonight. And Connor here was just telling me about a pair of foxes he saw in those fields out past the pond. If ye take the rabbits, then Connor and I will go and set traps for the foxes. They should bring a couple of nice pelts to warm someone's feet this winter," he said.

Jamie rolled his eyes. Maguire was about to start on their endless debate over Jamie's unmarried status.

These fine pelts, Jamie understood, were intended to warm the feet of the next lady of the manor.

"Being happily married," Maguire often promoted, "is the only way to find happiness." He spoke from experience, having a fine family with three grown sons. The oldest son's wife was due to present the Maguire clan with their first grandchild.

"Aye, Maguire," Jamie replied. "Fine fox pelts for someone's chilly feet this winter. And would ye be finding me the lady whose chilly feet concern ye so?"

Maguire's grin spread even further. "Well, I havna given up, ye know, and 'tis more than I can say for some around here. Ye need to get out a little more, lad. See what's out there and take advantage of the opportunities for happiness."

His grin expanded into an exaggerated leer. "Put a little joy into yer life, Jamie. Yer the laird of the land, and ye life is as boring as spit. I expect a fine, redheaded Irish lass would put some spark into yer nights. You havna given it a chance, Jamie."

"Give up, Maguire. There are plenty of warm beds in the village that welcome me, more than enough to keep me satisfied," Jamie replied with a meaningful waggle of his eyebrows.

"Baugghh," Maguire grumbled. "You know the satisfaction they provide is short lived. What I mean is a lass ye can keep near to your heart. A fine, redheaded Irish lass, 'tis what ye need."

Exasperated, Jamie responded with the sad truth. "Between famine and war, I see a shortage of life, redheaded or otherwise. Perhaps ye noticed? I fail to see any women, redheaded or not, I would be willing to 'keep.'"

Jamie shifted in his saddle, preparing to finally win their old argument. "Now, since fine Irish redheads are scarce about, I suppose ye expect one to fall out of the sky?" He allowed his grin to fill his face, for he felt he had finally bested Maguire.

Maguire answered, undaunted. "For shame on ye, lad, where is yer faith? What with the luck of the Irish, magic talking stones, and the wee leprechauns, who can say what might happen?" He passed the rabbits to Jamie with a toss and bounded away, young Connor fast behind.

Chagrined, Jamie sat as Maguire's laughter danced across the breeze. He pensively watched them ride off, and knew Maguire had managed to get the last word in again.

He sighed and shook his head. The truth was, a fine, redheaded Irish lass would be a welcome change. The only requirement was he had no urge to keep her, for keeping would require love and passion, which were strictly taboo. "Like I said, passion leads to insanity, and I refuse to participate."

With his resolution firmly secured with the fates, Jamie turned his horse toward the manor. He smiled and his mouth watered, not from thoughts of redheaded women, but rather visions of Cook's savory rabbit stew.

In the Greyhaven courtyard he dismounted and passed Pharaoh's reins to the young stable boy, Ian Moore. Snatching up the rabbits, he strode into the kitchen where Mary tended her fires.

"Maguire bid me deliver these to ye, Mary. If ye would, please take these bloody carcasses from me before the hounds attack."

Mary relieved Jamie of his burden, commenting succinctly as she did, "Aye, and I suppose ye have worked up a real appetite over at the neighbor's parlor, swilling Sir Eddie's fine port, seeing as how he willna drink real Irish whiskey."

Jamie guffawed, agreeing with Mary's assessment of Sir Edward. "Now Mary, ye know he secretly disdains of anything Irish. Ye should have seen the garb the man paraded in today."

Jamie pulled a face. "Could have frightened the birds from the trees, sure enough. But I always learn something from Sir Eddie. I shall have to recall how yellow with black stripes are fashionable next time I get a jacket made."

They laughed together while Jamie washed and dried his hands. "He offered again to buy Greyhaven for a princely sum. What say I take his offer," he said with a wink, "and we can all go away to a foreign land, leaving Greyhaven filled with naught but Irish whiskey for the man to choke on to the end of his days?"

"Nay, Milord," Mary said with a face of horror. "I have seen into the heart of that one, and 'tis black for sure. I canna go to me final rest leaving my beloved Greyhaven to the likes of him. My dear Harry would spin in his grave if Sir Eddie roamed the halls of Greyhaven. Aye, we make fun of Sir Eddie, but only because the man is so ugly inside, we canna understand him.

"I well remember the day he came and made an indecent proposal to yer mam before ye came back from the King's court. She turned him down flat, she did. He had barely gotten the words out when she turned around and told him to get out of her house."

Mary chuckled before straightening her face to a dour expression. "Yer mam is a great lady in her own right, Jamie, and to have common rabble the likes of Sir Eddie come into her own home and make a proposition like he did was an abomination.

"Sir Eddie took off out of here like a scalded hound with the Devil's own look on his face. He may act like nothing is amiss." She shook her head in sorrow. "I believe he holds a grudge. Watch out for that one, I say. He is a snake all right. You mark my word."

"I agree," Jamie answered. "The man bears watching and I will keep your warning close at heart. Sir Eddie lives among us but he can never be accepted. My fear is he returns the favor in kind ... and then some. I worry about what he wants to do with Greyhaven, such cannot be a pretty picture. We shall keep an eye on him. Now, about the evening meal, do ye promise me a fine rabbit stew?"

"Go on now, ye scoundrel, stew is coming, but not before ye go up and speak with yer mam. And change clothes before ye seek the lady's presence."

Jamie headed up to his chambers. Mary was right; his mother was a great lady and she had gambled much to keep Greyhaven for him. Even though he earned the new title of Earl of Greyhaven, he owed his mother for keeping the manor and lands in his absence.

Exiting his chamber cleaned and refreshed, Jamie went to find the Lady Kathleen. He approached the west tower and climbed the stairs to the top room. The room had great arched windows that filled the chamber with light from the south. The salon was his mother's favorite place in the entire manor.

Reaching the chamber, he saw her at the loom, working. "Good afternoon, Mother. How has this day been for you?" he said, standing at the threshold.

Lady Kathleen turned to see her son. Mother and son were cast from the same mold, both tall and lean with green eyes and black Irish hair as dark as midnight. She smiled at him and beckoned, "My son, the day has been exceptionally well, and is even better now I have your company. Come closer, Jamie, and share this afternoon light with me."

He came to her side and peered over her shoulder at the tapestry she was working on. "What is this, Milady? I see no St. Patrick casting out the snakes, nor St. George slaying the dragons. Tell me what you weave here, madam." He smiled, intrigued by his mother's mysterious talent with the loom.

Kathleen laughed lightly at her son's fierce look of concentration. "Nay, Jamie, if I tell you, where shall the surprise be? Such is the joy of the tapestry. Only the weaver knows the full picture until the piece is finished. I make this one especially for you, my son, and when the time is right you will know everything there is to know about the scene."

Giving him a slanted glance from beneath her lashes she added, "There is an event of tremendous importance coming to unfold in our lives. We shall see, very soon, if you are brave enough to ask again the full meaning of the tapestry."

With mock terror in his face Jamie begged, "Frighten me not, Milady. Tell me, or the secret of the tapestry shall haunt me 'til its completion. Sleep will allude me for wondering what you conjure on your magic loom."

Kathleen hugged her son and stepped back. "Tell me what you see now Jamie."

He peered closely. "I see the light blue of a daytime sky, yet with the moon and stars in attendance. But I cannot discern what this brightness is here," he said as he reached out to touch it. "You have placed the moon and stars beside the sun itself. Is that the riddle of the tapestry, Milady? Have you found a way to command the very heavens themselves into your own bidding?"

Kathleen looked away from the tapestry, lost on a distant scene. "If only I could," she whispered.

She turned back to him, her eyes brimming with mystery, or was that mischief he saw?

"I will tell you. Soon ... very soon, we shall see the tapestry's secret."

•

The Shaolin Academy of Arts, Bimthang, Nepal

Alex sat on a stone bench beneath the trees in the garden.

Four days passed since she had seen Master Chan. During that time she had thrown herself into a rigorous regimen of exercise, meditation and fasting. At first, so immersed inwardly, and with no clocks in the temple, she felt as though she had already stepped out of time.

But after four days, she was fiercely connected to the depths of her heart, feeling as though the wind blew through her soul. She held no connection to any schedule or routine. She was like ether, of no substance, existing with only one purpose—

Find Royce no matter what I must do.

Sensing movement, she opened her eyes.

Master Chan sat next to her, appearing without a sound. She felt comfort and security in his presence.

Without preamble he began.

"All creation has a primal purpose, a common journey, which is to return to its source.

"For humanity there is birth, life, and death, but for the soul there is infinity. With reincarnation, the experiences of many lives work to refine the soul so that it, too, may return to that place of its origin.

"Time is a factor created for this refinement process and has this basic rule: what once was, what is now, and what will be all exist together. The past, present, and future are quite interconnected.

"The soul travels these many lives collecting emotions. They may be positive or negative, and as such, carry the appropriately responding energies. This path is not easy for a soul as there are numerous obstacles along the way. These obstacles serve only one purpose, and that is to assist in refining the soul's emotions. For most, the journey is eternal.

"For some, refinement does come. This is true for very old souls who have been on their journey for many, many lives. You and Royce are an example of such a soul. For you to have been separated in this way indicates some event or a void must be altered to change the outcome of a path, or perhaps many paths, in this case.

"This void may exist in your life, or in Royce's. Perhaps it is pertaining to some event of which we have no knowledge. Or it may be a combination of all your lives, with only this exact moment in time holding the answer that will release all of you. I believe the solution to your problem is for you to erase this void.

"The future happens only after the past gets out of the way. You must go back to the time this void occurred and make a correction. This, my child, is what you would call your destiny. You have been chosen for this because you alone are uniquely qualified to accomplish this task. Only then, when you have served your destiny, will you and Royce be able to return to the current path. With this action, child, you embrace your destiny and ensure your future."

Alex had prepared herself to expect anything. Considering they were discussing a man born hundreds of years ago, the thought of time travel had crossed her mind. But considering it, and discussing her going, were two different things. She swallowed hard, not knowing what to say.

"Certainly, you have questions," Chan said. He looked at her expectantly.

Alex felt her eyebrows lift with concern, but she couldn't decide what words to choose. The first most obvious question was, "How Long?'"

But she knew that answer ... when bidness was finished.

What is the bidness?

"Save Jamie?" she whispered.

"Yes," Chan answered.

"And I save all?" she added. She thought of the portrait in California that looked like so much like her—and a chill settled down her spine.

What will be required of me to save Jamie?

She inhaled deeply, held the breath, and exhaled through pursed lips. At last she asked, "How?"

Chan pulled something from one of the hidden pockets within his robes. The object glittered and flashed brightly. She whispered, "Oh ..."

"You understand there is much ancient technology," Chan said. "Technology modern man is unwilling to understand."

Alex felt her mouth go dry. She hoped time travel came with a first class. She nodded for him to continue.

"I cannot tell you where this technology originated, only that within our most ancient of documents there is a diagram of this device." He passed the object to her.

The gold was heavy in her hand, but it was the most curious concoction of holes that made her think—

Why, it looks like ...

"A whistle," she said. "This is your ancient technology?" She turned the gold over in her hand, feeling it grow warm with her touch. Tentatively, she put what looked like a mouthpiece to her lips.

"No," Chan instructed, quickly reclaiming the device. He held it tightly in both hands. "There is some preparation."

Thinking she might be loosing her mind, Alex felt a giggle come to life. She suppressed it with considerable effort. "Of course," she said. "Preparation."

What am I getting myself into?

Suddenly, all her bravado left.

"Save Jamie, save Royce, save all," she chanted. "Save Jamie, save Royce ... save all."

So how does my being in Ireland in 1612 save Jamie? And who exactly are the "all" I must save?

She put her hands to her face, overwhelmed with questions.

I have no clue what I am supposed to do to save James Roy. But seeing as how this apparently is my only option ... I will go, however events play out.

"What do I need to do?" she asked.

"This device, a whistle as you call it, can access a portal through the timeless dimension back to the time you need. Your travel and direction is guided by your mind, your thoughts and emotional energy, your desire and intention."

He gave her a look of admiration and respect. "I would not give this device to just anyone. Only a mind highly trained and focused could successfully use this ... whistle. Knowing you, I am not surprised you have been chosen for such an adventure."

Alex choked back a complaint and waved her hand to ward off any compliments. She had yet to accomplish the mission. Finally she asked the only question left. "When? When do I go?"

"Before the morrow's dawn, come to my quarters. We will go then to a place where none can see us. Prepare yourself this evening, my child."

Alex spent the rest of the evening in her small room, deep in meditation to calm her excitement. As the bedtime bells rang, she lay down on her pallet, certain she would lay awake all night. She could not allow the enormity of what she embarked upon to enter her mind. The point of no return was long behind her, so she closed her eyes, seeking sleep.

A moment of stillness, and she slipped into unconsciousness.

The dream was a joyous collage of light and love.

In an ethereal place of no time, no substance, no motion, she was without a body, in a pure essence form. Another mind came near and she reached out, knowing this was Royce. The two combined into a form that knew no boundaries. She was complete, having come home at last. Peace, joy, and contentment infused her heart, giving her strength. Her resolve firmed and settled. She would go because this was the only way to free them from karma and bring Royce back.

Alex woke refreshed. She bathed from a bowl of water and donned her student's attire from the temple. Feeling her modern clothes inappropriate, she had nothing else to wear.

Dawn was still far off when she made her way to Chan's quarters. She raised her hand to knock when his voice called out, "Come in."

She entered, and Chan rose from his seat. A smile lit his face and the excitement glittering in his eyes was impossible to miss.

You would think he was the one going.

"What has you so pleased this early in the day?" she asked.

He passed her one of several packages from the table.

She took the paper wrapped package while eyeing the ones remaining. "What have you done?"

"Something to help you along the way," he said.

She tore open the paper. "Oh!" She pulled out a green long skirt, a white blouse and a leather vest. Undergarments followed, along with leather slippers and silk hose. "How did you get this so fast?" A memory sparked and she looked at his desk where a modern hard copy of *The Three Musketeers* lay. She and Royce had given him the lavishly illustrated book many years ago.

He pushed the other packages toward her. "Here are two more change of clothes for you," he said, smiling with obvious glee. A leather satchel was brought out. "All should fit in here for the trip."

She held up the clothes and saw the fit was decent. A smile tugged at her lips.

Chan nodded to a silk room-partition where she could change in privacy. Behind the screen, she dropped her simple cotton trousers and slipped into a chemise and silk drawers.

Where did he get the idea for these?

She stifled a giggle. The skirt fastened with buttons, and the leather vest fit snug beneath her breasts, making her chest feel excessively on display. A leather belt with an attached pouch finished the costume.

She smoothed her hands over the foreign clothing.

What the hell do I think I'm doing here?

Something extraordinary, something very few women could accomplish, came the quiet answer from within.

"Bidness," she murmured. "Momma Bear got bidness to do." She unwrapped the other packages, folded her student attire and placed all the clothing in the satchel. She stepped out from behind the screen. "How do I look?"

Chan looked up from the illustration on the back cover of *The Three Musketeers* and smiled. "You look perfect. You'll fit right in."

"We'll see how long that lasts." She opened the pouch on her belt and pulled out several gold coins.

"Mad money," Chan said.

"Ba ha!" Alex blurted. When she was fifteen and getting ready for her first date, her mother slipped her ten dollars. "In case it doesn't go well—you know, mad money—so you can get home." Alex placed the coins back in the pouch, nonetheless comforted by their heavy presence.

They left from a side door, silently passing down one long, narrow corridor after another, until they reached the garden. A few steps more and they came to a small gate in the back wall.

"Here," Chan said. He drew keys from a pocket and

stuck a skeleton key into the gate's lock. With barely a whisper, the lock's tumblers shifted, and he pushed through the gate swinging on silent hinges. "Come," he called.

Alex stepped though. "As long as we've been coming here, I never knew about this," she whispered. Beyond the gate was another garden, smaller, overgrown, silent and dark. She shivered as the cool air greeted her exposed chest.

"From the old days," Chan said. "Now, mostly forgotten as you can see." He stepped though an overgrowth of lilac tree and held the vegetation aside for her. Beyond was the garden's center, a clearing with a small statue of the Buddha and a pond long abandoned and gone dry. "We cannot be seen here, unless by satellite camera," he said, pointing straight up.

She looked up at the pre-dawn sky, feeling a disconnect settle around her. Where she was going there were no satellites, no TV, no cell phones.

A sudden panic filled her. *No cell phones!* How would she contact … anyone?

"You must not worry," Chan said, seeing her alarm. "Remember what Royce told you, that he is always with you. Have faith in his words, he would not have spoken this were it not true."

Alex nodded and sucked in the sharp mountain air. The night was still dark, and the sky yet glittered with the stars above, which, like her, were the creation of a higher power. She knew this.

She clung to the belief no matter where she was in all of existence this higher power was with her. And Royce, he was with her, too. She knew as much from her dream in California. Stiffening her back, she said, "I'm ready.

What do I do?"

He looked at her calm face and pulled out the gold device. He had placed it on a plain leather strip to go around her neck.

"In truth this does look like a whistle," he said. "But this device creates a certain vibration, and that vibration is the key that opens the portal for travel.

"By blowing the whistle, you will initiate an opening and you must prepare to be drawn into the timeless dimension. To control your path in and out of this dimension, focus on the person, place, and time of your destination. This is very critical, my child, for without this you will have no guidance and you will end up somewhere helter-skelter. Fix in your mind the name of the one you seek, together with the place where you must go, and the date in time you desire. Remember: name, place, and date. Do not waiver in your intent, Alex. You must commit to this with a master's skill."

She nodded, making the connection between Chan's instructions and cutting edge quantum theory, where the frequency of thoughts and emotions affect the behavior of matter, time and space via the electric universe. She looked wondrously at this fantastic man who appeared so simple, yet knew so much. Listening closely, she noted his instructions.

"Entering the timeless dimension you will experience some turbulence, a sense of disorientation, as though falling, but there is no pain. Do not be frightened because you are not actually falling. This is simply how your earthly senses perceive your movement through this dimension.

"This is the way you will go through time, and thus how you will return. Remember the focus and never loose your device for it is your only key. Do you understand these directions? Have you any other questions?"

Alex closed her eyes and breathed deeply. This was all about her strength and determination, and her faith in the unknown. For the briefest moment she quaked inside and wanted to bolt, but a soothing presence came to her. She heard Royce's voice as he said, "I am here, my love. I am with you … always with you."

She calmed her riotous thoughts and opened her eyes. "I am ready now."

With that Chan stepped back several feet and nodded, his eyes conveying to her great love, strength, and conviction … and no small portion of respect.

She placed the strap on the satchel over her head and across one shoulder. The whistle's leather strip was around her neck and she clutched the device tightly in her hands. She closed her eyes for several deep breaths. One, two, three. She felt the calm descend over her. Needing a final look, she peeked from one eye.

Chan nodded encouragement. "Blow on the device and keep blowing." The he smiled and waved as if she boarded a train.

She closed her eye tightly. All thoughts of Chan slipped away, replaced by a vision of the man on horseback. She slowed her breath and began counting down with successive deep exhalations, going into alpha and then delta levels of the mind.

Three, two, one—

A deep calm spread over her as her mind grew still. She posted the vision of Jamie McNeill on the screen of her mind and silently began the mantra: *James Roy McNeill, Ireland, 1612.* Cementing her focus through long practiced technique, she then took a deep breath and began blowing on the device. "James Roy McNeill, Ireland, 1612," she chanted aloud. "James Roy McNeill, Ireland, 1612."

She inhaled deeply and blew the gold device again with all her breath again and again and again. First she felt vertigo fill her ears and fought the desire to lurch for balance. Her eyes were tightly shut, for she didn't want to see.

"James Roy McNeill, Ireland, 1612."

And suddenly, she was falling, falling, falling—

As Chan watched, the hills that had begun to lighten with the coming dawn suddenly darkened. Quickly the air started moving, and below the chaos came a roaring sound and a quick boom of thunder. Chan looked down and saw the hairs rise up on the back of his fingers as a flash of bright green light followed the thunder.

When he looked up, all was still again. He was alone, waving at an empty space.

CHAPTER FIVE

Asked by the Wind:
Who are you? Where do you come from?
Do you dare to ride your dreams?

Greyhaven Lands, Ireland 1612

"What a fine and glorious day to be Irish," said Maguire, as he and Connor stopped their horses for a drink at the pond.

Connor lifted his young face to the sun and sniffed the soft morning breeze. "Yes, Uncle, 'tis a fine day. Do ye think those vixen will show today?"

"Aye, I do. We shall find something today; I feel it in my bones. Twas' Irish luck indeed ye saw them out in the meadow. Come on then, lad."

The two nudged their horses away from the sweet grasses around the pond and set off over the rolling and wooded hills on Greyhaven's southeast side.

The spring had been mild and the wealth and promise of summer was rich across the land. Crops planted early were robust with fields already green. Across the hillsides the maple, oak, and elm were well fleshed out with early summer leaves. Birds of all kinds flitted from branch to branch and the air was busy with their lively song. In the meadows left unplanted for grazing, wild flowers bloomed in great splashes of color.

They aimed for a meadow well east of the pond, and the land in between rolled gently. At the crest of each hill they stopped and searched for the vixen before going down into the next flowing vale.

The riding was pleasant work, their horses snatching at their bits to grab sweet grasses and flowers. Overhead, not a cloud was in the sky.

At the crest of one hill, Connor asked, "Uncle, do ye think my papa really loves me?"

Seeing the wistful look on the boy's face, Maguire's heart constricted in his chest. Connor was a good lad, but quiet and unsure of himself. Being the Earl's son was hard for the boy.

The Lady Kathleen, God bless her for being there for all of them, had stepped up gladly to care for the lad. Maguire knew raising Connor was her second chance to raise a son. It was Connor's father that shone in the boy's eyes like stars in the night sky. But the immense persona that was the Earl of Greyhaven was very intimidating to the boy.

"Ye know he does, son, he just has a hard time showing how he feels, just as you have a hard time showing him ye love him in return. Just between us, I can tell ye he once asked me the same about you."

He saw the doubt in Connor's eyes as he shook his head, disbelieving. "Do ye tell me true, Uncle?"

Solemnly Maguire nodded in the affirmative. He would do anything to see this family right, even if it meant telling a slight fib. Jamie had once asked Maguire the same question about his son.

"Aye, laddie. I tell ye, but only in extreme confidence, because I know you to be a man who can keep a secret. Yer da loves ye dearly son. Never doubt how much he cares."

"Thank ye, Uncle Robbie. I will keep in confidence what we have said." Connor turned his head to their left and pointed, indicating the hills just a few minutes ride away. "That way, Uncle. 'Tis where I saw the foxes. Come."

Turning his pony, the young boy cantered down the next hill with Maguire following his lead. They slowed their mounts to a walk, not wanting to startle any game they may come across. At the foot of the vale their horses stopped in mid stride, suddenly alert, with ears pricked forward across the hill.

Perhaps they smell the foxes, thought Maguire.

Sitting silently, with their breath held and heads tilted in that direction, they paused, horse and rider alike, listening. Presently a faint sound, unlike anything Maguire had ever heard before came on a sudden breeze kicked up from nowhere. He felt pressure in his head, and he and Connor both put their hands over their ears.

Beyond the crest of the next hill, the air grew dark as dusk on a cloudy day. Mystified, Maguire looked up and saw not one cloud overhead. Connor was still rubbing both his ears when a bright green flash came that made the horses dance, followed by a loud clap of thunder.

Maguire calmed his horse and saw the hair on his bare arm lift straight up. He and Connor looked at each other. Maguire knew not what to say. Connor's eyebrows arched far over bulging eyes. Wordlessly they cantered to the top of the hill.

"Do ye think the wee leprechauns are working magic?" Connor whispered.

At the top of the hill, they looked down. Maguire saw no wee leprechauns at all. Instead, there was a beautiful lady sitting in a field of flowers. Her red hair stood out, surrounding her face with a red halo. She held something gold in her hand. Her eyes were squeezed tightly shut, and she softly whispered something over and over. They edged closer and heard her voice.

"James Roy McNeill, Ireland, 1612 ..."

Maguire was dumbfounded. He looked to the lad, and the boy's expression was bright as daytime.

Connor spoke with a confidence born of seeing a miracle. "Uncle Robbie, look. 'Tis an angel lady, and she is come from the heavens to see us!" He grinned ear to ear with childish wonder.

"Aye, laddie, I believe ye may be right." Maguire could not refute the boy's claim. "She is lovely, even with her fine red Irish hair all sticking straight out."

He examined the angel lady whose eyes were still closed as she chanted the Earl's name. Glancing about, he saw no tracks through the flowers to where the lady sat.

Scratching his head, he looked up at the sky. Slowly, his grin began to spread. His shoulders lifted with glee. *'Tis more than I could have asked.*

•

Alex was falling, falling, falling. Pressure and a roar filled her ears and she dared not open an eye. She forced herself not to scream.

Without any impact, she was suddenly still. She felt

terra firma under her. She opened one eye.

Flowers.

Whew ... I didn't land in water.

She opened her other eye and saw a man and a boy on horseback. She tried to speak, but her vocal cords failed.

"Lassie, are ye all right? Are ye hurt in any way?" the man asked.

"James Roy McNeill. I must find him. Is he near here?" she croaked. When he answered, "Aye", she gasped. That she had traveled time and landed in the right place made her giddy with incredible relief.

Let's get this done. I have a life to return to.

Alex stood and brushed off her clothes. When she put her hands to her hair, she gasped. "Good heavens."

"Is that where you came from?" the boy asked.

Surprised at the boy's question, she looked up and realized what they were thinking. "Oh," she whispered.

Now what?

She thought of Chan's hopes that her costume would give her a chance to fit in, and squelched a chuckle.

Oh boy. Here I am outed before I got a chance to fit in.

"I'm Alexandra," she said. "But please, call me Alex. And no, I didn't come from heaven. Who are you?"

The boy looked disappointed, but eagerly offered, "Connor is my name, and the man you seek is my da."

She looked at the man accompanying the boy and smiled, prompting him. Abruptly he seemed to come from deep in his thoughts.

"Maguire, at you service," he blurted, smiling broadly. "Can ye ride, lass?"

"Yes," Alex answered. She took a tentative step, then another and felt her legs solid enough.

"Connor, give the lass your pony," Maguire instructed. "You come ride with me."

When Connor was seated with Maguire, Alex stepped into the stirrup and threw her leg over the pony's back to ride astraddle. "Ready," she announced. She glanced up, again catching the shock on their faces.

They'll just have to get used to me, she thought. She motioned them to lead and set the pony to keep up.

They soon cantered into a courtyard. Maguire made to help Alex from the pony, but she was already dismounted. She handed him the reins.

Connor jumped to the ground and immediately announced with childish excitement, "Mam will want to know about this." With that said, the boy was off and gone like a shot.

The two adults stared after the boy's quickly receding figure and then turned to face each other.

"I —"

"Ye—"

They both spoke at the same time and then chuckled.

Maguire asked, "If I might say, ye look as though ye could use a wee drink and a bite to eat. Will ye be staying with us here at Greyhaven for a bit, Lady Alex?"

Pensively, Alex looked around at the expanse of the Manor and its courtyard. She was being presumptuous, perhaps, but she had, after all, traveled four hundred years to get here. She hadn't met the Lord of Greyhaven yet, but she figured she would be here an indeterminate length of time.

Turning back to Maguire, she looked him clearly in the eye. "Yes, I believe I will be staying here for a while, if I am welcome, that is."

Maguire seemed pleased at her declaration. "Aye, lassie, Lady Alex, I mean. I believe you shall be welcome, very welcome indeed. I look forward verra' much to introducing ye to our lord Jamie. Come along now and we can show ye to Cook. A fine mug of cool ale on a warm day should set ye right. Jamie is out looking about the crop fields just now, but he should be returning soon. Come, and I can see ye get settled."

Alex was presented to Cook, and was whisked into a seat at a great table in the huge kitchen; a flurry of activity followed. Next came a mug of ale with a fresh baked pie, smelling, Alex sniffed, like beef and vegetables. A slice of hard cheese finished the meal.

She removed the satchel from around her neck and placed it on the table, eyeing the food with serious intent. When she broke open the crust on the pie, a plume of steam carried a savory scent.

Seeing she was in good hands, Maguire left the kitchen and headed up the stairs of the west tower to find Kathleen. She would no doubt be interested to see their visitor.

Reaching the uppermost chamber, he found her with the boy, who was telling the story so fast Maguire doubted Kathleen could unravel the words.

He entered the solar and stood behind Connor, his eyes meeting Kathleen's over the boy's head as the story was finished in one long sentence.

"So, Mam, an angel lady came to see Da!" Connor announced with a great gulp of air.

"Connor," Maguire said, taking the boy by the shoulders and turning him toward the doorway. "Will ye go down to the courtyard and tend the horses. I see young Ian is nowhere to be found, as usual, and the beasties need proper care. Go along now so I can talk to yer mam. Give the horses a small ration of grain while you are there. And remember to wash up when ye finish."

Connor nodded in agreement to all of Maguire's instructions, then turned to kiss his mam on the cheek before bolting through the chamber door. At the sounds of the young boy tearing headlong down the stone staircase, Kathleen grimaced.

Maguire rubbed his face, listening to Connor's flight down the stairs. Hearing no sound of the boy's tragic fall, he asked, "Did you understand what he was saying?"

She seemed not to hear his question. Instead, she walked to her loom and quietly resumed her steady work, weaving and pressing as though nothing had happened.

A prickle of goose bumps ran across the back of Maguire's neck. "Yer not surprised at all, are ye?"

Kathleen continued, nonplussed as she worked at her loom.

Maguire softly asked, "I take this to mean you have had one of yer visions, and the lady we found today is no news to ye." He was well aware of Kathleen's 'sight', for she had saved them and Greyhaven many times during the long years of war and turmoil.

She motioned to him over her shoulder, drawing his attention to her work. "Come, see a vision I had when Jamie was still a babe."

Maguire stepped up to join her before the loom. As he gazed at the work his breath caught in his throat. "Milady!"

A light blue sky curiously held the moon and stars, along with the brightness of the sun. Below, within a field of flowers walked a woman with red hair and green eyes. She was none other than their guest, Alex, the angel lady.

•

"Okay," Alex groused. "Where can a girl go pee?"

The directions she got to the 'necessary' room from Mary were delivered in such a heavy brogue Alex had no idea what the woman said.

What have I got myself into?

"Here," she grumbled, opening a wood and thatch door. Inside and around the corner she came to a bare room but for a table with a bowl and pitcher next to a stack of small towels. On the floor were two lids that looked like a pair of toilets without the seat. "A hole in the floor, just like India. Probably would be easier if I weren't wearing so many clothes."

Afterward, she washed her hands and tossed the dirty water down one of the holes, grateful for this much sanitation. Exiting, she speculated on where she was. Each direction she looked gave her another long corridor. She chose one and set out. "Well, let's see what Greyhaven has that requires my special talents."

The long stone hallways were covered with colorful carpets that ran the full length of the hallway in one piece, some fifty feet or more. Small side tables with candles punctuated the corridor, and there were several closed, large wooden doors. She stepped to one and pushed on the oversized handle. The room was a bedroom, done in light greens and deep purple. Alex sniffed spice and roses, and spied hairbrushes on a vanity table. Feeling an intruder, she closed the door.

After another long hallway, and another, and another, she began to feel like a rat in a maze. "Come on, got bidness to do," she complained. She picked up her pace, and soon was running. She reached up to pull her hair back out of her eyes as she rounded a corner and—

"Ooph," she grunted as she bounced off a large figure. Caught unawares, she landed on her rear on the carpet in a graceless tangle of long skirt.

A tall man similarly rebounded off the wall, and fell against one of the tables, scattering candles across the carpet. He bellowed out, "What in hell?"

"Good lord, man, don't you look where you're going?" Alex charged. Her legs seemed tangled in her long skirt and she tugged, trying to get her feet under her. She looked up from the floor, and her breath caught in her throat.

It's—

Royce was on the tip of her tongue, but this man was not Royce. He glared down at her. To her utter disbelief, he started yelling.

"God's teeth, woman, I could say the same to you! Who are you? What are you up to, sneaking about my manor?"

Alex jerked her skirt straight, deciding quickly ...

Not Royce.

"Lost yer tongue, have ye?" he growled. He towered over her, his hands planted on his hips and an inhospitable glare on his face.

She was unprepared for the hard line of his lips.

I traveled four hundred years for this?

Her indignation was short lived, for other emotions crowded quickly around her heart. She was equally unprepared for the love welling up at the sight of his familiar face. She wanted—

"Well?" he bellowed. "What are ye doing here?"

Alex put her lips in a hard line to match those of the lord of the manor. He reached down and grabbed her by the wrist. She let him help her to stand. Once she was upright, she tugged on his arm, pulling him off balance. She quickly pivoted, stepped back, and delivered a kick to the backside of his knee, buckling his leg.

He landed on all fours with a grunt of surprise.

She spun on her heel and left him. Sprinting down the long hallway, she slipped around the corner without looking back.

Fine, she thought. *Let him get used to that!*

At the end of the hallway she ducked through a doorway and into a stairwell. She bounded up the stone steps until she was breathless, wanting air, wanting light, wanting to be home with her husband, not rattling around this castle on a mystery mission to save a jerk.

She saw sunlight, and entered a room.

"Do come in, my dear," a woman's voice called.

The room was on the top floor, filled with large, arched windows, their shutters open to the summer air. A woman with black hair and green eyes that echoed the lord of the manor sat before a great loom.

Alex approached.

The woman rose and extended a hand in greeting. "I am Kathleen, Jamie's mother. Please come in; you have travelled far this day."

Alex tried to answer, but she seemed to have trouble with her own name. "A ... uh ... My ... my name is Alex," she stuttered. In Kathleen's eyes, Alex saw wisdom, strength ... and mystery, reminding her of Master Chan. But most of all, she saw warmth. "I am pleased to meet you, Kathleen." She gazed around the room, admiring the many tapestries that covered the walls of stone.

"So, you have met Jamie."

The tone of Kathleen's voice made the words less a question and more a statement, as if she already knew of their meeting. "Yes, I met ... Jamie, I believe. He looks like you, am I right?"

At Kathleen's smile of encouragement, Alex added with wry humor, "I don't think I made his Christmas list." She wasn't ready to reveal how she had left the lord of the manor.

Kathleen smiled, her eyes lighting with humor. "I knew you would be different. This shall be most interesting." She grasped Alex's hand, and her pale skin was smooth and warm, comforting. "Do not judge him by this first meeting. With time, I think you will see some of his finer points. Will you stay here with me for a while, that I may learn more about you?"

More like discover what you don't already know, Alex thought. She shrugged with determination. "Bidness, just focus on bidness," she mumbled under her breath. As she gazed past Kathleen, her eyes finally came to rest on the piece in progress on the loom.

"Oh my God." A chill ran down her spine as she walked to the loom. She touched the tapestry where a woman walked in a field of flowers ... a woman with green eyes and gold and red hair.

"That's me!"

•

James Roy McNeill, Earl of Greyhaven, examined the carpet from his position on all fours. Candles were scattered about, the side table was askew … and a twitch of laughter bubbled to his lips. "Ha!" he shouted out. "Ha ha—" He sat back on his haunches.

"Lord in heaven, she is magnificent." He stood and righted the table against the wall, retrieved the candles and set them upright. "I ha' never seen such glorious hair." He chuckled with the memory. "And she put me to the ground with just a wee kick."

Who is she? Why is she here?

This thought was immediately disturbed by—

Why does she seem familiar?

He turned and strode off to the kitchen, shouting, "Maguire!"

Downstairs, Jamie burst into the kitchen. "There ye are." His steward was pushed back from the table with a mug in his hand.

Jamie sat across from his steward. "Who is she?"

Cook stifled a snicker and turned away as Maguire looked up from his ale with a smug face and arched eyebrows.

"She? … Milord? And who might ye be referring to, sir?"

"I am not in the mood for games, Maguire. The little minx, whoever she is, just booted me to the ground. I want to know who she is and where she came from," he demanded.

"Ah, the little redheaded lass Connor and I found out in the wildflower meadow this morning. Well, her name is Alexandra, but her friends call her Alex. She is come from the heavens above, Milord, even though she denies it, and she has come here for you," Maguire said. He took a drink of his ale and set his mug down, a challenge in his eye.

"Aye, Maguire, but what do ye mean she came from the heavens? Tell me now, where is she from?" Jamie prodded.

At that moment, Connor entered the kitchen. To Jamie's amazement the lad came straight to him.

"Tis true as Uncle says, Da. We found her sitting in the field of wildflowers out past the pond this morning. We were looking to set traps for the foxes when the sky turned dark, and there was lightning and thunder without any clouds, and our hair stood up! We went over the hill, and there she was a pretty angel lady, and she was asking for you. She is an angel lady, and she came from the heavens to see you, Da."

Jamie was astonished. What had emboldened the lad? Before he could wonder at what brought such a change in the boy, his alarm was raised by the wild tale. They were all grinning at him like fools. Finally, he thought, *what I have long feared has finally happened— my entire house has gone mad.*

Looking over to his steward and good friend, he asked, "What is this story Connor tells?"

"Tis true as the lad tells it, Jamie," answered Maguire. "The lass appeared to have fallen straight out of the sky, just like Connor says. And any fool could look at her face and hear her lovely voice, and know she is an angel. Ask Kathleen what she knows."

Jamie felt goose bumps race down his arms. Where his mother was concerned, mysteries often arose. "All right, we shall see what the Lady has to say." Turning on his heel, he set off to the west tower to find his mother. What he discovered was even more disconcerting.

He found his mother and the angel lady descending the stairs arm-in-arm, chatting like old friends. He stepped aside to allow them passage, listening to the tinkling of their voices as they laughed and whispered.

They passed him by, but stopped suddenly as his mother turned to call him, "Jamie you are gawking, Milord. I have informed Maeve to put Alex's belongings in the room below yours in the east tower. We want her comfortable while she is here."

She promptly turned about, and with Alex firmly in tow they left him in the stairwell. His last glimpse of the lovely angel lady was of her green eyes looking back at him over her shoulder.

Jamie entered the solar and noticed his mother's loom. He approached, for much had been added since he last saw the piece. He edged closer, suddenly frightened.

I do not want to know.

There amongst the sun and the moon and the stars, was a woman surrounded by a field of flowers. Her hair was red with golden highlights, and her skin was tawny, unlike the popular pale skin so sought after by the women he knew.

Carefully he touched the figure, hesitant for he feared the flame of her hair would burn him right from the cloth. At contact with the silken fibers, there was indeed heat as he suspected. A searing wave of wanting and desire, of desperation and surrender—all came rushing, not from his fingertip, but from his heart.

"Yes," he whispered. "You would set fire to my very soul."

Suddenly, the thrill from their first encounter withered. He no longer wanted to know who she was, where she came from, and why she was here. Her very presence had the power to destroy his carefully structured life.

He pulled his hand back and turned away from the tapestry. Setting his mouth in his customary grim line, he marched from the room.

"Well," he growled. "Sorry to disappoint, but we canna have such a fire."

CHAPTER SIX

Baptist Sermon:
The trouble with trouble is it usually starts as fun.

Greyhaven Estate, Next Morning

In the early morning, Jamie brought his horse from the barn. "First I find where she came from, then I know where to send her back," he grumbled. "Back is where she must go. I canna have her here.

"Shall we see where the lass landed?" he asked his horse. Pharaoh nodded in agreement, and Jamie pulled the cinch tight on the saddle. "I think the story is malarkey," he added.

"'Tis not malarkey," Connor protested. "And you canna send her back."

Jamie jumped in his skin. Chagrined, he exclaimed, "Connor, son, you scared yer da." He looked over his shoulder to see the boy just inside the barn. "What are ye doing out here?"

"I would go with ye, to see where we found her," Connor said. He walked back into the barn and returned with his pony already saddled. "I knew you would want to go." He mounted and turned to face his father. With a steady look, he added, "But you canna send her back." A straight back and a sure seat on the pony displayed his determination in this announcement.

Jamie was stunned. His shy son was revealing himself to be surprisingly astute, and stiffer in the spine than Jamie expected. Was this sudden behavior an aspect of the insanity plaguing his family? Or was it the woman Alex's influence?

He shrugged, intrigued.

Connor led the way. They rode silently.

Nearing their destination, Connor called, "Stay with me, and you will see."

Jamie gave his son a slanted glance, but rode side-by-side with him. At the crest of the final hill they stopped; he looked down into the next vale.

A field of flowers bloomed in a riot of colors. In the center of the field, a circle of the flowers were flattened; he could see some of them lifting back up. Outside the circle of flattened flowers there was not one sign of passage. His and Connor's horses stood in the same trampled area that Connor and Maguire's horses occupied the day before.

Pointing, Connor said, "There ye see where she walked up to join us." When Jamie gave no immediate response, Connor probed. "Well?"

Jamie looked from the clear signs on the ground to the sky. "Well—" he started, scratching his head.

"Well?" Connor pressed.

Jamie wondered at the boy's grit this morning. "Well," he began again, clearing his throat. "I see how you would—"

"See her as an angel from the heavens?" Connor offered.

Jamie squirmed in his saddle. *This cannot be the answer. If she came from heaven, how do I send her back?* He shook his head, denying what he could not disprove, wanting to deny what he felt, needing to deny what he feared most.

"She canna stay," he stated.

"Why not?" Connor argued.

Astonished, Jamie drew back to examine his son. The two had spoken more this morning than in the last six months. "Ye like her, do ye?"

"Aye," Connor answered. "She is special, and she came here for us." Connor wrinkled his young face in consternation. "What do ye have against her, Da?"

Jamie turned his gaze back to the flowers where the angel lady first appeared. Was she an angel?

More likely a she-devil come to set us all afire.

Jamie thought of the losses his family had suffered these last years. This pain warred with his insane desire to bury his face in her hair.

Aye, he thought, *we will all burn in hell.*

He felt himself drawn in against his wishes. As with a riptide, he knew it was best to go with the flow ... for now.

"I have nothing against her, son. Perhaps you are right, and she is here for us."

They returned the way they came, the still morning broken only by Connor's chatter about the angel lady. "I know she is special, Da. One day you will know, too."

As they approached the barn, Jamie first heard the scream of a horse, followed by a great deal of excited voices. He cantered in, stopped and dismounted next to Maguire.

Ian the stable boy was backed into a corner stall with

a large roan gelding threatening him with bared teeth. The horse had lost its rope and stood, sides quivering and eyes rolling wide in fear.

Jamie started to go to the boy's rescue.

Maguire stopped him. "Wait."

From the shadows, Alex walked out, talking softly to the horse, walking in a wide circle, and drawing the animal's attention from the cornered stable boy.

"Come on, Blue boy, there's no one here going to hurt you, just be easy … that's it, over here. Good boy, good boy."

The horse flicked his ears back and forth, listening, calming at the sound of her voice. He took a step her way, head dipping, eyes down, stepping softly.

"That's my boy, come on, come on in," Alex spoke softly. She brought one hand up and the horse lifted its head, sniffing her flesh. She stepped closer and stroked the big jawbone, slipping her hand up to scratch behind one ear.

Ian saw his chance, and edged out of the stall and darted from the barn. He ran to hide behind Connor, who watched from behind his father.

"Watch," Maguire whispered.

Alex brought her other hand up carefully with a length of rope. She rested this hand atop the horse's head while her other hand came up the opposite side and slowly brought the end of the rope down. She whispered to the large animal, and he nuzzled her shoulder.

"We're okay now," she called out quietly.

"Have ye ever seen such a touch?" Maguire asked.

Jamie kept his eyes on Alex and the horse, ignoring his steward, but he clearly understood Maguire's pointed meaning. Clearing his throat, he asked, "Can ye handle him, lass?"

She walked out with the horse beside her. The length of rope was looped around the animal's head, but Jamie could see the horse had no desire to leave her side.

"Ye have a way with the beastie, I see," Jamie said.

She looked at him, and he finally noticed what she was wearing: snug pants that contoured her bottom, along with her blouse from yesterday and the leather vest, causing her breasts to—

He gasped and broke from his thoughts, feeling the heat of all eyes upon him. Maguire nudged him in the ribs.

"She should have a horse to ride," the steward said.

This was announced matter-of-fact, along with Maguire's eyebrows waggling in some coded message Jamie could not decipher. He frowned, fearing again he was watching his family go insane. At last he understood Maguire's intent. "Of course, would you like him to ride, if you are able to handle him, of course?"

Jamie cringed, hearing how he repeated himself. Maguire pulled back, looking at Jamie as though he was the insane one. At Jamie's side, Connor pulled insistently on his coat, shaking his head 'yes', while behind him the stable boy eagerly added his support.

In the midst of this clamor, Jamie dared to look into those mesmerizing green eyes. When she spoke, her voice caused silence to drop over them.

"I think we know each other," she said softly. The horse proved her words by giving her a soft push, ears flickering, the beast's expressive eyes seeming to show an interest in the conversation.

Jamie had seen enough battle to know when to call a retreat. While he would not admit defeat, he did have to concede there was nowhere to send her. Added to this, his son, along with his steward and his mother, seemed greatly enamored of the chit. Truth be told, even he held a desire to know more. He exhaled, feeling himself being swept aside.

She can stay for now. But she canna have my heart.

"Then the horse is at your disposal," he announced. Needing to assert his wishes, he added tersely, "While you are here."

He turned and walked off, not daring to look anyone in the eye.

One Week Later

"What do they do?" Jamie asked.

From the west tower windows of his mother's solar, he watched Alex and Connor enter the courtyard, their two heads close as they talked. They acted like brother and sister.

Connor had been Alex's constant companion since her arrival, and he insisted on referring to her as the angel lady. Much to Jamie's dismay, she managed to be everywhere he looked.

Yet, since their second meeting her first day, on the stairwell of this very tower, Jamie had not had one opportunity to be alone with the angel lady.

She was everywhere, but always out of reach.

Like now, he thought, as he watched his son laughing with her. The two were returning from some mysterious activity they did each afternoon after Alex completed her morning duties.

"Every day they go out in that strange outfit, and return all sweaty and boisterous. It is a mystery," he said.

He shrugged his shoulders and turned away from the window.

Kathleen sat at her loom, weaving the base for a new tapestry. "You could join them," she said. "I believe they would take to your company."

Jamie saw the teasing smile on his mother's face. She obviously knew much he did not, and her aptitude for mystery was a constant worry for him.

"If you would know more about our guest," Kathleen said, "Spend more time in her presence. I have a gift I would like you to present to her at the evening meal." She followed this with a too-bright smile reminding him why he worried about her. He left her to her weaving and her secrets.

Later, when Jamie entered the Great Hall for the evening meal, Connor and Alex were already seated at the table, whispering as though they harbored a great secret.

Jamie sat at the head of the table to their left, oddly feeling a little left out. "Well, Milady, you seem to have settled into our home with ease. I must thank you for the time you spend with my son. He blooms under your tutelage. I wonder what bewitchment you work here at Greyhaven."

"No bewitchment," Alex replied. "Only sharing what I know. I was a teacher, in a sense, before I came here." She smiled at Connor, who sat next to her on her right, his young face beaming his obvious adoration.

Jamie had it on his tongue to ask her what this teaching involved, when Kathleen entered.

"Good evening, Connor, Jamie." She took her seat on Jamie's left.

"Mother," Jamie nodded. He saw the glint in her eye

and knew she was up to something. Behind her back she secreted a package, which she placed on the bench out of sight, yet where he could reach it. He saw the bundle was the size of a small plate, wrapped in a rough spun cloth.

Kathleen asked, "And what have you two been up to today? I rarely see you these days Connor. Have you been busy showing Alex around Greyhaven?"

"Oh yes, Mam," Connor replied, turning to Alex. "We have become good friends and she is teaching me many new things. I have returned the favor by showing her all I know about Greyhaven."

He continued, looking directly at his father. "Da, Alex has been teaching some of the warrior arts she knows, and we would like to invite you to join us in our afternoon classes. If you would like to join us, that is."

Connor was breathless in his excitement, his face flushed as he peered past Alex. Jamie had never seen him so excited. His eyes sparkled, awaiting his father's answer.

Jamie saw they were all looking at him expectantly. He suddenly had a vision of himself and Alex, all sweaty.

He pushed the vision from his mind. Instead of answering the invitation, he picked up the mysterious package and passed it to Alex. "Perhaps, you might tell us what these objects are. If you know their purpose, then I would gift them to you." Arching his eyebrows, he awaited her response.

She took the bundle and carefully unfolded the wrapping, revealing a collection of gleaming objects, some like a knife without the tang, and others round with lethal sharp points.

"Oh!" she exclaimed. "They are oriental throwing

weapons—knives and stars."

Connor, like Jamie, leaned over to see. Jamie shot a glance at Kathleen. She sat back and watched with a smug smile of accomplishment.

"These are really nice," Alex said. "Where did you get them, Jamie?"

This was the first time he heard his name in her strange accent. He resisted the urge to smile. "First you must show us what they do, Milady."

Alex stood with one each of the curious items and moved a few feet away, looking about. She strode to the door providing entrance from the kitchen for the servants and looked inside before returning to the table.

She balanced the knife-like object on extended fingers, hefting it several times to measure its weight. She became very still, now holding the knife extended at arm's length, seeming to measure the distance to the door.

Jamie recognized in her posture many hours of practice to attain such a level of supreme confidence.

A soft step and she flicked the knife, sending it sailing end over end to sink solidly into the wood of the kitchen doorframe. She then held the round object tucked into her right hand, curled into her body, and spun. As she turned, she extended her arm, releasing the silver circlet to fly and embed itself in the doorframe just below the other piece.

Jamie felt his mouth go dry. He had never seen such lethal grace, such calm confidence, such deadly determination. He did not envy anyone crossing her path.

He cleared his throat. "That was … interesting. I see you have some experience with them. I would gift them to you with one stipulation." The words came out heavy with meaning he did not intend.

Or did he?

A wave of tense anticipation crept around the table. Kathleen leaned forward, a smile blossoming; Connor looked ready to jump out of his chair. All of this Jamie perceived through his peripheral senses, for Alex held him with her cool green eyes. He leaned ever so slightly her way for he could almost hear her whisper, "Anything, just ask."

With a snap, Jamie corralled his thoughts. "These devices, the star and knife. Do you think you could teach me how to use them?"

Connor jumped from his chair and ran to stand by Jamie.

Alex laughed. "Come with us, Jamie, and I will teach you how to throw a star."

The enormity of her words washed over him.

Of course she knows how to throw a star, she came from—

He caught himself before he finished the thought, but without a doubt she intrigued him like no woman he had ever met. She unearthed in him the desire to do something ... wild. This frightened him deeply, yet he was drawn to her. He could not decide whether to run from her, or join her.

What else can she do?

He had to know more about this woman. Hesitant, his normally stiff lips melted into a grin. "Yes. I would like to know ... how to throw a star."

•

Alex donned her jeans, blouse and vest and headed for the barn. She had some time alone as Connor had contrived to be off with his father on some errand. Everyone else was busy with preparations for the Midsummer Eve celebration later this week.

"Come on, Blue." She swung her leg over his back and gave him a click. He started out at an easy canter.

She rode east, down by the stream, past the mill, and skirted the crop fields till she reached the pond.

"Nice," Alex said, admiring the solitude. "Finally, some alone time."

She dismounted and unpacked a saddlebag. First came a blanket she spread close to the bank of the pond. Next she brought out a small bottle of wine, an apple, hard cheese wrapped in a cloth, and fresh baked bread with a small tub of butter.

"That's what I'm talking about," she said with a gourmand's delight. "No fast food out here." The cheese was sharp, and the wine sweet. "Oh my God, nothing tastes this good in the future." She sipped her wine from a clay cup and leaned back. "I miss the future, Blue," she said. "Did I ever mention I have a horse just like you in Santa Barbara? Yeah, he's just like you."

That's not all.

Her two lives were hauntingly similar. "The parallels," she told Blue, "are undeniably spooky."

The horse flicked his ears her way, but continued grazing.

"Thank heaven I have you to talk to. Kathleen seems to know so much, I feel like I'm wasting my breath trying to tell her anything.

"There's Maguire, but he has only one thing to say, and we all know what that is." She rolled her eyes, feeling sympathy for Jamie, who was literally surrounded.

"And what about the lord of the manor," she asked, raising her cup of wine. "To the lord of Greyhaven."

She sat back propped up on her elbows, watching the clouds scuttle about in a perfect blue sky. "He paces, you know, at night. I hear his steps, even through all that stone. Sometimes ... sometimes I can't sleep either, knowing he's so close."

Blue had grazed his way around the pond and back to the blanket. Alex tossed him the last piece of her apple. "I stopped carrying the whistle everywhere; I think its safe in my room." She closed her eyes, feeling drowsy. "But I still don't know how I'm supposed to save Jamie."

Or do I?

"Don't ask that of me," she mumbled. She rolled onto her side and pulled the saddlebag under her head. "I want to go home. I want my husband. I want Royce."

She drifted asleep, relaxed in her heart, her mind, and body. The sun passed in the afternoon sky, slowly bringing long shadows. Suddenly she jerked, hearing Royce's voice from within her mind.

Wake up Alex! Beware!

She sat upright, instantly alert. A man knelt by her blanket and the sight of him launched a shiver of revulsion down her back. She had awakened just before he touched her. "Get off me," she hissed as she rolled away and jumped to her feet.

The man was startled and fell back upon his haunches in the grass. "I was not on you," he protested.

"Who are you?" she demanded. She didn't bother to ask what he wanted, for she saw in his aura what he was.

One very sick and twisted man!

He was absurdly dressed, about thirty-five, with pale blue eyes and blond hair. He grazed her with a speculative expression she didn't like.

"My dear," he protested. "I am Sir Edward David Hamilton Burke, Master of Montrose Court," he said as he stood up. He tsk-tsked and brushed the grass from his costume.

Assuming a much-aggrieved expression, he said, "I am neighbor to the Earl of Greyhaven. I was just passing this way after visiting the Earl when I saw you lying here. I thought perhaps you needed assistance." He finished with a sniff.

Her skin crawled, knowing he watched her while she slept.

I know what kind of assistance you were about to offer.

"You have nothing I need," she stated bluntly, lip curling with disdain. Keeping him in her side vision, she began collecting her blanket and stuffed the remnants of her meal in the saddlebag.

"You dare speak to me like that!"

He lunged and grabbed her wrist. Before he could continue, with a small movement of her hand Alex reversed their grip so she now held him. She reinforced this position with her other hand and spun, twisting his arm so his body had only one place to go—facedown ... with his fancy boots in the muddy pond.

"Never touch me again," she said.

She held his arm with the elbow locked, pinning his torso to the ground. Keeping his locked elbow braced against her leg, she leaned on the arm, applying weight to the joint.

"Stop," he cried, his voice muffled against the ground.

Alex put a little more pressure on the bent wrist; Sir Pervert paled and looked ready to pass out. Staring

down into his contorted face, she said, "Do you understand?"

He winced and attempted to wiggle away. She
pressed harder.

"Yes," he screeched.

She released him quickly and stepped back.

He rolled away clutching his strained wrist; his
screech had faded into sobs.

Alex tied the bag to Blue's saddle and mounted the
tall roan. Seeing Sir Pervert whimpering in a huddled
position, she gave a snort of revulsion. "You like to dish
it out, but you can't take it, can you?"

I'm keeping my eye on you.

She rode off, leaving him on the ground.

•

The Next Afternoon in a
Wooded Glen Near Greyhaven

Alex surveyed her two students, Connor and Jamie, and remembered how much fun it was to come to
class and learn new things when she was a student. She
always left the dojo a bigger person, figuratively, than
when she arrived. She always left the dojo smiling.

Can I get the lord of the manor to crack a smile?

Jamie fidgeted in his newly made outfit of baggy
pants and a wrap around jacket tied with a rough length
of cloth.

"It's called a gi," Alex said.

"My feet are getting dirty," Jamie protested. He
tugged on the rough belt knotted at his waist.

Alex grinned. "You're going to have so much fun you

won't notice these little inconveniences, I promise."

They did a series of warm-up exercises to get the heart pumping. Alex noticed Jamie kept up well. "Looks like the lord is in pretty good shape," she mumbled.

They practiced walking and kicking and punching moves punctuated with a kei yell. "Haiee," she demonstrated. "Be ferocious. Startle your opponent into a split second of hesitation, then use that second to your advantage."

Connor needed no encouragement. He set the example for Jamie, and soon they were practicing a truly bloodcurdling shriek.

Alex put her hands over her ears and shouted, "That's good, you got it. Now I'd like to move on to something else." They paused, their faces red and sweaty with matching grins. "Connor, come and we will show Jamie a two-person drill in hand-to-hand combat."

"This is fun, Da," Connor said. He jumped up and stood in front of Alex.

"No one gets hurt because we go in slow motion," she instructed. "Think about your move; is it a block or a strike? Your opponent will respond with two counter moves. Ready?"

Connor nodded. They squared off and bowed to each other. Alex sent a slow punch to Connor's face. He did a body change and evaded her move.

"Yes, very good," Alex said. She stepped to the side and executed a kick. He did another body change and finished with a strike to a pressure point in her leg she had shown him the day before.

Alex stepped away, saying, "Excellent, you remember what I showed you. Now, you and Jamie begin."

"I canna strike my son," Jamie said.

"Well, you won't really hit him," Alex said.

"I canna do it."

"It's all part of the training," she explained. "Eventually we will make solid contact in these drills because contact helps toughen important body parts used for blocking and striking. It's really a lot of fun, something you'll get used to doing. But we won't make you do anything against your will on your first day.

"Instead," Alex continued. "I want to show you a joint lock, a very valuable tool. Jamie, come here."

He gave her a skeptical look. "I am beginning to see why you wanted me to come ... " He stood in front of her.

"Grab my wrist," she instructed. At Jamie's look of resistance, she repeated, "Come on, grab my wrist. I won't hurt you." His gaze deepened, giving her a second evaluation, as though the thought of her hurting him had just now occurred to him.

He grasped her left wrist.

She held their hands up for Connor to see. "All I have to do is bring my captured hand up and over going around Jamie's forearm and suddenly my hand is on top and now I am holding him."

Her other hand came to his forearm to reinforce the grip, and she gave Jamie a smile of warning. Before he could react, she spun, twisted his arm, and he leaped forward and plunged face first onto the ground.

Just like Sir Pervert did yesterday.

"Like this, you can control with just a little bit of pressure." She braced his locked arm against her leg and leaned on it gently. Jamie howled with pain just as she released him.

Jamie clambered from the ground, holding his wrist.

"Ow. Ye said ye wouldna' hurt me—"

She took Jamie's arm and rubbed his wrist top and bottom. Her thumbs worked a pressure point that flooded the area with healing fluid. She rubbed briskly, forcing the fluid back out and returning the joint to a healthy state. "There, you'll live."

They practiced standing forward rolls on the soft forest floor, laughing at one another in their clumsiness and hesitation. Soon, the movement smoothed out, and they progressed to a running forward roll.

Alex did the move, her hands barely touching the ground, as she came up in a crouch, hands raised and ready for defense. "You want to come up hands free, see?"

Connor and Jamie practiced, over and over, until their gi outfits were soiled and their faces smudged with dirt. At last each one executed the move perfectly, coming up with hands ready delivering a Viking worthy kei.

"Very good," she exclaimed. "You both did very well today." They finished class by bowing to each other and reciting, "O ne gash e mash."

Walking back to the manor, Connor asked Jamie, "Have ye ever had so much fun, Da?"

She looked to see Jamie's reaction. Their eyes met over the boy's head. She saw respect, surprise, and ... curiosity. But most of all, she saw a smile. His perpetual grim line was relaxed into an engaging smile, making him very handsome.

"Aye, son. Never have I had so much fun."

"Your neighbor didn't think it was much fun yesterday," Alex mentioned with a grin.

Jamie stopped. "You met Sir Edward?"

"Yes. I was napping out by the pond when he crept

up on me."

Connor asked, "What did you do?"

"I gave him the wrist lock you saw today, and instructed him to never touch me again. He did not take it well." She glanced at Jamie. The rigid set of his lips was back.

"We suffer his presence, thanks to King James," Jamie said.

"He must be watched," Alex replied. She arched one brow, giving Jamie a sharp look. "There's a word for him—"

"Dangerous," Jamie silently mouthed.

Alex took Connor by the shoulders. "Run up and ask Cook to heat water for me, please?"

"Plenty of water," Jamie added. "For all of us."

Connor bolted down the path, pausing periodically to practice his Viking yell. They heard his progress until his cry finally faded away.

"The man abuses women," Alex said. "Do you know the sickness I speak of?"

Jamie gave her a shocked look that turned into a furrowed brow. "How do you know this?"

"I can see his aura, the energy coming from his body and soul. And his is dark, darker than anything I've ever seen. Only one other time have I seen such evil, and that man was a convicted sociopath. What lives in your neighbor's mind is not … normal."

"Yesterday, you actually did that … that joint lock to him?"

"Yes, and I wasn't gentle. He squealed like a pig," she said. "When I took him to the ground, his feet landed in the water. I'm sure his pretty boots were quite ruined."

"Ha ha," Jamie barked. "I would pay for such a show."

Alex allowed herself a brief smile, but the memory of the man's aura stifled her humor. She caught Jamie's attention with her serious look. "We have to be very careful of him. Watch him, Jamie, never trust him."

Was this the danger she was here to save Jamie from? How is Sir Fancy Pants a threat to Jamie? She looked down the path recently taken by Connor, considering all those she had come to care about.

"If he touches anyone from Greyhaven," she announced, "he'll get more than a wrist lock."

•

Mid-summer's Eve dawned clear and warm with a light breeze out of the south, perfect for a party. Alex woke to the sounds of happy people being busy. Immediately, her nose was fully awakened by the heavenly smells that filled the air. She jumped out of bed and went to the opened window.

A panorama of tents, vendors, animals and flags spread below. "Oh!" she squealed. "Gotta go, gotta go—"

She washed her face, and brushed her teeth and her hair. At her armoire, she paused, excited. Inside was her new outfit, presented to her by Kathleen last night after the evening meal.

"Your wardrobe is meager," Kathleen said. "I think this might fit. Please, will you wear this tomorrow?"

Alex pulled out the dress. It was pale yellow muslin with gold satin trim, and pale green ribbon accents on the short sleeves, at the waist, and lining the open neck. The two colors perfectly accented Alex's red and gold hair.

She slipped the dress on over the chemise from Nepal, and in a daring move, pulled on her modern thong panties.

"There," she said, smoothing her hands over the dress. The sparse coverage of her panties beneath the long dress left her feeling slightly wicked and a little horny. "Maybe, just maybe, if I'm a good girl, perhaps someone will kiss me today."

"Oops!" She covered her mouth in mock rebuke, watching her reflection in the tall slender mirror. The dress was very flattering; just knowing Jamie would see her this way made her stomach flutter with ... anticipation?

"I can't help being young and healthy, or that the Earl is looking damn good these days."

Is he Royce, or is he Jamie?

The question had given her no rest these last few days. Since Jamie started coming to class, she saw her husband in small facial expressions and hand gestures. Even the things he says sometimes—

Are so like Royce.

"Face it, I'm attracted to the man, whether it's 2017 or 1612."

She took the extra ribbon that came with the dress and wove it thorough her hair, working it into a French braid. Satisfied with the way she looked, she went to join the party.

The manor's approach was turned into a renaissance faire similar to the renaissance festivals she and Royce attended in California.

"Oh, but this sucker is real!"

The road was lined with vendors selling everything imaginable, from jewels to fabrics, arms and armor, leather goods, cooking implements, and spices from the orient.

Food was on display in more varieties than she had ever seen, and every stock animal possible was here for sale or breeding.

Along with the horses, cattle, pigs, chickens and rabbits she expected, there were surprises. "Llamas, in Ireland?" she murmured.

Everyone from the village had turned out for the affair. In addition, a band of gypsies made camp, and out came jugglers, men breathing fire, and sultry eyed women taking coin for palm readings and fortune telling. A magician pulled rabbits out of a tall hat, and the wind crackled from the whip of dozens of multi-colored flags. Musicians filled the air with song, making Alex's feet want to dance. "I love live music," she exclaimed.

Flanking the road to the east was a great bonfire fed by logs the village men had been gathering all week. The fire would stay lit for the day and night and into the next morning. Anyone passing the fire must walk in a clockwise direction, going east to west, imitating the passage of the sun.

Banners in every color were strung from the trees. Around the huge bonfire was a brilliant row of jousting pennants brought down from the Great Hall. Games and contests like arm wrestling elicited loud cheers as villagers attempted to best their neighbor at an array of unimaginable feats. All were singing, drinking and laughing. Children ran amok, their infectious squeals of joy punctuating the air as they darted from one game to the next.

Alex drank ale and stout. She ate until she couldn't swallow another bite, so she sang and played their games. No one seemed troubled by the fact that she knew none of the songs and none of the games. Her unrestrained exuberance to participate more than made up for what she didn't know.

Connor ran up and tugged on her hand. "Come play blind man with us, Alex." She let him pull her along, laughing at his excitement. When they held up the hood for her to wear, she said, "Sure," and slipped it over her head.

For a moment she stood, collecting what was around her, weeding out the big noise, tuning her senses to the smells and small sounds around her. Now came the auras, and she had a thermal scan of everyone within twenty feet.

First Connor tried to tag her, but she faced him every time and evaded his every move. Next came Maguire, but he soon gave up, winded and laughing.

Alex knew when Jamie entered her circle. He smelled of a particular spicy soap Kathleen made, and he moved with a distinctive quiet step. She pretended to not notice him, allowing him to sneak up on her.

"Got you!" he exclaimed.

The hood came off. Alex knew she was red faced, her breath smelled of Irish stout, and her hair was probably a mess. But when she opened her eyes, his face filled her vision, his scent curled her toes with sweetness, and all she wanted was for him to kiss her.

She took a step toward him and her leg brushed up against his thigh, making contact with a solid hard on.

"Oh," she gasped. She looked into his eyes and saw no apology. Heat bloomed across her chest and she suddenly wanted to rip the smothering muslin—

"Milady," he said, a seductive hum underlying the word.

"My lord," she blurted.

"Do you need assistance?" he asked. His gaze poured over her exposed chest before fixing on her lips.

Her thoughts were stuck on the bulge in his pants.

Before anyone could move, Connor arrived and interrupted.

"Come Alex, and see the dragon cake Cook Mary has made. There are flames coming out of its mouth. You must come quick if we want to get a piece." He tugged on her hand, insistent. With no room for rebuttal, she passed the hood to Jamie with a wink.

"Ha!" he cried good-naturedly, but Alex saw the desire smoldering in his eyes just before he slid the hood over his head.

After the next game, Alex begged off from Connor and left him as she searched for a mug of ale. Seeing Kathleen, she joined her under a broad oak tree as dusk settled on the revelers.

"Kathleen, this is wonderful. Everyone is so exuberant and robust. They are serious about having a good time," Alex said as she sipped her ale.

"We provide all this, for the people are an important part of the land. Their happiness is important. Greyhaven would be nothing without its people, and the people would be nothing without their lord to watch over them.

"I see Jamie joining into the festivities this year for the first time. He normally shuns excitement, seeing passion as a dangerous weakness, a taint to be excised. I wonder what has changed him?"

Alex kept her recent encounter with Jamie to herself. Softly she said, "Passion is a gift from God. Humankind was meant to be passionate. It is one of the things that makes life worth living."

Kathleen responded, "I quite agree with you my dear. Perhaps you can convince Jamie of such wisdom."

Jamie could be seen from where they sat, and Alex's heart constricted when she admitted how handsome he was. Tonight he wore tan leather breeches with a white linen shirt that complimented his physique. He was the living, breathing epitome of tall, dark, and handsome.

Is initiating Jamie to passion how I save him?

A coil of heat opened deep in her core and she admitted she wanted him. But her heart pulled her first one way, then another. She had not forgotten about Royce by any means, but Jamie was so like him she sometimes forgot they were different men.

Am I ready to give my heart to this man?

CHAPTER SEVEN

Celtic Wisdom: Brave the Unknown; Believe the Impossible; Embrace the Questionable.

Monet's Garden

"Do you understand?" Andros asked.

Royce cringed, for as badly as he wanted to understand, part of him didn't want to know. At last the image he saw in the white frame had to be confronted. "I am Jamie, but why is Alex there? How is she to save him … me?"

"You do not remember," Andros stated.

Believing in reincarnation was one thing, but seeing one of your past lives played before your eyes was agonizing. Watching his life from the audience made him want to shout, "Stop. Let's rewrite … Can we edit— How about a re-take?"

This is why I am here? To watch a past life I screwed up?

"Alex, she's there to fix me in that life?"

Andros waved his hand, and the waters shifted.

Royce leaned forward, straining to see.

Show me. I just don't remember.

•

Montrose Court, Ireland, 1612

Sir Edward paced back and forth in his parlor, his agitation growing by leaps and bounds. "Oh sit still, and cease your sniveling," he growled.

Standing before the fireplace was Ian Moore, the young groom from Greyhaven. "I can still have you sent to prison," Sir Edward threatened. "Think about what they will do to you there. By forcing you to spy on the Earl I am doing you a favor. You should thank me."

Ian cringed. The boy was typically Irish. He had a runny nose and he always smelled of horses and manure. Sir Edward made the boy take his shoes off before entering his home.

But that did not mean young Ian could not be used.

"Who is she? The red-haired woman at Greyhaven, where did she come from?" he barked.

Ian wrung his hands. "She came from the heavens. She is an angel lady."

Sir Edward swung at the boy, cuffing him on the ear.

"Ow, I tell ye true," Ian cried. "She came from a field of flowers one day. Her name is Alex."

Squatting down to look the boy directly in the eye, Sir Edward said, "Listen to me, you little thief, I have kept your identity from the authorities all these months on your promise to provide me with the information I require. And what I require right now is who that woman is and what she is doing at Greyhaven. You will tell me the truth and not this ridiculous story about an angel." He thought about the new boots she had ruined, and rubbed the wrist still sore from his encounter with her. Abruptly he stood and lashed out, striking Ian across the face. "Wretch, I have met the wench, and I assure you she is neither an angel nor a lady."

Ian struggled to stand. "They are good to me at Greyhaven. I dinna feel right about spying on them." He sniffed and wiped his nose on his sleeve. "She always talks nice, and one day she saved me from a big horse. Ye can beat me all ye like, but ye will not change what I tell ye."

"Stop whining and go. Remember, I know you for the little thief you are, and mayhap I will go and talk to the authorities about you and your crimes after all."

The boy ran from the parlor and ducked out the door, barely escaping Sir Edward's poorly aimed boot.

"This woman, who is she?" Raol mused. He spoke from a high-back chair, hidden from the boy Ian's interrogation. "She is an unknown factor, potentially disturbing our plans for Greyhaven."

"And I owe her a reckoning for ruining my boots," Edward said.

Not to mention the nightmares plaguing me since we met.

"I have to break this hold she has on me," he blurted.

Her voice! To hear her beg for mercy would free me.

"I must have her," he said. His foot tapped the carpet. "Taking Greyhaven from the Earl is not enough. But taking Greyhaven and the woman—"

"Then you shall have her, my friend," Raol confirmed. "We will take them both."

"How?" Edward asked. "The Earl must be disposed of first."

Raol smiled and stared out the window toward Greyhaven. "When we burn the barn, he will come." He shrugged, nonchalant. "Then I will kill him."

◆

Alex followed Jamie and Connor as they entered the woods on their way to the glen for her class. Connor chatted excitedly with his father. And Jamie ... Jamie looked just like Royce.

His step, the tilt of his head, even the color of his hair when the sun hit it was achingly familiar. Alex swung from hating being here, to wanting to run her hands through his hair and put her arms around his neck—

"Can I please have an afternoon without this horny-toad on my back?" she mumbled.

"Did you say something?" Jamie asked. He had stopped on the path and was staring at her.

Alex shrugged off her wayward thoughts and mentally put on her Sensei hat. "Are you ready for today?" she asked Connor. The boy was so wound up he ran a circle around her and Jamie.

"Yes, Sensei," he shouted with exuberance. "I willna let you down, Sensei." With a whoop, he jumped and took off, racing the last fifty yards to the glen.

Alex laughed and glanced at Jamie. His return gaze was warm, and his eyes sparkled with joy; a ready smile graced his normally stern lips. The level of transformation made her breath catch in her throat.

"You have made quite a change in my boy," he said. "A change much for the better, I might add."

"The potential was there. I just gave him an outlet," she said. "Studies show the benefit of highly developed eye-hand coordination goes beyond good balance, especially in juveniles. It nurtures the psyche with confidence, stimulating social skills."

At her words, Jamie's first expression was a deep frown that slowly went blank. "Aye," he said slowly, as though deciding whether to agree with her. His quick laughter followed. "Ha! Well, I havna clue as to what ye just said." He looked up the path where Connor was warming up for class. "But ye have worked a miracle. Perhaps Connor is right to call ye an angel lady."

They arrived at their meeting place and quickly began with warm up exercises. When they moved on to two-person stretches, Alex worked first with Connor, then Jamie. At one point she realized Jamie was staring at her chemise through the gap in her gi jacket.

She shifted her gaze to his eyes; the lust burning there was impossible to miss. An accompanying ripple of heat shot down her spine, momentarily making her legs feel weak. The prospect of joining with this man frightened her, even as it thrilled her. She lowered her eyes, unwilling to reveal her vulnerability. Their stretching was completed and she stepped to the head of the class.

"Sensei, what have you brought?" Connor asked.

"This is called a jo. Maguire made it for me," Alex said.

She showed them the smoothly carved four-foot staff, and gave it to Connor.

He exclaimed, "This is my size. I like it." He passed the jo to Jamie.

Jamie inspected the staff, looking down its straight, solid length. "Oak," he said. He passed it back to Alex. "And whose hard Irish head are ye going to straighten out with this little toy?"

"Whatever hard Irish head I see needs straightening," she quipped. She took the staff. "The farmers of Okinawa converted many farm implements into weapons—" She was ready to say, "In the mid-sixteen-hundreds." Instead she asked, "Would you like to see what this little 'toy' can do in the right hands?"

They backed up, giving her space.

She bowed, indicating the beginning of a kata. The series of steps, punctuated with several chilling kei, displayed a variety of strikes with the jo—coming overhead and down, from the ground up, and forward. She spun, she stabbed. She jumped and kicked. She made the stiff oak sing like a leather whip. Signaling the end of the kata, she finished with a bow. "That my friends, is how to cause a lot of damage with one little stick."

Connor's mouth was stuck in a little O.

Jamie's eyebrows peaked over bulging eyes.

Alex smothered a grin. "I have asked Maguire to make another jo, for you Connor. For you, Milord, he is making a six-foot version called a bo."

Connor looked ready to lift off the ground.

Jamie, however, suffered from another form of excitement. Alex realized the location of his discomfort, and couldn't help but glance at his pants. He attempted to cover the bulge in his crotch with his hands.

She looked away, feeling her cheeks burn. This sexual tension, she thought, is getting unbearable.

He should just kiss me and get it over with.

•

Deep asleep in her bed, Alex dreamed of fire. She felt it in her heart, her body, and her soul, and now fire had invaded her dreams, complete with smoke.

She sat up in bed. "Fire," she croaked from a dry throat. She reached for the pitcher of water at her bedside and gulped enough to loosen her vocal chords.

"Fire," she repeated, louder. Getting out of the bed, she ran to the window. The pitch black of night was lit with an orange glow of fire. "Hay barn," she exclaimed. She dressed and grabbed her jo and throwing weapons. Just as she pulled the door open, Jamie was descending the stairs.

"What do ye think yer doing?" he asked.

Alex had in her mind to say "preparing to save your ass," but she saw the normally tight line of his lips flatten further when he eyed her attire and the jo. She threw back her shoulders and proclaimed, "I'm coming with you."

Without a word he reached in and pulled her chamber door shut.

Alex stared at the back of the door that suddenly filled her vision.

Perhaps this commanding technique works well with seventeenth century women.

"Well, it doesn't work with me."

She exhaled deeply, counted to thirty and exited her chamber, arriving in the courtyard in time to see the retreating backsides of Jamie and Maguire with a small troop of men.

Seeing Connor, Alex shouted to him, "Get Blue for me; go now." With this directive, the lad ran to do her bidding. Alex went to the barn and collected Blue's saddle. Connor came running up with the horse.

Alex saddled Blue and slipped the bridle in his mouth. She took the reins and mounted, instructing Connor, "Stay here."

She and Blue bolted out only minutes behind Jamie and the others. She knew exactly where to go, so she gave Blue permission to fly. Racing along the path through the trees, her heart ramped up with adrenaline. Her emotions were super-charged and she forced herself to focus.

She reached the hay barn, and her worst fears came alive as she made out the distinct sounds of combat within the chaos of shadows created from the light of the burning barn.

"Jamie, where are you?" She saw him on foot, slashing and fighting with a sword against two men. A riderless horse broke between him and his attackers; Alex saw her opportunity. She chose her target and charged into the melee.

Blue bore down on the man and Alex struck his head with the jo. He dropped his sword, wavered and fell to his knees, holding his head. "Ahhhh," he cried.

Turning about, she saw Maguire also fighting two men, and went to his aid. She rode between them and swung the jo, cracking the antagonist's hand. He dropped his weapon and fled, following the other attackers into the woods. As he disappeared, Maguire felled his other attacker with a sword thrust through the chest.

Wheeling Blue about again, Alex saw the man she had struck in the head was gone. Suddenly, the fight was over as quickly as it began.

"Who are they?" she cried. "Why burn a hay barn? This makes no sense."

Maguire poked his dead man with his foot. "I dinna know this one," he said.

Jamie walked up, his brow furrowed in worry lines

as the dead man was loaded onto a horse.

Alex dismounted. She clutched Jamie's arm, searching his body for wounds. "Are you all right? Have you been hurt?"

Silence, brief but hard was her answer.

"Why are you here?" he demanded. "I instructed you to remain at the manor."

Too many emotions were raging inside her. The adrenaline of battle, the fear of Jamie being hurt, her desire to see him safe, all tumbled through her heart. That he chose to reprimand her added anger to the list.

"You did not," she spit. "You actually said nothing beyond slamming the door in my face. You're lucky I was here. And I don't see any gratitude." She stuck her chin out, indignant at his words.

They argued toe-to-toe. In her peripheral vision, she saw Maguire slinking off. She brought her focus back to Jamie.

His face was flushed and smudged with soot from the fire, and his eyes glittered, not with hard rage, but liquid and molten with—

"You could have been hurt," he said softly.

"As could you," she protested weakly.

His hands grabbed her shoulders, seeming ready to shake her. She went soft, all angry resistance melting. Before she could react, he bent down to kiss her. His lips were crushing in their need. She parted hers, acquiescing, allowing his tongue entrance.

With all the longing of her body and her mind, she met his need. She moaned into his mouth and pressed herself against him. Their breaths mingled and they clutched each other frantically as the fire surged through them.

She had wanted this so badly for so long, and now it was finally happening. Struggling for air, she broke away and gasped the name in her heart, "Royce!"

Heat turned to ice, and they both froze.

"I ... I'm sorry," Alex sputtered. She wanted this man, Jamie. But she was so used to saying Royce.

Jamie's expression told her nothing. His face was immobile, his eyes inscrutable.

His hands dropped from her shoulders, but he stared deep into her eyes, as if to read all that had not been spoken. He held her in his gaze as if unable to let go.

She twisted free and ran. Grabbing Blue's reins, she mounted in one smooth motion. "Hya," she cried and kicked the roan in the flanks.

The light of the smoky fire became a blur in the fading darkness. She and the horse flew, with her concentrating on the task of staying alive on the back of this big animal. She put her face to the wind, letting it rip the tears from her eyes before they could fall down her face.

Like all good horses, Mister Blue knew to end a run at the barn, which they approached. By the time they came within sight of the manor, Alex had the horse slowed to nearly a walk, and they both arrived with a steady heart.

"Take him, and make sure to walk him before you water him, he rode hard tonight." She passed the reins to Ian, the groom, who, oddly seemed to avoid looking her in the eye. "Whatever," she mumbled.

She went straight to her chamber, throwing off her pants and shirt and changing into a sleep chemise Kathleen had given her. Flinging open a set of shutters, she sat down on the padded bench seat and propped her chin on her knee. Glancing up she saw her reflection in the mirror. "Oh, my God, look at the mess," she gasped. She took the hairbrush and began to straighten out the wild tangles that came from her frantic ride.

Royce always did this chore for her, teasing her about how impossible her hair was. Once, she threw her hands up and declared, "Well, hell. What am I supposed to do with it?"

His response had been to pull her close and gently wrap his arms around her, his lips on the top of her head. "This," he said. "This is what you do." He kissed her hair and rubbed his cheek against the top of her head. His gesture had been so sweet she remembered how her insides melted with a rich, satisfied feeling.

She hugged herself, remembering the sensation. "That's why I called him Royce because he made me feel the way Royce does. But tonight, my feelings were for Jamie ..."

I thought I was supposed to protect him ... to save him.

"But who will protect me from him?"

What a fool she had been to think she would just show up here, take care of bidness and be off without any complications. When did the universe ever move your life around and keep things simple?

Well, he will certainly have questions now. A confrontation I cannot avoid is coming.

"Don't think about him; just handle events as they develop." She rolled her shoulders and exhaled deeply, trying to relax. She picked up the brush to braid her hair while she waited.

♦

The hay barn smoldered behind him, but all Jamie could think about was:

"She called me Royce."

He heard her say Roy, and thought she was calling him.

"Now who the hell is Royce?" he asked.

He wanted to hold on to her, but she was too swift. As soon as she spoke the name, she twisted free and bolted.

Maguire came up behind Jamie with the dead man's body loaded on a horse. "She is one mighty warrior," he said. "Too bad ye let her get away."

Jamie shook his head and rubbed at his face, wishing to dispel the forces constantly nipping at him. "'Tis the insanity, I know," he mumbled under his breath. "Another McNeill drawn in to the depths by weakness ... and well meaning friends."

Maguire ignored Jamie's comment. "The boys have the fire under control," he said. "They will search around for some clue as to who these hooligans are."

"Aye," Jamie answered. He collected his horse and followed Maguire. Once they reached the manor, Jamie went straight to the library and poured a glass of whiskey. He took the decanter with him, and dropped into a chair by the fireplace. Thankfully, the fires in a great stone house were never out. The flames were a diversion for his busy mind.

"Who are they? And why burn a hay barn?" he wondered. The season was early enough for them to replace the hay. And a hay barn was easily rebuilt. He drained his glass and refilled it.

"Such men should be interested in thievery, not burning a barn." Since the English Crown had confiscated almost six counties in Northern Ireland, local people, mostly Catholic villagers and servants, were ejected into the countryside without home or lord to care for them. Rather than serve newly appointed English masters, they joined lawless bands that left mayhem in their wake, much like what they just experienced.

"But why here at Greyhaven?"

If these marauders are locally organized, Jamie wondered, who would be interested in supporting this type of activity? He and Maguire must speak with Sheriff Morton.

"Now, about the redhead," he said. He emptied his glass of whiskey and left the library. Behind the Great Hall were stairs to the chapel. He ascended them slowly, thinking about what he must say to her.

In the chapel he looked around. The heavy wooden doors bolted from the inside, and the walls were three-foot thick.

"In here, the truth will be heard ... the whole truth."

Pulling the bell cord, he summoned a servant to fetch her. While he waited, he recalled their kiss, where she had scorched even him.

Lord let me be insane. Just let me kiss that redheaded woman again.

•

The summons wasn't long in coming.

"Yes?" Alex answered the knock at her chamber door.

"His lordship would see you in the chapel, Milady."

Wanting to get this over with, she went directly to the chapel. Upon entering, she turned to bolt the door, immediately understanding why Jamie had called her here.

The truth, she thought. *He means to have the truth,* and here they could speak openly without fear of being overheard.

"So be it," she whispered to the closed-door panels. She straightened her shoulders and turned around to face what was coming.

God help me ... I have never been good at secrets.

Looking into his searching eyes, she took a deep breath and put on her best smile. "So, what would you like to ask first, Milord?"

His inspection of her was a scorching examination. "I do not care for that hair style," he said bluntly.

Alex almost laughed were it not for the intensity of Jamie's gaze. "It is called a French braid, Milord," she returned just as bluntly.

"I am aware of what it is called. I only meant the style does not become you."

"Then I suggest you speak more clearly."

A silence stretched between them. She walked to him, closing the distance. "You have questions, Jamie. I am here to answer them. Let's get on with it, shall we?"

His gaze raked over her, head to toe. She was simply dressed in one of her day outfits of a light wool skirt that was split, her soft leather vest, a silk blouse, and ankle boots. "The day you arrived I inspected your belongings before they were taken to your chamber."

He shifted foot to foot before continuing. "I noticed your clothing was strange, different in a way not clear to see."

She frowned. Clothing? *What the hell is he babbling about?*

Clearing his throat, he added, "There was a small garment, pink, I believe, that … mystifies me."

She lost her frown when her mouth dropped open. Of all the things in the world he could ask, this is on his mind? She felt the corners of her mouth twitch. "The garment you refer to is called a thong. Where I come from many women wear them."

"Where I come from" echoed through the chapel. Jamie looked to have not heard.

"I see," he said slowly. He seemed to ponder carefully his next words. With a deep breath, he asked, "Who is Royce?"

She answered carefully. "Royce is my husband." She continued in spite of his quick intake of breath. "He was involved in an accident and disappeared. He is presumed dead." These last four words came in a rushed whisper as she rubbed the empty finger on her left hand.

He reached out to gently lift her chin, capturing her gaze. "Where do you come from, and why are you here?"

She cleared her throat and slowly licked her lips. "I am from the future. I was sent to find you, to protect you … to 'save Jamie and save all' in some way, although the details were not made clear to me." She held his gaze, wanting him to see she hid nothing.

The look he returned was all she feared, and nothing she hoped for. "You do not believe me," she blurted.

During her confession, his mouth had gone from a small O to a larger vacant opening. He clapped his mouth shut with a visible effort and then opened it again, perhaps to speak, but no words came. All he produced was a frown.

"Your story is too preposterous to consider, yet I

canna refute what you say. From my mother's tapestry, to the bent flowers where you arrived in a field with no other tracks. There are many pieces that now fit: your language is different, the clothes." He turned away, rubbing at his face. He heard confusion in the exhalation that rattled from his chest.

"Jamie," she said softly, reaching for him.

He spoke, a confession whispered, the words breaking her heart. "Mayhap I am insane, after all, but I find I can not help myself." In a sudden movement he grabbed her by the arms.

Alex jumped, for his actions startled her, but she didn't resist. Very slowly and with clear intent, he lowered his head, giving her ample time to accept or reject what he was about to do. But she didn't move, in fact couldn't move, such was her anticipation of what was imminent.

She leaned toward him. Barely inches from her face, he challenged her, daring her to turn away. In response, she gazed back at him, her eyes speaking all she couldn't put into words before she closed them, and offered him her lips.

The contact came like lightning from a spring storm, streaking from one to another.

She made a small moan of acceptance.

Gently ... slowly ... he captured her.

First her mouth, sweetly, lovingly, his gentle actions spoke of love. Next, her body was claimed as he tightened his arms, bringing them loin-to-loin. Her heart followed, capitulating when he released the tail of her braid and brought that hand up through her hair, destroying the braid and freeing her curls. He cupped her head, drawing her in, deepening the kiss, and branding her soul.

She had to give all of herself for him to believe her. She clutched at him madly, willing him to accept everything she gave—her story, her life, her heart ... and her soul. She wanted to hide nothing from him ever again if he would only accept this one gift ... the 'preposterous' truth of who and what she was.

Suddenly she realized she lay herself open to this man like she had never done before, not even with Royce.

It will be all or nothing—else I am wasting my time here.

What have I done? she wondered.

What would be worse, for him to reject me ... or accept?

The intensity of Jamie's possession, the enormity of her actions, the confusion in her emotions came crashing together, and it was too much. A single tear escaped one closed eye.

"I can't," she sobbed. She withdrew from the warmth of his embrace, wrenching her face away, ending the heat and passion in his kiss. She stepped away from him and the emotional chaos he brought to her life.

She slowly backed up, shaking her head. More tears came pouring and she swiped at them angrily.

I am a warrior—

Never have I been so afraid!

Wiping her mouth on the back of her hand, she tore her eyes away from the incredulous expression on Jamie's face. Continuing her retreat she backed up until she bumped into the closed doors. Turning about, she stopped with her hand on the bolt. Before releasing the doors, she spoke over her shoulder.

"And who ... who is supposed to protect me from you?"

With these words left softly behind, Alex threw open the doors and ran for the second time that day.

Jamie was stunned when he heard the pain and fear in her plaintive cry. She was proud and fearless and she had lain herself bare to him in a way he had never done. If only he was as brave as she.

I am ashamed.

His chagrin was closely followed by a smile and a grimace.

"From the future," he snorted. "Aye, and my name is—"

He threw his hands up and resisted the urge to bang his head into the wall. "Just as I thought, we are all doomed, the whole McNeill family. I am simply the last to fall prey to this weakness." He looked at the door and, following her lead, wiped his scorched mouth on the back of his hand.

"Save me?" he asked, perplexed.

Whatever doubts and questions he had earlier were now replaced by other concerns far larger. He rubbed the bridge of his nose and moaned. "Lass, how do ye save me when you are the insanity?"

He, too, exited the chapel in a hurry.

•

Monet's Garden

Royce viewed the scene. The truth gnawed at his heart.

I have to face this if I am going to understand.

"I was afraid," he blurted in a hushed whisper. "More afraid than I ever was on a battlefield." Ignorance and fear came heavy with sorrow. He wiped a tear from his eye. "Good thing she was there," he declared. "Or I would have really made a mess of things."

"So you are beginning to understand?" Andros asked.

Royce felt his eyes glaze over as his mind raced through bits and pieces of two very different lives. Try as he might, he still did not understand why he was here.

Or why Alex was in Ireland.

"No," he said.

Andros gave no response as his hand moved to clear the water.

•

Montrose Court

Edward paced his parlor, waiting for Raol to return with news of the Earl's death. Below in the courtyard, the sound of a horse running broke the still of night. He ran to look out the window, and recognized Raol's horse.

"Damn!" he cried, and bolted out of the room.

The horse had stopped suddenly, pitching its rider to the cobblestones. Edward went to his knees, turning over his friend. A large bruise covered Raol's left temple.

"What happened?" Edward cried. "Who did this? What of the Earl? Can you stand?" He placed an arm around Raol and helped him up. The Spaniard was wavering on his feet.

"Easy, compadre," Edward murmured. Panic rose in his chest as he assessed the extent of his friend's injury.

"The wooo-man," Raol spoke with a slur. "La Diabla. She did this to me."

"We will take care of her," Edward said. "First we must get you inside.

Edward closed his eyes, the fear of being alone filling his chest. He and Raol had been together for years. What began as debauchery developed over time into specialized kidnapping and holding captives briefly ... or indefinitely.

How will I continue without you?

Raol's head lolled. Edward bent and picked up his unconscious friend, taking the stairs as fast as he could, panting by the time he reached the parlor where he laid Raol out on a couch.

Edward soaked a cloth with water and applied the compress gently to Raol's temple. The bruise was turning black and swelling. He feared his friend's skull was cracked open.

He tried to wake him, but was equally concerned about jostling the damaged head. "Wake up, Raol." When no answer came, Edward bowed his head and held his friend's hand.

Edward's dry eyes burned as though he had cried all through the day. As Raol's hand grew cold and stiff, an accompanying pressure took up residence in Edward's head. His mind raced with visions of all the victims he and Raol had enjoyed—and all the victims they would never acquire now that Raol was gone.

"You were the only one who understood me."

Only Raol appreciated Edward's exacting process for

picking their victims; only Raol understood Edward's exhilaration when planning an abduction; only Raol relished the suffering of others as Edward did, finding mutual sexual satisfaction within their exploits.

Night fell, and the French servants came to light the lamps. Edward was still holding Raol's hand.

"Mon Dieu!" Jean cried when the lamp revealed Edward sitting with Raol's body. The servant stepped back and crossed himself. "Monsieur Raol!"

"Bring the shovels," Edward commanded, praying the Frenchman understood. Raol would not receive burial in consecrated ground; he would not even get a grave marker. He could not afford inquiry into the Spaniard's demise.

Jean returned with the boy Armand and helped Edward carry Raol down the stairs and out to the garden behind the kitchen. Edward picked up a shovel and broke ground, feeling the pressure in his head escalate. When he and Jean and Armand had the grave deep enough, Edward jumped down and positioned his friend and companion's body. He whispered, "I will avenge your murder."

He climbed out and stared down at Raol's body, seeing all his dreams of filling the dungeon rooms of Montrose Court destroyed. He could not carry on by himself.

"Then your murderer," he choked, "will have to last me a very long time. I promise she will beg for death every day." He looked off in the direction of Greyhaven, bitter bile filling his mouth.

"Nay," he added. "She will beg every hour."

CHAPTER EIGHT

Anonymous: To change, find courage within.
To grow, reach above.
To endure, search deep and persevere.

Five Days Later, Greyhaven

Alex woke to the sound of birds outside her window. She rolled over to face the window reluctantly, her heart as heavy this morning as it was last night …

"I don't think this is working," she told the birds. "I am not getting bidness done, and I … I want to go home." Tears sprouted at the thought of home.

Royce, where are you? Help me!

She gave in to the flash of tears, sobbing silently into her pillow, her body racked with remorse and grief. "What if I can't do this?" she whispered into her wet pillow. "How do I get you back? Oh Royce, I miss you so much."

The last five days had been hell as she and Jamie actively avoided each other. She cancelled the afternoon classes, telling Connor she wasn't feeling well for a few days. "I expect you to go out to the glen and practice as though I was there. You know what to do, and I will know if you haven't practiced," she declared.

She remained sequestered in her chamber when

not at her duties or out riding Blue. Whenever she did exit her room, she would look furtively in all directions, making sure she didn't run into Jamie. Avoiding the lord of the manor had not been that difficult.

Meals were a silent affair with "Pass the salt, please," the only words at the table. After one night in this fashion, Jamie began taking his meals in his study. Alex took her meals in the kitchen, the last to eat.

"I want to go home," she moaned into the pillow.

The tears ran dry, and she sat up, needing to blow her nose. "Kleenex," she complained. "I frickin' miss Kleenex." She crawled out of bed and rummaged in the chest for a handkerchief. A glance in the mirror did little to lighten her day. "Great, I look like a red-eyed, red-haired, snotty nosed frickin' dragon."

She returned to the bed and crawled back in. "Well … I refuse to participate any more. I'm gonna stay in here until I starve to death," she announced.

Her stomach rumbled.

She ignored it. "I happen to admire anyone smart enough to know when they are not fit for company," she mumbled, pulling the pillow over her head.

Voices intruded on her solitude, coming from the yard. Male voices. She pulled the pillow aside and listened for—

His voice, she prayed.

"I expect to be gone most of the day," Jamie said.

Alex pushed her face into the pillow.

He's going to be gone all day.

Her shoulders slumped and more tears gathered in her eyes.

Outside, their conversation continued.

"I have the snares ready at the house," Maguire said.

"To your house," Jamie said. He resisted the urge to glance up at Alex's window to see if she was watching. To see if she cared.

To see if she was still here.

I have not seen her since the day we talked in the chapel.

He put his back to Greyhaven and headed for the stables. "Huh," he grunted. "An outlander in my own manor." He kicked at a stone in his way and stomped down the path. "Here to save me she says," he complained. "Sure … and what do ye mean by 'save'?"

He entered the stable and grabbed Pharaoh's halter. "Come on big boy, we have traps to set. Mayhap when we get back, that red-haired minx will have—" He stopped and snapped his fingers. "Disappeared, just as she came."

Pharaoh nodded, seeming to agree. "Aye, gone, like the wind, taking this insane maelstrom, this … this storm … " He tapped his forehead. "Taking this storm with her."

During the brushing and saddling process, Jamie grew quiet, feeling he had adequately vented his spleen. But while his earlier rant gave his mind a small measure of satisfaction, he gained no relief in his heart.

He walked his horse outside and mounted. Being up on Pharaoh's back gave him a sudden view—

Of her window.

"Does she suffer as I do?" he said to his horse. "Chaos between her heart and her mind? What would she gain by a liaison here when she belongs … somewhere else?"

A nudge with his heel and Pharaoh turned away. Without looking back, he said, "I think it would be best for all if she went back to where she came from."

•

She listened to Jamie's footsteps going off toward the stables. "What a great mess this is," she exclaimed. She rose and half-heartedly splashed water on her face. After dressing, she hid her disappointment at Jamie's day-long absence behind a false smile.

Reluctantly giving in, she admonished her reflection, "Starving never helped anything."

At the kitchen, the smell of fresh baked bread greeted her growling stomach. She picked up a cloth napkin and selected a biscuit from the warming station next to the fireplace. A crock of butter and one of jam was already on the table. She sat quietly, not wanting to attract attention.

"There ye are, Lassie," Maguire boomed as he sat next to her.

Alex jumped in her seat. "Morning," she mumbled with a mouthful of biscuit. Seeing he planned to stay and chat, she gulped from a mug of cider and wiped her mouth. "Aren't you supposed to be off somewhere?"

He pulled back and took her measure. A great grin came to his lips. "Aye, that I am, and so 'tis why I look for ye. We have the new gran' baby, and seeing how I expect to be gone all day," he said with a great movement of eyebrow, "I thought you might take the time and stop by for a visit with Annie."

She noted the emphasis Maguire put on 'expect to be gone all day' and wondered what he was up to. But the chance to get out and away from her problems was an escape she couldn't refuse. "I would love to. Tell Anne I'll come by after midday."

Maguire rubbed his hands together reminding her of a mad scientist in an old movie. Before she could challenge him, he added, "She's baking today, ye know."

Her mouth watered in immediate reaction, drowning any objections. Anne spent many years in France before becoming a member of the Maguire family; she was renowned for her fine pastries.

"I'll be there," she confirmed.

•

That afternoon Alex approached Maguire's cottage on foot, grateful for the change of scenery and curious to see the new baby.

"Hello inside," she called out, eager for a reprieve from her worries.

The door opened, and Anne Maguire invited Alex in. "Come along in, I have been expecting you. And ye look like you could use one of my pastries, or two."

Annie was fifteen years Maguire's junior. With her brown eyes, curly red hair and round cheeks, she looked to Alex like she came from Middle Earth.

Alex entered, offering the contents of her basket. "Cook sent along a loaf of her dark brown bread and a crock each of strawberry jam and sweet butter."

"Wonderful," Annie exclaimed. "I have the water on; sit while I make tea." While she worked, she added, "We can chat until Maggie Grace wakes, then she can wrap you around her little finger like she does the rest of us."

"She is the first born of your first born, is she not?" Alex asked.

"Aye," Annie answered. "And my next oldest is getting married next week."

The mention of marriage cast a shadow on Alex.

Marriage ... Royce ... Jamie.

She set the remnants of her pastry aside, avoiding Annie's eye as the woman warmed to the subject of her second son's coming nuptials.

"My Brandon and his sweetheart, Megan Gordon, will have their official ceremony after being handfast for this last year."

"So Brandon and Megan have lived together and she is happy," Alex stated with a smile. She could only imagine joy for such a couple.

Why can't I imagine such happiness for myself?

A robust cry came from tiny lungs.

"Oh, there she is," Annie said. "Let me tend her feeding and bring her out."

She waited, hearing Annie collecting the babe for its mother, Erin, who was still bedfast. The sounds stirred Alex's long banked desire for a child. She and Royce had not conceived, although they tried.

"The time is not right," Royce would say.

She always wondered, how do you know when the time is right if the timing isn't under your control?

Soon Annie returned with the babe, a tiny but robust bundle. "Oh! I see you," she whispered. Maggie's eyes were blue, and her head boasted plenty of soft, pale gold hair.

"Oh, my," Alex cooed. "Won't you be a heart breaker one day." She stroked the soft cheek, bringing a quick smile to Maggie's tiny face. "It's no wonder they are all wrapped around your little finger."

She took Maggie to the open window so she could see the child better in the light. "Wow!" Alex exclaimed. The color in Maggie's eyes brought a song to mind.

"Amazing Grace, how sweet the sound," Alex sang.

She hummed the tune and held the babe close, picking up the words with more vigor. "Amazing Grace, how sweet the sound that saved a wretch like me. I once was lost but now am found. Was blind, but now, I see."

This child holds a fresh start, Alex mused. *How can I do that, how can I make things change between Jamie and me?*

Cause I sure ain't getting any bidness done here.

•

Jamie watched Maguire set the last trap, sad to see the day's work end so soon.

Now I have to go back to the manor.

He took the empty snare sack and tied it to Pharaoh's saddlebag before swinging up into the saddle.

Maguire mounted his horse and joined him. "We finished early enough, you should come by the house, see Annie and the babe."

Jamie was not fooled—every nuance told him Maguire was up to something. The steward's tone was a little too insouciant and his eye contact too deliberate. "Why?" he challenged, curious to see Maguire's reaction.

Maguire pulled back, indignation, or guilt, bringing color to his cheeks. "I was not aware ye needed a reason. But if you must," he declared, drawing up with full offense, "Ye could come by to check on the health of your people, Earl."

"Ha!" he blurted, now certain Maguire had more reasons up his sleeve for Jamie to come by than he was revealing.

Anything, Jamie thought, *to keep me from going home to that redheaded—*

"To your house it is, then. Lead on," Jamie encouraged.

They reached the village barn and left their mounts to be cared for by one of the village lads.

"We can break open a new cask of ale," Maguire said.

They walked up the hill to Maguire's large cottage. As they approached through the trees, Jamie stopped suddenly in his tracks. He dropped in a hunch and flattened his back to a tree. Coming from a window on the top floor of the home was Alex's voice.

No!

His shoulders sagged and he dropped into a soft crouch, loving the sound of her voice. She sang a melody he did not know, the words haunting him.

Amazing Grace, how sweet the sound; how sweet the sound that saved a wretch like me; I once was lost but now am found; Was blind, but now, I see.

Jamie's throat constricted. "I canna live with this any more," he whispered. Before Maguire could object, Jamie gave his steward the signal for silence.

He backed up enough to turn and slip away, unseen.

•

Alex put her nose to Maggie Grace's soft down curls and inhaled her fresh scent. In pondering how to proceed, she instantly thought of her sister Fallon, and *What would Fallon do?* came to mind.

"Fallon would say exactly what's on her mind," Alex whispered to Maggie. "And to hell with anything called correct."

Anne came and collected Maggie. "She is a dear one," Alex said before Anne could speak. She then abruptly stood and brushed off her skirt. "Anne, don't think me rude," she said in a rush. "But I have to go." She crossed the room in quick determined strides and picked up her basket.

"Maggie Grace has given me an idea," she said. "An idea to help solve a problem." While Anne's mouth opened in surprise, Alex skipped to the door.

"Thank you, Maggie," she called as she opened the door and left.

•

Jamie rode Pharaoh back to Greyhaven, wiped the stallion down and released him into a pasture. He came back into the cool barn. "Where to go and be alone," he said. "Where to go where she canna find me ... " He looked around and his eye came to the ladder up to the hayloft. "Ah, I havna been in those rafters since I was a lad."

He climbed the ladder and pulled it up after him. "There," he said, brushing his hands together with satisfaction. "Good. Absolute isolation," he announced. Surrounding him were fresh bales of hay stacked across a solid floor above the stalls. He gathered loose hay into a comfortable pile and stretched out with a self-assured, "Ah."

He heard footsteps as someone enter the barn.

"Here is Pharaoh's halter and gear, so he is back," Alex said.

Alex's foot began tapping, and Jamie could imagine the fierce look on her face at the mystery. He stifled the urge to call her up.

"I have looked everywhere," she said. "Dammit, where could he be?"

The horse just below Jamie moved, responding to her voice.

"Hey, Blue. How are you, big fella?" she asked.

Jamie closed his eyes, seeing her in his mind's eye as she stroked the horse's long face, rubbing behind his ears. Hearing her voice today after five days of abstinence made the closed gates of his heart fall open.

How I wish she would touch me with such care ...

His thought made him cringe. He wanted her so badly, yet he could not seem to breech his fear ... of passion and the responsibilities therein.

"Well, hell," she complained.

A smile erupted even though Jamie held his breath; he strangled an accompanying chuckle. More of her voice came and he strained to hear every word. She sighed, and he shared the frustration he detected in her exhalation.

"How can love be so difficult?" she asked.

Afraid to move and disturb the revelations coming from below, Jamie kept still.

"I think it's best to just get it out in the open," she continued. "Just say it. Jamie, I love you. In fact, we are old souls who have loved each other in many lives, and I just need to tell him. Oh, for Christ's sake, I traveled through time, and now I'm here and—"

His need for air was desperate, but his need for the truth was more important. He held on, silent until—

"I can't continue hiding my love," she finished.

Above, he put his arm to his mouth and exhaled into his coat sleeve. Down below, she huffed, snorting through her nose.

"Wait until I get my hands on him," she declared, and stomped from the barn.

Hearing her steps fade, Jamie gasped, filling his lungs with air as he reviewed what he just heard. A broad grin filled his face, coming all the way from his heart.

"Going to kiss that redheaded woman again," he whispered.

•

A Week Later, Greyhaven

Alex lay in her bed, hearing the busy work of the manor's inhabitants.

Wedding day, she thought. How would this day's events differ from what the ceremony had become in modern times? A quick trip to Vegas? A multi-million dollar affair yielding to divorce in a couple months?

"Not likely," she whispered.

Today's wedding would require nothing less than the commitment of a lifetime, lasting truly, she finished aloud, "Till death do ye part."

She couldn't think of marriage without thinking of Royce, and thinking of Royce always brought her mind back to Jamie.

"Jamie," she said. She had yet to 'speak her heart and mind to him' since coming back from seeing Maggie Grace, as he had managed to avoid her earnest efforts at tracking him down. "He's hiding from me."

Alex jumped from her bed and began washing. "Well, not today, mister. You are in my sights." She began pulling her hair back as she was prone to do when she had bidness to tend to, when a knock came at her door.

"Alex," Kathleen called.

Alex opened the door. Kathleen smiled, her eyes mysterious, and reminding Alex of Master Chan. Instantly she knew the woman understood Alex's heart and mind.

"May I come in?" Kathleen asked.

"Of course," Alex mumbled, feeling goose bumps race up her arm. She was instantly both wary of and excited for what had brought Kathleen to her door.

"I have a present for you," Kathleen chirped. She held out a bundle of green and lavender muslin.

"Oh!" she exclaimed. "The colors are perfect."

"They should go well with your hair, do you think?" Kathleen finished.

She felt more goose bumps dance across her shoulders. For a moment she suddenly felt disoriented, as when she passed through time. For this instant she was adrift, as insubstantial as a flash of green light—

"Let me help you," Kathleen said.

The words came from a distance, but they drew her back. She felt her bare feet on the Persian carpet on her chamber floor. The breeze through the window brought odors that spoke of activity in the manor's massive kitchen.

"Yes, please, I would love your help," Alex responded softly.

The dress was laid out on the bed. The light green muslin was adorned with purple ribbons and embroidery. The neckline allowed a generous view of her chest. Alex dressed and sat before the mirror as Kathleen picked up the brush.

"I thought to wear my hair up," she began. The strange sense of disorientation rose again, drawing her eyes to the mirror, leaving her mesmerized by her reflection.

Jamie would prefer my hair loose.

Kathleen's eyes met Alex in the mirror. "Oh, leave it down," she suggested. "Your hair is far too lovely to contain."

Alex felt the room pause and she was again timeless, recognizing how this mundane decision—

—is my moment of choice, more monumental even than traveling through time. By wearing this dress and leaving my hair down today something in my life will change as a result. Am I ready to go through with this surrender?

Kathleen held the brush. She tilted her dark head, her green eyes waiting for Alex's reply.

The answer to the question rested in Alex's soul. Her heart softened, her body warmed, and her mind rejoiced. "Yes," she said softly. "I think I'll leave it down."

Kathleen brushed Alex's hair vigorously, bringing a shine and fullness that surrounded Alex's face with color. Once her slippers graced her feet, she was ready to go.

"I have one more thing," Kathleen said. She pulled from her pocket a necklace and fastened it behind Alex's neck.

"Freshwater pearls, they are beautiful," Alex whispered.

"They are beautiful because you are wearing them," Kathleen added. "Now come, we will have to catch up." She grabbed Alex's hand.

Downstairs Connor waited for them, anxiously pacing. "Come on. They left already," he declared, and bounded out the manor door.

Kathleen pulled Alex along as they darted down the road to the village. They caught up with Connor who had joined the crowd in front of the bride's home.

Alex strained on her tiptoes looking for Jamie.

"He is in the front, with Maguire and Brandon," Kathleen said.

"Megan, as Lord of the Land I am here with your betrothed, Brandon Maguire. Are ye ready to become his wedded wife?"

Megan stood outside on her doorstep, waiting for them. She wore an ivory muslin gown with small pearls sewn to the bodice; Irish lace covered her hair. With a smile that filled her face and eyes, she opened the door.

The smell of cooked goose wafted out the door and the crowd gave a collective "Ahh … "

"Aye, my Lord. Brandon's goose is well cooked," Megan spoke loud enough for all to hear.

The crowd erupted into cheers and applause. Alex was so caught up the jovial atmosphere, she forgot about looking for Jamie. She cheered as Brandon swept Megan into his arms and they kissed before Maguire and Megan's father separated the two for the ceremony to proceed. The lovers waved to each other as if they couldn't bear being separated for a moment.

"What's happening?" Alex asked Kathleen. The crowd was surging into the small home, and Alex thought of sardines in a can.

"The ceremony is here, the celebration outside," Kathleen shouted over the raucous cheers and laughter. They were crammed tightly together.

Suddenly, silence descended. Alex was trapped behind a large man and could see nothing but his back. "Darn," she muttered.

"For Megan and Brandon Maguire," Jamie called out to the crowd. "And all who are here, may wealth, health and fertility bless us all. Let the ceremony begin with the Lord's approval."

She tried to locate Jamie by the sound of his voice, but by the time she squirmed into a different vantage point, he was no longer in the front. She scanned the crowd.

And found him ... staring at her with such intensity a shiver shook her legs. "Oh," she mouthed silently. The sudden feral heat between them surprised her. She forgot about the wedding ceremony droning past her ears, for her entire being was focused on the message coming from across the room.

Heat ... possession ... surrender.

She licked her lips.

He gave her one slightly raised eyebrow, a challenge.

Her body quickly responded. She was warm, and not only on the outside. A flicker of desire came to life deep in her core. She wanted—

Jamie tilted his head, questioning.

What do you want?

This answer is easy, she thought. "You," she whispered silently through pursed lips.

He smiled in return, not quickly, as with conquest. But slowly, taunting Alex more than his words could ever say.

What is he thinking?

Alex parted her lips. The house was too warm and she needed air and ... something hard and wet sliding—

Her knees went weak and she closed her eyes. Were she not locked in the crowd she would have gone to the floor. She was so incredibly filled with desire, all she need do was press her legs together and she would orgasm in the middle of all these people. Sweat trickled down her back, and she groaned inwardly as she resisted.

She opened her eyes.

He was gone.

She exhaled in a burst, not realizing she was holding her breath. Her breasts tingled and she refused to hold them, to place her hand under her skirts and relieve this fire coursing through her core.

"Are you ready?" Kathleen asked.

Alex jumped and knew her cheeks flooded with color. Her sudden embarrassment effectively shut down her near orgasmic state. "Ready?" she choked.

Kathleen smiled as though she noticed nothing, yet knew everything. "Time to go outside, to celebrate," she answered.

The room was half empty. Everyone was exiting; the sounds of cheering outside finally entered Alex's ears.

Oh my, I missed the entire ceremony.

Fresh color rose, heating her face anew. She fanned her face and smiled back at Kathleen as though nothing were wrong. "Of course, if you will lead the way," she said. She stepped aside with one thought.

Where is Jamie?

Outside, the wedding party was well on its way back up the hill. On the east flank of the manor, tables were set up under the trees. Already, kegs of poteen, ale, mead and wine were opened and ready for drinking. Streamers of cloth in all colors along with lanterns were hung from the lower tree branches. Bunches of flowers were tied with bright ribbons as a centerpiece on the tables. Other tables were bare, awaiting the arrival of food.

A mug of mead was pressed into her hand as Kathleen propelled her into the mix. Children ran laughing. A great deal of backslapping was going on between the men, and the women chatted gaily.

Music began, coming from a group of village men playing a fiddle, bagpipes and a flute. Dancing needed no encouragement.

"Count me in," Alex exclaimed. The excitement was contagious. The mead was sweet and spicy and her feet soon began to tap to the music. She was thinking about looking for him when Maguire stepped in front of her.

"Will ye do me the honor of a dance, Milady?"

Alex set her mug on a nearby table. "The honor is all mine," she responded. Maguire took her out to the dance area where they joined the step in progress. They separated and turned, coming back to separate and bow. As their heads came together he whispered, "Ye look lovely. And yer step is fine, I might add."

"Connor taught me."

They turned around and stood back to back. She added lightly, "Would you know where Jamie is?" They stepped away and came back to join hands. He held one hand up and she passed beneath his arm.

"I am here," Jamie said.

She stepped right into his arms, having been effectively passed on from Maguire. Her breath jumped and adrenalin rushed. She stepped on his toe and nearly stumbled. He caught her with a firm hand at her waist.

"Milady?" he asked with a concerned tilt of his head.

Alex saw the heat smoldering beneath the polite inquiry. She gained her equilibrium and smiled back, letting suggestion slant her eyes. "Milord," she responded coyly.

He dipped low and whispered into her ear, "Do you know what Leonidas said to Xerxes on the plain of Sparta?"

They separated and stood ready for the next step. She tilted her head, uncertain if she had heard him right. As a nobleman, he had studied the art of war, and the battles lost and won from the past. She knew the answer, the true words, not those uttered in the movie.

She curtsied into a bow as he returned the gesture. They stepped together and hooked arms. "Are you preparing for battle, Milord?" she asked, catching him directly with her eye.

They parted and walked the length of the line of dancers, returning to stand before each other. Alex searched his face. His eyes were warm and soft, reminding her of Royce. There was no hint of battle visible.

Had the battle already been fought and lost, or won?

Her stomach felt giddy and she tingled down her arms and legs, alive with desire for this man. She was failing at containment and feared what she might do, even in such a public forum.

The music ended and they bowed politely.

Alex couldn't move. Her eyes were riveted to Jamie's face, seeking more nonverbal messages, wanting to fan the simmering heat that now filled her being. Her need for this to happen had climbed to a painful point, making her desire all the more sweet for its postponement.

More music began, and he reached for her hand. His eyes were inviting, his smile engaging, and his warm scent intoxicating. She took his hand, and the dance began.

As before, when she lost track of the wedding ceremony, she was captive to a spell, oblivious of the celebration proceeding around them. Through the twirling, the steps, the brief contact and then separations, all movement fueled her intoxication with Jamie.

When he laughed, her heart expanded to capture the sound. When he squeezed her hand, she squeezed back. When his eyes blazed down into her face, she returned the look.

Suddenly, the music ended and Alex, flushed with excitement, looked about for her mug of spiced wine. Not seeing it, she grabbed a fresh one from a passing tray and gulped. Winded from laughing and warmed from the dance, she fanned her face. Before she could get her breath, Jamie stepped beside her.

"Now, while everyone is busy with their drinks, go to your chamber. I will come to you there," he whispered.

Alex swallowed hard around the accelerated reaction from her heart.

Yes, dear God, yes!

She pulsed with desire, her nipples hardened, and her knees went weak. With a surprising, stately grace, given her current body-on-hormones condition, she turned from him and slipped through the crowd and into the manor.

Once inside her chamber, Alex pressed her back against the door, adrenaline flooding her body. Her heart raced from the sprint up the stairs, and she felt her damp clothing cling.

"Wash," she commanded, adding, "And slow down

before you look like a fool."

She exhaled, bringing a small sense of calm. Fresh water felt cool against her skin as she held the wet cloth to her face. "What are you doing?" she asked her reflection.

The face that gazed back at her was at peace. Internally she felt her pulse continue to race with excitement. On the surface, she was like still waters.

Know your heart, be true to yourself.

She was giving herself to this man, and he was Royce, and he was Jamie, and—

Who else? Under how many other names have we loved each other?

She stripped away her clothes and bathed, watching in the mirror. When she drew the cloth over her breasts, her nipples puckered exquisitely, and she let her head fall back, giving in to the sweet heat already building between her legs.

"Ohh," she moaned, feeling her earlier near-orgasm rise. She breathed through pursed lips, panting, and continued her bath, letting the fresh air cool her heated skin.

With a last look in the mirror, she smiled at her reflection. Anticipation had placed fire in her eyes and brought an attractive flush to her skin. "Huh," she grunted, remembering an axiom from her dating days.

Never go drinking when you're ovulating.

She fluffed her hair and climbed into bed.

CHAPTER NINE

"Molon labe!"

Jamie watched as Alex twirled around in the last step of the dance, and knew that single image of her would remain in his mind till the day he was gone from this world. The music faded away, leaving him with one thought clearly prominent.

My beautiful angel lady, I can no longer deny my love for you.

She gulped from a mug of wine and smacked her lips.

Holding back a grin at her antics, he stepped close and spoke. "Now, while everyone is busy with their drinks, go to your chamber. I will come to you there."

She was breathless from the dancing and her eyes were bright, her lips pursed just as he imagined they were when he kissed her in the chapel … and as they soon will be when he finally takes her in his arms.

With no reaction, she turned from him and easily moved through the crowd. He watched her back, so slim and straight, so sure and … safe.

"Ha!" he laughed, shaking his head.

When was passion ever safe?

She would take him into the very insane territory he swore to avoid, but in her arms was a safe harbor he would find nowhere else.

With steady restraint he went to the manor and slowly climbed the stairs past her door and up to his chamber. Even though he had not rushed, his heart was drumming too fast, and his breath caught in his throat.

"Aye," he said. "She makes me as excited as a young lad." He stopped in front of the mirror and saw the truth in his reflection. "She is an angel, and I canna understand how and why she is here … but from the heavens she has come."

After bathing he chewed a mint leaf and rinsed his mouth. He wore clean pants and a fresh washed shirt with the laces open.

"Are you ready for this?" he asked his reflection.

He saw no turmoil in his visage.

"Huh," he grunted. "You know there will be no turning back."

One eyebrow lifted in recognition of this fruitless argument with himself. Within, his heartbeat was steady as his body yearned for the touch of her skin, the smell of her hair, her voice saying "I love you."

"Well, then," he said. "Here we go."

●

Alex heard his earlier footsteps as he passed by her chamber, and had waited patiently, knowing he, too, needed to slow down in order to appreciate what was happening. He came to her now, silently, without a knock. Her chamber door opened, and in the full light of mid-afternoon, her soul mate arrived.

"Jamie," she said. She pushed the covers aside and rose up on her knees. All she wore was the pink thong.

She heard a quick intake of breath.

He crossed the room in long strides and stood by the bed, yet out of her reach. "I never dreamed any one could be so lovely," he whispered with a voice broken on gravel.

Alex's heart melted at his simple words. "I am here, Milord. Molon labe," she whispered. She held her arms up. "I offer you my surrender." She felt his hands at last against her skin, warm and exciting. In his eye she saw a sparkle of humor.

He shook his head slowly, negating her offer as he ran his hands up her back. "Nay, 'tis I who surrender."

She shivered as his lips made the slow descent, coming closer. His breath fanned her face, smelling of mint and making her mouth water with anticipation. At last, the first tentative touch of his lips came so soft and gentle, loving and kind, unlike the hard possession of their kiss in the chapel. This one moment, Alex thought, is worth the trip through time. The simmering sweet heat rose from her core into her belly, making her tighten her muscles in pulses.

"Ohh," she moaned as he took full possession of her lips. His tongue slid gently across her lower lip and she parted them for him. Their tongues met, and their bodies pressed a little harder, arms hugged a little tighter, breath came a little faster.

He pushed her back to arm's length and ogled her. "Lass what are ye wearing?" he exclaimed in brogue. His eyebrows wagged with wicked admiration.

She was alive with wanting this man. At this point, this was her mission, to save him through a very carnal act. She was going to give him a twenty-first century adventure.

She flicked her hair over her shoulder, exposing her breast. The cool air tightened the already hard bud, and the heat in Jamie's eyes told her not to stop.

"I see now," he managed over a choke, "What this little garment is for." He reached to touch the pink thong.

"It looks like this," she said. She turned quickly around and presented her bottom for his view, knowing how her butt cheeks looked being separated by the little pink material. She looked over her shoulder. Jamie reached out and cupped one cheek before smoothing his other hand over her waist where it flared into hip.

She spun around to present him with a pout. "Are you going to take your clothes off?" she asked, pointing. "Or are you just here to tease me?" She hooked the top of the thong and tugged on the elastic fabric.

He pulled his shirt over his head. Next his britches were hastily unlaced and tossed aside. When he stood up, the evidence of his desire was impossible to miss.

He gave her an unapologetic look of pride.

"Thank you," she prayed silently.

He does look just like Royce.

He climbed into the bed and she took him in her arms. "Kiss me, kiss until I can take no more," she pleaded.

Their lips met and she inhaled his scent, soaking up the pheromones, feeling them fan her already ignited hormonal state. Her legs sagged open as her knees went weak. Her breasts raked his torso, sensitive to the light hair scattered across his chest.

She broke from the kiss and drew her lips along his neck, sucking, licking her way across his collarbone. His hand came from her shoulder to the nape of her neck and up into her hair. Slowly he lifted her back up, and returned the favor by taking her down a similar path of pleasure.

His lips kissed her shoulder, her collarbone, and the top of her breast before taking her nipple into his mouth. As he gently kissed her nipple, a flood of heat and surrender opened in her. She gasped, for air, for relief, for more. "Oh," she moaned. She was desperate for the release of this heat, this orgasm that had begged for her attention all day. She pulled off the thong and reached for his hard-on, pulling him down on top of her. "I can't wait," she breathed throatily. It was her turn to be unapologetic.

"Aye," he answered, his voice as raspy as hers. He reached for her and found her already wet.

She almost came at this first touch. Her lips were swollen and wet, eager for penetration well before he touched her. His fingers were warm and strong and she arched her back, rubbing her chest into him. "Please," she begged. She grabbed his shoulder, feeling him position himself for entry. She pushed against him, relishing the smooth round head about to plunder her body. She pushed, and he entered her just through her lips.

"Ah," he moaned. "Yer killing me." He shifted his hips and Alex hung onto his shoulder. He slid in with one long steady thrust.

Tears sprouted in Alex's eyes. The joy and the relief were exquisite. The battle was fought and the final surrender behind them, a battle fought and won on both sides.

Now all she had to do was enjoy the ride.

They held each other still in tight embrace, relishing the sensation of entry, the sharing of heat and the exquisite sensation of wet on wet sliding deep—

"More," she whispered. She tilted her hips and he pressed a little deeper.

"Ahhh," came a communal sigh.

Nice and easy, they drew back, just a half measure. And came together again.

"Ohhhh, that was nice," she panted. "Again, please."

Out he slid, a little farther. He came back, wet, hard, throbbing within her.

She rolled her head in ecstasy. She had so much pent-up sexual energy she was sure she couldn't get enough. "Again," she breathed into his ear, lifting her head to kiss his neck, clutching at his back now. Her thighs had broken a sweat and their bodies were sliding against each other in a slick of passion. She knew she didn't have long. She quickened the pace.

He was kissing her neck and nuzzling her ear; her breasts were flattened into his chest, and their pelvises were pounding one another. Sensations of her coming orgasm began reaching out from her belly.

"Coming," she moaned into his ear. She was consumed by her orgasm, feeling multiple waves of incredible ecstasy rip through her body.

He tucked his hips and pressed into her with increasing intensity before stiffening with a groan. "Oh," he gasped, and pushed up on his arms, back arched while thrusting deeply into her.

They lay with labored breath while he held his weight off her. He kissed her neck, brushing away the hair from her sweated flesh, then blowing lightly to cool her down.

"Oh my," Alex breathed heavily.

He rolled off her and lay close, holding one of her hands. She turned to face him, winding her feet through his legs. She smiled, feeling her contentment roll off her in waves of sated energy. She took his free hand and brought it to her lips, kissing his fingers.

At last their breath slowed and Jamie's eyes locked onto hers. "What have we done?" he whispered, and kissed the back of her hand.

"It's called—"

He gave her a soft shake to stop her. "I know what to call 'it,' but what else have we done?" he reproached.

"We did what we were supposed to do," Alex said calmly. She let him look deep into her eyes, for she had nothing to hide. Bidness was being done.

"And what do we do next?" he asked.

Alex took one of his fingers with her teeth and drew the digit into her mouth. She thrust her hips at him, drawing her legs up so they slid through his.

"I have duties to attend to as Lord of the manor," he said with a dour mouth. "I canna stay all afternoon, much as I care to."

"You will come back," Alex said. It was a statement.

"Were I not concerned about your social standing—"

She interrupted him with a "pffft" of disdain.

Jamie drew back. One eyebrow went up. "What does 'Pffft' mean?" He withdrew his legs from hers and sat on the edge of the bed.

"It means I care not what people here think of me."

He slid on his pants and laced them before speaking. "We have our ways 'here,' and I, especially, care about what people think of you." He pulled on his shirt and came to kiss her. "Worry not. I will take care of everything," he stated.

Alex wondered what "take care of everything"

meant, but let the concern go. She had not had a man in what seemed forever; she didn't want to risk another dry spell at this moment.

Let him take care of everything as long as he comes up here and takes care of me.

"When?" she asked. Still on the bed, she pulled him over and playfully tugged at the laces on his pants.

She noticed he had gone still, and looked up. The heat reflected there, the promise, the love ... brought a shiver of passion up her spine.

As she kneeled on the bed, he pulled her up into his arms, her naked body pressed against his chest. He was Rhett and she Scarlett in that famous pose. His voice was husky, and the intensity of his expression made her breathless.

"I canna say where you come from, or how long you are here, but as long as I am allowed to see your face each morning, you are mine, and I am yours."

He kissed her, his lips coming quickly, allowing her no escape. She was crushed in his arms, bringing their hearts to beat barely inches apart as he spoke his love with this eternal declaration.

His hands stroked her back, and he ended the kiss. She was immobile, emotionally spent, dazed and sated in both mind and body.

"Will I see you tonight?" she whispered.

He was at the door. He looked over his shoulder, and answered softly, "Only death could keep me away."

She sighed when the door closed behind him. "Wow!" she whispered into her pillow. She rolled over onto her back and hugged the pillow close as she brought her knees up. "He is the same," she stated. "Only different."

Royce or Jamie, there were subtle similarities in

both. Jamie kissed like Royce, but Royce was less … traditional.

"Does this mean bidness is concluded?" she asked in a hushed voice. "Is this how I save him?" She shrugged, unable to answer. "Seems like a lot of bother just to get laid," she mused. Outside, the sounds of merrymaking and festivities came to drift in her window, beckoning her to participate. "Come, be part of life here," she heard.

With a sudden declaration of autonomy, she blurted, "No, bidness is not finalized." This announcement led to the next inevitable question—

Then what else is required?

Suddenly her mouth went dry and her heart hammered with a silent fear. A shadow loomed, and she was forced to acknowledge the specter in her mind. Her hands came to her throat in a defensive gesture.

"How long," she whispered. "How long am I supposed to stay here?"

I don't want to leave!

Suddenly every moment was precious and fleeting. She jumped from the bed, splashed a little water on her face, freshened up and redressed. She looked out the window and saw a party she didn't want to miss.

"Wait for me," she cried as she dashed through the door.

She joined the crowd of revelers, grabbing a mug of ale from a table. She sipped and smacked her lips at the bitter tartness. The music stirred her feet, and the sound of laughter surrounded her, bringing a smile to her face and her heart.

Today is for living!

Maguire waved for her to join in the beginnings of

a new round of dance. She emptied her mug with an unladylike gulp. "God, how I love these people and this place," she mumbled, and plunged into the dance.

One dance became a dozen. Food and drink was without end as the lanterns were lit. Alex partied like a rock star, indulging every moment of fun, whether it was gastronomic, another dance, or joining in telling jokes. Just before sunset a cake was brought out, carried by eight strong boys, for it was a five-tiered masterpiece.

Meagan and Brandon held the knife together as they cut the first slice and set it aside. "To the bride and groom!" rang the toasts. No sooner had the cake been cut than the bagpipes came up again.

"I have to sit," Alex complained. She took her piece of cake, marveling at the fine texture of the white cake and the delicate marzipan and sugar flowers adorning her slice.

"I have been watching you," came a voice at her shoulder.

Alex smiled wondering when Jamie would approach her. "I know," she responded tartly as she nibbled at the cake. She gave him a quick, playful glance.

"You are wicked."

"I am," she agreed sagely. She licked the sugary confection from her fingers.

He came around and sat across the table from her. "This is exactly why I have stayed away from you this afternoon," he mumbled under his breath.

"I know that, too," Alex offered without commiseration. She delicately pulled off a bite of cake and popped it into her mouth and licked her lips. "Oh," she moaned with a face of exquisite pleasure.

"Perhaps I should leave before you make a spectacle," he complained in a hushed voice. He eased out of his seat and leaned over the table. "I will see you—"

"I know," Alex finished with a wink.

"Wicked—"

"I know—"

He turned and melted into the crowd.

She sucked the remnants of the cake from her fingers. A feeling of rightness, a rising sense of well being flowed through her. She was crazy content. "Yes," she said with conviction. She stood, dusting crumbs from her skirt. "I believe I will stay."

She retreated to her room even though the hour was early. "A nap," she suggested, feeling the excesses of the day. "Yes, a bath and a nap." She rang for bath water and was soon sitting in the tub with hot water and scented oil up to her collarbones.

"Oh, how good this is." She slid down even farther, letting the warmth of the water work its magic. Her head rested on a folded towel, and she sighed deeply. "Ummm, so glad to be here."

The water wrapped her with comfort. Peace was all around her. She felt complete, in perfect harmony with the universe. Her mind drifted. She was in a cocoon, suspended by a thread. Above her, a small tear opened the cocoon, drawing her attention, begging her to explore.

"No," she implored softly. "Not yet."

She woke as the water came cool. "Oh," she mumbled, climbing out and wrapping in a towel. "I wanted the nap after the bath, not in the tub." She dried and dressed in a thin chemise, her heart beginning to quicken with thoughts of what this night would bring. "Jamie," she said with a sly smile. Knowing her power over him was a heady rush. "He will come."

Her desire for this man, whether he was Royce or Jamie, was a part of her and impossible to deny, as impossible to deny as the color of her eyes. She looked in the mirror, barely recognizing her reflection.

"You ... have changed," she said softly. She couldn't put a finger on exactly how, but she was certainly not the person she was the day she arrived.

"What is the mission, now?" she queried. She touched one breast and her nipple hardened immediately. A soft molten river of desire worked through her loins, and she closed her eyes.

She saw not Royce, but Jamie.

"I want you," she whispered. "You are the same, but different, and I want you no matter who you are." She knew she would never be complete until she fully connected with this man ... there was more bidness to come.

Feeling as if in a trance, she asked her reflection, "What are you doing to me?" In her mind, she saw the cocoon on the slender thread. "Not yet," she whispered softly. "Not ready to fly ... away ... not yet."

Suddenly Alex started. She glanced into the mirror, and as though she had just now noticed her reflection, blurted, "Oh hell ... look at that hair!"

She took her brush and went to the window seat. Beginning at the tangled ends, she worked the brush through, at last reaching her scalp. A sudden draft and squeak of hinge told her Jamie had arrived.

"Milord," she said, glancing over her shoulder. He was behind her, his hands stroking her arms, pushing her hair to one side. His warm lips kissed her shoulder, and she closed her eyes. "Uummm," she exhaled, feeling shivers dart down her arms.

"May I?" he asked, taking the brush from her hand. He drew the brush from her scalp to the ends until her hair crackled and snapped, alive with fire in its red and gold depths.

Alex was in a state of semi-euphoria, luxuriating in his touch, mesmerized by the similar behavior between Royce and Jamie. She took a deep breath and turned toward him so he could see her eyes. Reaching her arms around his neck, she said, "I love you, Jamie." Before he could react, she pulled his face down for a kiss.

With their lips and mouths locked in passion, he carried her to the bedside and set her down, breaking the kiss. His breath came ragged and he paused while they faced each other, touching forehead to forehead.

"I love ye, Alex, like I never thought possible for me in this lifetime," he said, his voice husky.

Tears sprouted hot and burning in Alex's eyes. In that instant of hearing his words, she suddenly understood. "I know," she said, half-sobbing. "That's why I'm here."

She pulled back to see his face. His eyes glittered with unshed tears ... tears of joy. The intense emotion in his face broke what little control Alex held. A watershed of emotion let go. "I'm here," she cried. "I'm here, my love." She began pulling at his clothes. When he was stripped bare, she pulled off her chemise.

They raked each other with a hot gaze.

Her nipples hardened and puckered with expectation when she saw his erection. Without words, each knew the other's heart and mind, and they were one.

They came together in a hot rush of give and take.

She felt his teeth graze her shoulder. An insistent press of hard flesh against her thigh made her knees go weak. She returned the favor and nibbled at his neck while rubbing her sensitive nipples across his chest.

"Aagh," he cried. He scooped her up and tossed her on the bed, diving on top of her.

Jamie's fingers played up and down Alex's ribs as he positioned her, moving her higher in the mattress so he moved down her torso.

"You have the most beautiful breasts I have ever seen," he murmured.

She meant to tease him with, "How many breasts does that include?" but he was licking her and sucking on her already sensitive nipples. Her hips arched in a silent call of need.

"Aye, lassie, I know," he said.

She knew he mocked her earlier words, but she had no complaint. A finger slid inside her, drawing the slick of her wetness across her lips to moisten her clit.

"Aye, lassie, I know." He dipped his head, and while the one hand played, his lips suckled and licked and circled her. Slowly, her hips began to pulse.

"Oh," she moaned. She could not hold back. She wanted to wait for him, but he was calling up an orgasm right now. She brought all her focus to the flickering beginnings. His tongue was warm and wet, his fingers, probing and stroking. His free hand came up and began to massage her breast.

"Bingo," she grunted. The flickering grew to an inferno of exquisite pulsing as her hips began jerking in erotic spasms of release. Her back arched as the orgasm exploded through her body. She inhaled with a gasp and went limp.

Breathless, she lay inert while he stroked her thighs, her belly, her arms. He kissed her stomach and inched up her body, slowly bringing her back to life.

"I love you," she whispered. Jamie's face came into view as he came to lie over her. He kissed her collarbone, her chin, and the end of her nose. He nuzzled her neck and kissed her ear. Softly he answered, "I know."

Alex smiled.

Perhaps he isn't so traditional after all.

She shifted her weight, opening her legs, and his hot flesh dropped to nudge her wet opening. A tingle raced from her breasts, through her hips and down to her toes. She opened wider, and he pushed in. "Oh," she moaned, biting into his shoulder. She was already wet, and he slid in, filling her. She retreated, feeling him leave her, then came back to have him fill her again.

His muscled chest moved across her breasts and his thigh muscles bunched into powerful cords when he returned the thrust.

Deep and slow they became one. Touching, exploring, tasting, creating a crescendo.

"Take me now," she begged.

"Aye," he agreed.

He held his weight off her while he pressed deep between her thighs. She knew another orgasm was building; she brought her focus to that warm and tingling spot that was getting worked so sweetly with each stroke. Back and forth, wet on wet, his hardness rubbed her slick and swollen flesh.

Ignition came.

"Now," she whimpered into his shoulder. Her hips jerked and she pressed into him taking him deeper, feeling the exquisite electricity race along her nerves from her core to the ends of her body.

Jamie clenched against her in a frozen grimace of passion. They collapsed in a gasping, sweating, twitching and pulsing heap.

"Whoa," Alex gasped. She grabbed his hand and kissed his fingers. "I love you."

Jamie's eyes closed and a blissful expression shot across his face, making Alex tingle all the way to her toes.

He pulled her to him, wrapping his arms around her as if to keep her in that moment forever. "Never leave me," he said. "Do you promise?"

Alex heard the desperate edge in his voice.

He worries about me going back!

She held him tight, her ear to his chest, hearing his heart beat so strong and solid. She worried, too, about how long she would be here. She considered melting down the gold whistle from Master Chan, effectively closing that door. But Kathleen had found it in her chamber one day when she delivered clean clothing.

"Is this how you traveled?" she asked. With a mischievous look in her eye she put the whistle to her mouth and filled her cheeks with air.

"No!" Alex had to shout to stop her.

Kathleen looked at the gold device with speculation. "Perhaps I should keep this for you," she declared, and tucked the whistle away in a pocket.

She knows something.

Alex decided she didn't want to know what Kathleen knew. She was happy to let her keep the whistle.

Now it's too late to go. I want to stay.

She held Jamie tight, suddenly fearing their fate.

I will save him and I will stay. Period.

"I promise," she whispered. "I promise."

•

Dawn came, bringing the song of birds and the rose colored tint of early light. With the shutters of Alex's chamber open, cool air moved through the room. She stretched slowly and reached out, but her hands met only empty bed linens.

"Gone," she said.

She sat up in the bed, sighing with joy that comes from a night of good loving. She was not surprised he had left; there were many reasons why he should not be found here this morning. This newly discovered relationship was something she wanted kept quiet for a while before revealing it to the world.

"Food," she said, sitting up. She saw her reflection in the glass and covered her face with her hands. Ringing the bell for bath water, she set about straightening her chamber before the men arrived. Once the tub was filled, she sank down, letting the water rise over her head.

She drifted with her face submerged, afloat in the tub, disconnected, alone, a heart beating slow and steady, confirming her thoughts.

I am here to stay ...

She sat up, letting the water stream from her hair. "I am here to stay," she said, liking the sound. The words made her happy, the solid conviction in her voice strengthened her resolve, and the thought of living a long, rich life with this man enticed her.

"Well, it's settled then," she announced. "But let's just keep it quiet for a while."

After toweling her hair partially dry, she dressed and went to the kitchen.

"Ooohh," she said with a squeal of delight as she found still-warm brown bread, fresh butter, and a platter of fried pork slices. She grabbed a piece of the salty pork fat, and sucked on the crisp edges as she sat at a table alone. It seemed Cook Mary and one of her kitchen lads were the only ones up.

"Well, lass, you look fit this mornin'," Mary quipped. She eyed Alex like she was inspecting a haunch of venison.

She forced herself not to cringe from the inspection. As it was, she felt like she was wearing a sign proclaiming Freshly Banged. "Ooumphed," she mumbled. She gulped her morning tea, struggling to continue. "Oh," she said, wiping her mouth. She displayed her most innocent smile and said, "I had so much fun yesterday."

Mary's inspection continued in silence, and Alex's smile became plastered on her face.

"Aye, well, 'tis good to see ye with such a spark in your eye," Mary said. She extracted a final, deep, once-over before turning back to her duties.

"Whew," she slowly exhaled, whistling her relief. She finished her meal and headed for the stables. Seeing the boy Ian was nowhere about, she collected Blue and saddled him. Before anyone else could 'inspect' her, she mounted and urged the horse into a cantor.

Greyhaven Manor was a ghost town. She brought Blue to a walk and they crossed the stream and passed through the village without seeing a soul. On they went, skirting the mill and quietly walking past lush fields.

"This is what I need," she said, pulling Blue to the pond. "A little more space and a little less inspection."

She dismounted and looped the reins over Blue's neck, knowing he would not go far.

She dropped to the ground, lush with late summer grass, and lay back, scanning the clouds for images. Her heart was at peace. The constant wonder of why she was here had finally been answered; she would love this man and live here with him to the end of her days.

"And have a child?" she asked hesitantly. She shrugged, not needing the answer to that question to-day.

"I am happy here," she announced. She put her hands behind her head and closed her eyes, imagining the birthdays, the Christmases, and many New Years she would have with Jamie. She saw their children rac-ing through the manor. Maguire would have his hands filled with a new generation.

"Ah," she sighed. "I have never felt so right in all my life."

•

Jamie left Alex's chamber well before sunrise. Tear-ing himself away from her warm bed had been nearly impossible. He watched the soft rise and fall of her breath as she slept, and a knot of intense emotion filled his chest, cutting off his air and filling his eyes with hot tears.

I love this woman more than life itself.

The realization hit him, both hard and soft at the same time. While having such a goddess in his life, a time traveling one at that, made him feel invincible. Loving her made him vulnerable.

In his chamber, he bathed and dressed, eager for a

day that now held more meaning for him than any other day in his life.

Breakfast was a cold slice of ham and bread, which he took to the library. Thankfully, few were about and he was able to slip into his sanctuary unobserved. He nibbled on his breakfast while his mind wandered over last night's events.

"Aye, she is a firebrand, all right," he whispered. "And she is mine," he added, feeling the joy and utter amazement rise in his heart. "Whatever have I done to deserve such an angel lady?"

He heard the sound of hooves in the courtyard and went to the windows to see who was able to move this early after yesterday's festivities.

"None other," he muttered, seeing the only person not invited to the wedding—Sir Edward, fashionably dressed and bright as a bed of spring pansies, dismounting down below. At this very moment, Sir Edward looked up and waved to Jamie.

"So much for hiding out," Jamie complained.

A knock came at the door, and Mary called out, "Someone here to see you, Milord."

"All right," Jamie said. "Show him in."

•

Sir Edward entered the Great Hall into Greyhaven with his usual sense of longing, now expanded by the recent death of Raol into a seething hatred for all things Irish, in particular ones with red hair.

Greyhaven was stately, dignified, and historic. Here, he would avenge Raol's murder and, as lord of the land, be able to continue with his exploits. He looked around, seeing himself ensconced as lord, the servants lined up before him for morning review. He smiled, feeling a brief bubble of delight surface through his smoldering rage.

You will be mine, along with those who deserve punishment.

He entered the Earl's library with a swirl of his new deep blue and burgundy cape. Noting the Earl's casual attire, he asked "Did I catch you at an inopportune time?"

The Earl responded curtly. "We had a wedding here yesterday."

"Oh," Edward answered, pushing his cape off his shoulders. "I was not invited."

"Yes, it was a local affair, you understand," the Earl said. He tilted his head, one aristocratic eyebrow lifted, silently asking, "Why are you here?"

While not interested in any affair of the peasants, Edward was on a mission. "Milord, I have come to ask you about the incident I hear you had recently. I wonder, have you determined the source of the riffraff who have been terrorizing us these last several months? Did you take any prisoners?"

"No," the Earl replied. "The only one captured died before we could interrogate him." He turned away from Edward, walked to the windows and looked out.

Edward frowned. The Earl practically ignored him, and was staring out the window. He followed the Earl's gaze, stifling a hiss of repugnance.

Raol's murderer, the red-haired woman!

A haze of red obscured Edward's vision, making him choke. Every time he saw this witch, something dreadful happened. The pressure in his head expanded, bringing a buzz into his ears. He saw Raol's lifeless body lying in the dirt, and the buzz turned into a roar. He choked and blurted in frustrated anger, "Milord, will you make up your mind and sell me this estate?"

The Earl pulled his attention away from the window and stared at Sir Edward. His gaze shifted and went distant for a long moment. When he answered, his aristocratic eyes were cold and threatening. "Greyhaven is not for sale, at any price, especially to you. Now, please leave."

Sir Edward clamped his mouth tight as he was immediately bustled down the stairs and out the door. With a snort and a 'humph!' he stormed to where his horse was tied, mounted and rode off without so much as a look back.

"Unbelievable!" he ground out between tense jaws as he rode through the village. By the time his horse raced past the mill, his rage filled his mind and his vision. Once out by the fields, he pulled up on the horse. The animal came to a sudden stop, pulling back against the hard metal in its mouth as Edward jerked cruelly on the reins. "Stop!" he shouted. He reached forward and thumped the horse between its ears.

"I will not be thwarted," he fumed. "I am destined to avenge Raol's murder. I am the rightful Lord of Greyhaven Manor," he insisted. "I—"

He spotted a horse … and a red-haired figure on the ground.

It is she!

Suddenly, the opportunity at hand was too much to pass up. He thought of his poor Raol murdered at her hand and he knew this chance was his to take. "I will be lord," he said with all the animosity his hatred of this woman could muster. "And I will give them what they deserve."

He dismounted and dropped his horse's reins. Silently he crept again to the very same pond where he had last crossed paths her. Remembering his ruined boots, he shrugged off his new cape and left it on the ground, safe from the muddy pond.

And my wrist hurt for a week.

Barely a few feet to go ...

•

Alex drifted in her good dreams. She was happy, the children were happy—

"Ooph," she grunted. She opened her eyes and almost laughed. Sir Edward Fancy Pants sat upon her abdomen. With one hand he held one of her hands pinned to the ground.

"You! Again?" she said, incredulous. "Not very smart, are you?"

"Eh?" he responded.

"I said, not very smart, are you!" Alex shouted. With her free hand, she fixed her fingers into a tiger's claw and struck Sir Edward straight into his eyes. He screamed and covered his eyes with his free hand while trying to keep her pinned with his other. She grasped this hand and braced it for leverage. With the strength of her legs, she flipped him up and over her so he landed behind her on his back.

She jumped up to deliver a robust kick to his groin, but she was stopped short by the sudden appearance of Jamie.

He stepped into the fray and crouched over Sir Edward, pressing a knife into his throat. Looking down into the wounded man's already streaming eyes, he said, "I should kill you for accosting my fiancée like this."

CHAPTER TEN

Celtic Love Song:
Everyday Know Laughter, Silence, and Song

Kathleen's Solar, Greyhaven

Alex parked her hands on her hips and glared at Jamie. One part of her wanted to throttle him, one part wanted to throw her arms around him.

"What were you thinking to make such an announcement without discussing it with me first?" she blurted. She spun on her heel and returned to pacing. "I can't believe you did this!"

Kathleen sat silently working at her loom.

Jamie leaned against the fireplace mantle with his hands stuffed into his pants pockets. "I canna see why you are so upset," he offered. "The man was on top of ye, and I was ready to kill him."

"Fine, kill him," she argued. "But leave out the announcement we are engaged!" She stepped close, pointing with her finger. "Because we ..." She waved her finger rapidly between the two of them. "We have not discussed marriage."

"You being my fiancée gives me more right to kill him," Jamie answered, sounding smugly logical.

Kathleen stood. "Alex, he was acting in your defense, thinking you needed help."

"I needed no help. I had the situation under control," Alex grumbled. She wanted to shout, "My being in danger is not the issue." She was being childish, she knew, but the anger and disappointment rising inside was alive, and she couldn't let it go.

"No harm in him wanting to help," Kathleen coaxed and pried. "So I wonder why you protest. Are you saying you do not wish to marry Jamie?"

She stopped, feeling the air of her indignation whistle away, leaving her collapsed, defenseless. She looked up. Jamie stared at her intently, as if she might actually refuse his offer of marriage.

If he doesn't know any better than that.

"Huh," she snorted. "I'm not marrying anyone who hasn't the decency to ask first."

There, she said it.

She turned and marched past Jamie, giving him a lethal look. "Ooooh," she sputtered as she stormed from the solar.

She marched off to her chamber. "Make me the last one to know," she muttered. She was being ridiculous, she knew, and it damn well felt good. She was tired to taking care of everyone but herself. "Damn it," she fumed.

Their beautiful secret was out.

He hasn't even asked me, and now everyone knows.

After his arrival at the pond, Sir Edward scrambled off, his imminent death postponed by the eruption of their argument. The discussion followed the two of them all the way home.

Connor overheard them. Once he discerned their

topic, he jumped straight into the air with an excited hoop and ran off toward the village to spread the word.

Alex was surprised the entire population wasn't at the door already, clamoring with the news. She could just see the look on Maguire's face . . .

"Ooooh!" she spit and barged through her chamber door, slamming it behind her. She renewed her pacing, fuming, until her gaze came to the tumbled bed where she and Jamie had found ecstasy only hours ago.

A deep exhalation took the angry wind from her sails. She sat on the rumpled covers, her hand caressing the sheets that had held so much loving.

"No one likes being taken for granted," she grumbled.

•

Monet's Garden

Royce smiled, remembering the day. "I have never seen her so angry," he commented.

"She is not an easy woman, is she?" Andros asked.

"No," Royce agreed. "But where would be the fun in that?"

The water's surface swirled with more revelation. Royce leaned forward to see, even though he remembered well.

•

Jamie watched as Alex stomped out of the solar, her exit leaving a vacuum of silence as strident as her rather vocal tirade. With her storm of emotions gone, he was finally able to take a breath. "Well," he exhaled with amazement. From a dry throat he added, "I have never seen anyone ... so upset."

He knew no other twenty-first century women, so their nature was a mystery to him. "I ... I thought she would be happy." He frowned with dismay. Looking up he saw his mother's eyebrows furrowed in astonishment at his words. Before she could say anything, he quickly exited the chamber.

"Time for Maguire," Jamie said. "'Tis all his fault anyway, what with his incessant chatter about me needing a fine, red-headed lass and all."

He bounded down the stairs and entered the common room just as Maguire burst through the door. "Is it true?" Maguire shouted. He rushed over and clapped Jamie soundly on the back. "Well done, man!"

Jamie scowled. "'Tis all your fault, you know."

"Eh?" Maguire grunted. He pulled back, confused. "What did I do?"

"All this talk of red-headed women," Jamie protested. "Now I am affianced to one who willna speak to me." He glared at Maguire. "You should have seen the stink-eye that woman turned on me." Feeling Alex's recriminations were undeserved Jamie prepared to unleash his rising ire on his friend. Before he could begin, Maguire burst into laughter.

"Ha ha!" Maguire began. He gave Jamie the once over before throwing his head back. "Ba ha ha ha," he howled. His humor grew until he bent over and put his hands on his thighs, belly laughter rocking his body. He looked up, eyes streaming before he bent over again and succumbed to his laughter once more.

"Verra funny," Jamie commented drily. He stood

with his arms crossed, waiting.

"Oh, ho ho ho," Maguire groaned. A ripple of lingering guffaws burst loose as he stood up and wiped his eyes. Finally composed, he motioned for Jamie to continue.

Jamie ignored Maguire's twitching lips that threatened to release another outburst. "So I have a problem and need your help," he said softly.

"Aye, laddie, and so you do," Maguire said, nodding sagely. He draped a fatherly arm about Jamie's shoulders. "Come then," he coaxed. "Over a pint ye can tell me everything."

•

Alex woke the next morning feeling cranky and miserable.

She wanted Jamie in her bed.

"We need to talk," she said. "All we have to do is talk, and then all this ... unhappiness will go away."

She climbed out of bed, thinking how big and lonely it was without Jamie. "Of course I want to marry him, but I'm old fashioned and I want to be asked." She washed and dressed with a mind to find him and settle their affairs. Feeling bidness on her schedule, she was tempted to put her hair up. But one glance in the mirror and she knew loose curls would serve her purposes better. She fluffed her hair, and, feeling like Scarlett O'Hara, pinched her cheeks.

"Look out, Earl, I'm coming for you."

Down in the kitchen she picked up a chunk of ham, a slice of deep yellow cheese and a fluffy biscuit with butter and jam. Hearing voices from the great dining room, she took her plate and mug. As she entered the room, Jamie's voice caught her attention.

"Make your lists, ladies. Mary, whatever the kitchen requires for the feast. Mother, fabric and such for the wardrobe. And Connor—"

Alex approached and set her plate on the table. At the mention of 'feast', Cook Mary squealed and darted into the kitchen. Kathleen was grinning broadly, her eyes sparkling. She grabbed Alex's hand and winked.

She lifted her shoulders in question, suddenly catching the infectious delight. "What?" she mouthed silently, looking at Jamie.

"Connor," Jamie announced with suspense, "will be going with me."

At this, Connor brightened. "With ye, Da?"

"Yes, son. 'Tis about time you went to town. But you have to conduct yourself as a man, understand?"

"Yes sir," Connor answered.

Jamie finally turned his gaze to Alex. She felt a tingle race through her limbs, for his eyes were warm and sparkling with mischief. "Alex, make sure whatever you might want gets on a list."

She was speechless. While she was a little put off to hear he was leaving when they had bidness to settle, his generous offer in the nature of shopping was exciting. She couldn't imagine what there was to choose from; the truth was all she wanted was him. "Yes, Milord," she answered. "When do you leave?"

"In the morning." With that, he collected a suddenly mature Connor and they exited, heads together in discussion.

The next morning came with a flurry of lists and laughter. Alex joined in the crowd seeing them off. She saw only one packhorse and, considering how many lists she saw change hands, wondered how they were going to fit it all on the one poor animal.

"Milady," Jamie said softly. He stood before her, having already spoken with everyone else.

"Milord," she answered with a little more sauciness than was needed. Her anger from the day of the pond incident had dissipated, and all she wanted was to have him in her arms, whether they were married or not. From his announcement yesterday about the feast Alex knew he intended to marry her. She had to admire his confidence, seeing as how he had not yet asked, and she had not yet agreed. She had sweet anticipation as to how he was going to pull off such a feat. Wanting him to carry her best image with him while he was away, she smiled.

Jamie gazed over her face. With soft words just for her, he said, "You will be here when I return ...?" He took her hands and held them to his chest.

His words struck deep. Thinking she might leave in his absence wounded her. She felt her throat tighten up, but she swallowed and pushed the emotion aside. "If you promise you won't run off on a ship bound for the orient." She winked to further lighten the moment, and squeezed his hands. His slow smile made her heart bang against her chest with crazy love.

Suddenly, a bubble of quiet surrounded them. She knew nothing but the intense emotion in Jamie's eyes. He pierced her heart with a look.

"I wish to spend the rest of my life with you, woman," he growled, his voice shaking. "Are you ready for that?"

A deep, exciting energy pulsed around them. Alex felt as though their two life forces were joined and entwined. She was a part of this man. Existence without him was not possible. "Yes," she answered without hesitation.

He released her hands and enveloped her with his arms. His lips came down and she closed her eyes. The hormones of love made her heart beat fast and her knees went weak. He held her tighter and their lips parted. All she could think was "molon labe."

Jamie broke the kiss, but held her close. Groggy with passion, Alex opened her eyes. His breath fanned her face as he kissed her chin, her nose and her forehead. "Stay safe. We will return post haste."

"Be careful," she said.

He released her and walked to his horse, mounting quickly. "Ladies," he said with a gallant sweep of his hand, as Kathleen had come to stand with Alex.

Maguire handed the lead rope for the packhorse to Anson, the man he selected to accompany the Earl. "Keep them safe, lad," he ordered.

Connor was on his pony, looking oversized on the small horse. But he sat tall and patiently waited on his father. With a tap of Jamie's heels into Pharaoh's flanks, the procession wound down the hill.

As they rounded the curve and were gone from sight, Alex realized he just asked her to marry him in not-so-many words. And she said yes. She grabbed Kathleen's hand. "They will be all right, won't they?"

Kathleen gave her a smile free of concern. "Of course my dear. Have no worry." She placed her arm over Alex's shoulder as they turned to enter the manor. "These are golden days for Greyhaven."

She took Kathleen at her word and relaxed. He and Connor would return and their days together will be golden, as Kathleen said.

That night Alex joined Kathleen in her solar.

"'Tis quiet without them," she said, watching Kathleen balling yarn to use in her tapestries.

"Aye," Kathleen answered. "When the Earls fled in September of '07 the entire countryside went quiet, mourning the loss of our men. But life goes on." She exhaled hotly with frustration.

"The stupid fools played right into English hands. With no nobles to thwart the Crown, the English invasion began in earnest." She put down her yarn and looked out the window. "I suspect all this matters not, for the English crown will prevail in the end."

Kathleen said this with a tone of resignation, telling her Kathleen knew much of the future. Alex hunched her shoulders, not wanting to ever know such a gift. "Tell me about them, the Earls," she said.

Kathleen looked up, surprised. "'Tis naught but musty old history."

"I'm going to be part of this family. I deserve to know what I'm getting into," Alex said.

Kathleen rose. "Then we must see where all the McNeill secrets are held."

They went down stairs and across the great hall and up more stairs to Jamie's library. In the corner was a nook filled by a great desk.

"Oh," she exclaimed. "We have this desk." She pulled up a chair and watched as Kathleen burrowed through the piles of ledgers and papers covering the top of the desk.

"This was made by my father, Rory McNeill," Kathleen said. "He made it out of the hardest Irish oak, proclaiming it would outlive the English Empire." She pulled back and looked at Alex. "Was he right?"

"I always suspected there was a story behind this desk," Alex said. "And yes, your father was right. For the most part the great English Empire is gone. But the desk is intact at one of our homes."

Kathleen pulled from the pile a rolled up piece of soft leather. She spread it out across the desktop. "The family tree," she said with satisfaction. She ran her hand across the leather, pressing it flat and smoothing out the folds.

She moved closer to see. "This is still in the desk, Kathleen. I looked at it to find where Jamie was before coming here." She saw the oxblood leather-bound book, unearthed in Kathleen's rummaging on the desk. "And this." She opened the familiar ledger with the family crest on the front.

"Here is where we will record your marriage to Jamie," Kathleen added with an encouraging tone that half questioned.

"Worry not," she said. "I intend to marry your son, but he's going to work for it. No one likes to feel taken for granted." She glanced through the family ledger and noted no pages torn out. The last recording was *The Abandonment.* She closed the book and handed it to Kathleen. She wanted no mysteries to derail her golden days here at Greyhaven.

Let Kathleen be the keeper of secrets.

"You said the desk holds the family secrets?" Alex asked.

"Have you not found the hidden compartment? Look here," Kathleen pushed the clutter from the top right side and reached behind a drawer. A section of the desktop popped up.

"Oh!" she exclaimed. "How cool is that?" She peered into the open compartment some three inches wide, a foot long, and over a foot deep. There was nothing inside. "No secrets today?" she asked.

"No secrets," Kathleen said as she pressed the wood panel back into place.

Alex watched Kathleen and knew the woman held more secrets than the CIA. Alex's gaze swept the nook, and landed on an ornate gold clock on a side table. A chill skittered down her back. She had not seen a time keeping device since she came here.

It's just an old clock.

"Why am I afraid of it?" she whispered.

Kathleen came to Alex's side. "'Tis an old clock Jamie brought back from one of his military excursions." She peered at Alex closely. "You are disturbed by this?"

Kathleen's voice barely reached Alex, sounding muffled and far away. The room faded from her senses; Alex was all alone, more alone than when she traveled through time.

"Alex? Alex?"

She shuddered and shook free of the chill. Kathleen had a hand on her arm and squeezed gently.

"Golden days, Alex. These are the golden days of Greyhaven. You are the golden days of Greyhaven."

Alex nodded, but the feeling of being so alone was a memory she held now. "Golden days," she said, mustering confidence. "Golden days."

•

On the expected day of their men's return, Alex sat watching at her chamber window, for the elevation gave her a greater line of sight.

"Come home to me," she whispered. She recalled sitting on the deck of their house in California and speaking those same words. She felt cursed. "Once they get back, the man is never going out of my sight."

Golden days.

She longed to feel his arms around her. Her woman's core ached for his return inside her, completing her, making them one and thereby invulnerable. Without him, she was lost.

A shout came from down in the village. She saw people running, and more shouts.

They're here!

The urge to dart down the stairs was fierce, but she stayed rooted at the window, for she would see him sooner from up here.

More auditory excitement came from the village and she could hear footsteps down below as some rushed out. She fixed her eye on the point where the land rose high enough to reveal travelers. Her gaze was intense and she was reminded of looking for the green flash on the horizon.

A horse's head came first.

"Pharaoh," she said, breathless.

An instant later Jamie's face broke into her view.

Her vision blurred, flooded with tears hot with joy and relief. She dashed her hand across her eyes and turned from the window. "He's home," she said, and ran from the room.

She bolted down the stairs, but stopped before running outside.

Slow down.

She paused, collected herself, and gracefully walked

across the great hall. Hearing Jamie's voice from outside, she gave up the pretense and ran headlong for the outer door. She burst through, breathless, and drawing everyone's attention.

Jamie dismounted and handed Pharaoh's reins to Maguire. Suddenly he was before her, and the eagerness in his face melted her already squishy insides. "Milord," she said, searching his eyes, her heart running fast at the joy she saw on his face.

"Milady," he whispered. "You are here."

"And so are you, Milord," she answered.

He took one of her hands and kissed the knuckles. "You will not be sorry," he said. He wagged his eyebrows with mischievous intent.

Before she could respond, he waved to the others and called out, "Come, we have much to unload." He joined the crowd, leaving her with flushed cheeks and a heart overflowing with high expectations.

Alex pulled her eyes from Jamie and finally saw there were two pack animals and a wagon filled with goods.

The man Anson was climbing down from the wagon seat and ripping off the cover. Squeals of joy and hoops of laughter filled the air.

"Alex," Connor shouted.

She looked up at a Frisian horse with long black mane and tail reaching the ground. "Oh, Connor, he is beautiful."

He dismounted and walked the gelding to her. "This is Xander. I named him after you."

The gelding reached out to poke at Alex's pockets with his soft black nose. "You have spoiled him already," Alex admonished.

"No," Connor said. "'Tis father doing the spoiling." He looked at Jamie overseeing the unloading of goods.

She followed his gaze. Jamie was passing out bundles like St. Nick on Christmas day.

"He is different," Connor said. "I have never seen him so happy."

She felt the love for this boy, his father and this land swell in her heart. A flash of tears rose in her eyes and she groped for Connor's hand. "'Tis I who is spoiled. Greyhaven has given me so much."

"You ha' seen nothing yet," he whispered sagely.

"Did you get what I asked for?"

"Of course." He reached into a pocket and drew out a pouch. He passed it to her with a look that bragged. "Getting his ring size was tricky." He nodded, his smug expression showing his pride. "I slipped a potion Mary gave me into his drink."

"Ha!" Alex crowed. She clapped her hand over her mouth to stifle any more outbursts. She palmed the pouch, feeling the weight inside. "You did good."

"The engraving is there like you asked."

She hugged her soon-to-be stepson. She stepped back and looked him over. "Did you grow a foot while you were gone?"

"I hope so," he said, smiling. "Excuse me, I must show Xander his new home."

Connor walked off. Alone, she pondered everything happening around her.

These truly are golden days.

•

The next morning Alex lay in bed late, dreaming

of the Renaissance Hotel on St. John where they had a great chocolate bar with rivers of chocolate, pots of mousse, crusty soufflés, and crunchy chocolate toffee. The dream was so real her mouth watered at the thought of a spoonful of dark, creamy chocolate pudding. She could smell the chocolate.

"What?" she grumbled, half awake. She opened one eye and sniffed.

"I definitely smell chocolate."

She opened the other eye and brought both into focus. The first thing she saw was a tray on the dresser.

"Oh boy," she murmured. She stretched with joy before sitting up in the big bed so she could stare at the tray, wondering at the secrets possibly harbored there.

"I smell chocolate," she said. "And I see a gorgeous rose."

What else?

Unable to hold discovery off any longer, she climbed from the bed and approached the tray. "Oh," she exclaimed followed by a flurry of child like applause. She picked up the tray and took it back to bed. From back beneath the covers she luxuriated in the wonderful feeling of being spoiled.

"Connor did warn me."

Beside the steaming mug of hot chocolate with cream on top, no less, lie a blood red rose, thorns removed, and a white linen napkin. A heavy gold chain spilled from out of the napkin folds. She pulled until the chain fully emerged bearing a large, rose-colored baroque pearl. "Oh, oh, oh," she squealed. She put the necklace on, slipping the long chain over her head. The pearl nestled just above her breasts.

She sipped her chocolate and smacked her lips like

a princess. "Golden days, indeed, " she murmured. She picked up the napkin to wipe her mouth, and saw the folded card beneath.

It was a simple, white card with the McNeill crest in gold on the front and a single horizontal crease. She opened the fold, inside was written, *Will you marry me?*

"Yes," she whispered. "Yes." Suddenly suspicious of the absolute quiet, she got out of bed and looked out her window. In the grassy clearing was a message spelled out in flowers. "He must have picked every flower in the county."

Marry me?

She laughed. "Yes," she said. "Yes, yes, yes!"

She bathed and dressed in a hurry. The kitchen was deserted. She ran to the common room, but no one sat at the great table. "Outside," she said, breathless. She ran through the door and out to the proposal in flowers.

"Yes," she said, laughing. She picked up a small bundle of wild flowers tied with ribbons and noticed a trail of flower petals going off toward the barn. She skipped off, following the petal trail.

"Now what could he possibly have in here?" she asked rhetorically, ducking into the cool darkness of the barn. She hunched her shoulders with excitement. When her eyes adjusted, she saw a black horse's head peering over the stall door in front of her.

"Oh, my," she said in a hush of amazement.

The horse looked Frisian, like Connor's. A long, wavy black mane was silky to the touch, the soft nose inquisitive, searching. Alex giggled when the horse nudged her in the ribs. "You are a beauty."

Beside the stall hung new riding gear of soft leather and gleaming brass. A note was propped up in the leather.

"Ride with me," she read.

She spun and ran back to the manor. Still no one was in sight as she took to the stairs. She reached her room; on her bed was a large box with her name on it.

"Alex," she read. She ran her fingers over the fine cursive hand; it was strong, yet elegant. "Like he is," she said. She removed the top of the box. Inside was a black riding outfit.

"Huh," she inhaled sharply.

She pulled the jacket and riding habit from the box and held it up, twirling around to loosen the folded skirt. A quick glance in the mirror and she stopped.

"I know this, I know this."

A man rode a horse through green woodland, followed by another rider. They stopped to dismount, laughing gaily. The woman, her face hidden from view, reached for her companion and pulled him in for a kiss.

"They are in love," Alex whispered from memory. "Royce showed me this scene in a dream at La Casa."

Where I was told to save Jamie, and I save all.

Had it already happened? Did Royce know he was Jamie? Did Jamie know he was Royce? Where was her choice in all this?

"Stop it!" she commanded. "I will not let ... anything ruin my happiness today."

Quickly she stripped and put on the riding habit. It fit perfectly. The white ruff at her neck worked with the black fabric to accentuate her hair color. She put the pearl on, and it rested seductively in the V-neckline above her breasts.

A glance in the mirror was startling. She did not see the Alex Martine McNeill she knew ... and it was not just because of the outfit.

"I've changed," she told her reflection. She thought how Jamie and Royce were the same, yet different.

"Like me," she announced. She picked up the gloves and rushed out the door.

At the foot of the stairs she slowed to collect her composure. She waited inside the great door, her hand ready to open it. Once more a threshold lay before her, and she paused, understanding each portal required a metamorphosis in her for passage.

I do not recognize myself any longer.

Suddenly Master Chan's words echoed through her memory. "The journey is not about what you were, but what you become."

She thought of all that had happened at Greyhaven in the brief time she had been here, especially the changes evident in Jamie, and in Connor.

Could this be the "saving" she was intended to do?

"I honestly can't conceive an alternative to opening this door," she stated with sincerity. With the path so clear, she followed her heart's desire and turned the handle. She stepped through, and knew she was uniquely blessed.

The many bouquets that had made up her proposal had been collected and set by the door in an enormous vase, filling the air with the intoxicating scent of flowers. The morning was cool, the sky peppered with clouds, and her handsome man waited.

Jamie held the reins to her beautiful new horse. "Do you like her?" he asked. He looked at the horse, then back at her, expectant.

"She is beautiful, and elegant ... like you," Alex said softly. Everything was surreal, as though she lived the dream. When she stepped through the door she must have entered some alternate dimension. Everything was high-def perfection.

Let me live in this perfect state forever.

She smiled and reached for his hand. The touch was pure 'coming home' magic, as if all eternity had prepared for this moment. "Shall we go?" she asked.

They mounted and turned to go down the hill, but instead of going out toward the pond, they went off into the woods bordering the ocean cliffs.

Within the woods the air smelled of rich forest earth churned up by the horse's hooves. The path was wide enough to canter side by side. Every time Alex looked over, he turned and smiled, his face alive with love and happiness. Her heart took a bow for accomplishing this metamorphosis in him.

Their path took them to the forest edge. A grassy plain bordered the woodland to the cliff's edge, reminding her of the cliff edge at La Casa where she had heard Royce's voice. "With you, my love," he said. "Always with you, as I promised."

He dismounted and came to her side. He smiled, his gestures saying more than words could, and reached for her hand.

She jumped down into his arms, laughing with the thrill, the beauty, and the impossible moment, for this is the scene Royce showed her in the dream. She pulled his head down for a kiss, whispering, "I love you."

His lips answered her beckoning, warm and demanding, yet gentle, vulnerable. He broke the kiss, breathless as he asked, "Will you marry me, bear my children and live your life with me here at Greyhaven?"

The rush of emotion swelled through Alex's throat

and brought tears running from her eyes. "Yes," she de-clared. "Yes, a thousand times, yes!"

His kiss was an act of possession firing Alex's heart. She belonged to this man, and she would live her life here with him.

Abruptly, Jamie pulled free with a great smile and shout of joy. "Does this mean … ?"

He stepped back and pointed his finger at her, rap-idly waving the pointer back and forth between them, mimicking her gesture in the solar the day he an-nounced their engagement to Sir Edward. "Does this mean we have talked marriage and can now make the official announcement?"

Alex laughed and her eyes watered at his imitation of her. "Aye," she said in her best brogue. "Ye can shout it from the rooftops, Milord."

•

Montrose Court

Sir Edward walked the subterranean chambers be-low the house proper, scowling at the well-appointed prison cells.

"These rooms were supposed to house our harem of delights," he grumbled. "Do you see any delights here?" he asked the silent walls. He inspected the rooms where the beds had fine linens, with accompanying manacles attached to the walls. Out of sight were spaces desig-nated for bathing and relieving bodily demands.

"Long-term," he announced with pride.

"First I will kidnap that red-haired witch. When the Earl fails to find her, he will sink into despair." He closed

the door to the first chamber and threw the latch, filling the room with the harsh finality of metal clanging
against metal.

At a second chamber he swung the door wide. "Dear
Kathleen, I even have a place of honor for you." Next
to the manacles, a black leather whip hung on the wall.
"Just for you," he said, and closed the door.

He walked past a third and fourth chamber with a
happy step. The keys jangled together at his waist and
he whistled lightly as he climbed the stairs.

"There's even a room for the boy," he ruminated.
He stopped and cocked his head as a solution came to
mind. "Or ..." He brought one finger to his lips, pondering the answer. "Off to London he goes. I'm sure someone will pay for his smooth cheeks."

He walked toward the stairs, speaking to his lost
friend. "Raol, I am vulnerable without you. But your
murder has forced me to be ... more daring, more determined." His jaw clenched tight with his desire to see
Raol's death avenged; a new strength and commitment
was created from his grief.

"I will watch them just as you always did, and I will
plan. I may be alone, but I learned well. You will be
proud."

He whistled as he climbed the stairs.

"I am more deadly than ever."

CHAPTER ELEVEN

Pilot my dreams on the crest of a wave;
give me safe haven in my lover's arms.

Alex rode next to Jamie back to Greyhaven, unable to take her eyes off him

I am so happy.

Jamie was her Royce, and yet so much more. Her time here with him allowed her to see the development of a side of Jamie's personality that wasn't so visible in Royce.

I have brought change in him, and he has brought change in me.

They rode up to the manor, laughing with joy. When they crested the hill, everyone from the manor and the village were congregated outside.

Before she could say anything, Jamie protested. "Ye said we could make the announcement."

Her chest grew tight with love for this man. He had obviously gone to a great deal of effort to orchestrate this morning's events. And it appeared all of Greyhaven was part of this moment. She could see the hope and expectation on their faces. Even though she came here a stranger, they had made her family.

How am I so blessed?

She brought her horse to a stop, and Jamie pulled up next to her. She smiled and took his hand. Raising their clasped hands up high, she cried, "Let's have a wedding!"

The eruption was immediate.

Maguire rushed at her and pulled her from her horse, laughing. He hugged her and swung her around in a circle with her feet flying off the ground. "At last," he cried, tears making his eyes shiny. "An angel ye are, lass. An angel, indeed."

Next came Connor, grabbing Alex's hands and laughing. "Maguire's right. By bringing life to Greyhaven ye have saved us well enough."

While the comment was meant in jest, Connor's words brought a chill to Alex's shoulders. *To save them all*, she thought. That was the mission.

Beyond Connor, she saw Kathleen, standing by the great door, a smile on her face. As if sensing Alex's distress, she mouthed the words, "Golden days."

She shook off the ominous flash and smiled her best at Connor. "'Tis all of you who have saved me," she said.

A sudden shout from deep in the crowd. "When, Milord? When is the wedding?" came Cook Mary's voice.

"Marrying this woman is the greatest gift a man could have," Jamie announced. "Let us marry on my birthday, August thirty-first."

Alex pulled back and looked at Jamie with amazement. "That's the end of the week, Milord! What about the banns?"

"I will pay the fee for the license," he said. He squeezed her hand and gave a look deep with longing.

His voice was husky when he said, "I canna wait thirty days, so aye, we marry at the end of the week. And it will not come soon enough."

"Is the Earl gone mad?" Mary groused. She turned and marched off to the kitchen, mumbling, "We must have a great cake, and the boys have to go hunting right away."

All of Greyhaven joined in the wedding preparations.

Each morning the men went out hunting. Maguire and Connor were busy setting and checking their traps. When not involved in outdoor activities, Maguire was all about the manor, his joy and approval evident. He wore a constant grin as he stayed at Jamie's side, keeping him busy until the big day. This time of brotherly fellowship provided the opportunity for an endless flow of advice on the management of redheaded lasses.

Jamie finally told him, "Enough!"

The greatly anticipated day arrived.

Alex sat before her mirror with her hairbrush in hand. She had breakfast earlier and had bathed. Her wedding dress hung ready for her to step into. The jewels she would wear were laid out.

Is this the last portal?

She held the gold ring Connor brought back from Donegal, the only item on her list. The ring was smooth rose gold, a plain circle with no adornment except for the word *forever* engraved on the inside.

This was a duplicate of the ring she gave Royce when they married. The parallels in this life and her modern life still left her with chills. "I am here by my consent."

Yet nothing that happened here was in her plans.

"Who was on the planning committee?" she asked

her reflection.

She smiled in return. Questions like how and why these fantastic events were happening in her life had fallen by the wayside.

And what about Royce? Where is he?

"Royce is here ... He is Jamie, always with me as he promised, even here," she whispered.

A knock came at her door.

"Yes," she called out.

Kathleen entered. "I thought you could use some help," she said.

The knowing, sympathetic wisdom in Kathleen's sudden presence made tears shoot into Alex's eyes, burning her nose. She dabbed at her eyes. "I'm ... I'm overwhelmed Kathleen. I want this wedding, but something in me ... is afraid." The tears came in earnest, and Alex bowed her head, letting them fall into her lap.

Kathleen rushed to her side. Kneeling on the floor, she took the cloth from Alex's trembling hands and lifted Alex's chin. "You must not cry. Do you want him to see you with red eyes?"

She sat immobile while Kathleen dabbed at her face, accepting the ministrations as if she were a child.

"Who is he?" she blurted. "Am I marrying Jamie or Royce?" She gave a snort of hysterical laughter. "Ha! I mean, what am I doing here?" She shrugged with angst, and more tears fell.

"I thought you already answered these questions?" Kathleen probed. She pulled a clean cloth from her sleeve and offered it.

She mumbled, accepting the handkerchief.

"Then what are you afraid of?"

She knew the answer deep in her heart. At first she

was afraid to quantify the fear by speaking the words, but the fear pushed into her mind and flitted through her thoughts. Now she had to say the words in order to purge the fear.

She took a deep breath and rushed. "I don't know how long I'm supposed to be here ... I mean, I left a life behind. These vows are a life long commitment and I already made them once in my other life. Can I say the words again when I don't know how long—" She gasped and looked away.

"Ah," Kathleen cooed. "I see."

"You do? Because I—"

"Alex, life is an uncertain adventure."

"Ha!" Alex blurted. She gave Kathleen the no-shit look.

Kathleen continued, waving Alex's reaction aside. "You have no more uncertainty here with this marriage than you would with any other marriage. Every day can bring joy or pain. The day is what you make it."

Alex felt her throat thicken up. She choked, "But how many days will we have? I have gone so far to be with him. I am afraid of still losing him."

There. I said it.

Kathleen shook her head. "No one can answer how many. Who would want to know?" She peered into Alex's face. "If you knew how long you had with someone, would you do things differently? Would your days be more precious? Or would your time be tainted?"

She hunched her back with fear. "Do you know something?"

Kathleen put an arm around Alex's shoulders. "I know these are golden times, and you should put on your lovely dress and marry my handsome son."

Alex released a slow exhale. "I have never been so afraid of loosing someone," she confessed. "He is a part of me. Without him, I do not exist."

"Then you should marry him and let joy fill your heart," Kathleen coaxed. "Because he feels the same."

"He does?"

"You have made him whole." This announcement was said with a soft smile of amazement. "Golden days, I promise."

"Golden days," Alex said, mustering confidence. "Golden days." She felt her doubts evaporating. "Okay, then, you're right." She stood and looked at the dress. "Will you help me?"

When the dress and all it's adornments were in place, Alex felt like a princess in a fairy tale. The mirror confirmed her thoughts. The bodice was form fitting ivory silk covered in an intricate floral design of tiny pearls and diamante. The sleeves were elbow length in the lightest chiffon. From the waist flowed a full skirt of silk in alternating panels of cream and ivory with more of the pearl and diamante detailing. The entire ensemble reflected light, and she glowed like an angel.

Kathleen dressed Alex's hair simply, pulling it back in a loose French braid, with a feathering of loose tendrils framing her face. In place of a veil, Alex wore a garland of lavender and rosemary. Her only other adornment was the pink pearl Jamie gave her and matching pearl earbobs.

"Are you ready?"

Gone were Alex's fears and doubts. She was here and now, and in this moment she would marry the man she loved. She nodded.

"Remember, golden days," Kathleen said. She gave

one last squeeze of Alex's hands and left.

Alone again, Alex caught her breath and stilled her thoughts. She bowed her head and gave thanks for Kathleen and Master Chan, and to Royce. "I looked for you," she said. "Here is where I found you."

Standing at the threshold, she paused and cocked her head, listening for the sound of faraway temple bells, the sigh of the wind, or the sound of Royce's voice. But only silence came, and she exhaled with a bitter-sweet mix of relief and regret.

"Some paths are not easy," she said, and stepped across the chamber threshold. She walked the long corridors coming at last to the stairs leading to the great room. She took her steps carefully.

Do not trip and fall.

As she rounded the final curve, the congregation came into view. Below her was all of Greyhaven, the people whose lives had become important to her ... the people who made her life important to them.

Her gaze swept the crowd until she came to Jamie.

Oh! He is so handsome.

The moment moved into her heart and she felt the expansion of love rise from her chest to bathe the room in a wave of love.

"This is what I was meant to do," she whispered.

As she began her descent, the bagpipes started playing. At Jamie's request, she had taught the pipe player the song Jamie heard her sing at Maguire's house, *Amazing Grace.*

At the bottom of the stairs Maguire waited.

Alex stifled a chuckle. Maguire's beaming smile was infectious. He was, Alex believed, hovering a nano space off the floor.

"Lassie," he said reverently. "'Tis the finest day Greyhaven has seen in many a year."

"Will you walk with me?" she asked.

"It is my honor."

The walkway was outlined with fresh greenery and filled in with the still fragrant dried flowers from her flower-bouquet proposal. Lining the aisle were the people of Greyhaven, showing Alex the happiest faces she had ever seen. Each one nodded and cried openly with joy, or crossed themselves for the blessing of this day.

Alex held her head high and trained her gaze on Jamie.

I would marry him in any life.

The parish priest began the ceremony. Alex heard the words, made the motions, and spoke the vows, but it was as if she and Jamie were the only ones in the room.

She felt like an angel. He was her heavenly mission.

I will love this man for all of my many lives.

She remembered the panic she felt when she discovered Royce was nowhere to be found. The cryptic message from Chan turned her world upside down, and agreeing to leave her life and cross time was the hardest thing she ever attempted. But her love for her mate would not let her rest until she found him.

And here we are.

Alex brought her gaze to Jamie. His eyes are happy, she thought. His warm hands squeezed her, bringing a shiver of anticipation for those hands touching her a lifetime. Her heart swelled, and tears flooded her eyes. Suddenly, she realized, they wore each other's rings.

I missed my wedding!

"You may kiss the bride," the priest declared.

"Damn, and no video," she muttered.

He came to her to claim his kiss and heard her words. "Stop cursing and kiss me, woman." His hands held her face and his thumbs wiped the tears from each cheek.

She laughed. "Yes! Kiss me, and never let me go," she commanded.

He held her face gently, as if already fulfilling her command. His lips touched hers, his breath against her face. She closed her eyes and reached around his neck, holding him, drawing him closer, wanting them to be eternally fused together. His hands moved to wrap around her, tightening the embrace. He stepped in, leaning her back.

His lips ravished hers, and she opened them for his loving assault. When he stepped in between her legs, she moaned, "Oooh."

The priest smacked the bible together with a loud slap. "Ahem," he coughed.

The kiss persisted, but began loosing steam. She opened her eyes as Jamie pulled his lips from hers. Her face felt flushed. Her flower wreath was long gone, and she felt the French braid had come loose and her hair was trailing down her back.

His eyes filled her view. They burned with an intensity of emotion that made her heart flutter. "Never leave me," he whispered softly.

"Never leave me," she returned.

The intensity in his look softened. He smiled. "Agreed."

They straightened and stepped apart, hands held.

"Now since you have, ah, kissed the bride," the priest continued, clearing his throat. "Know ye' are married before the eyes of God. Let the celebration begin!"

The crowd erupted in a chorus of exclamations.

Jamie grabbed Alex's hand. "Come, we must be the first to leave." They ran for the great door. Just as they reached it, the bagpipes began again and two men opened the doors.

Alex and Jamie ran out into the sunshine.

Close behind came the crowd showering them with wheat. Alex threw her hands up to ward off the wheat fall, laughing. Jamie pulled her into his arms and whispered, "May this marriage bring ye joy for all your life, Milady."

She brushed the wheat from his hair. "The same to you, Milord."

As with Megan and Brandon's wedding, the lawn before the manor was filled with linen covered tables that spread all the way into the trees. Each table had a flower bouquet and greenery centerpiece.

In the midst of these tables was one round table set for two. Two silver goblets and silver place settings waited for the bride and groom.

Alex caught the smell of food. "Oh, my goodness!"

Several tables under the trees presented a variety of cold foods. Alex saw bowls of artichokes and new carrots and peas. Baskets of breads sat with crocks of sweet butter and strawberry jam. There was a great wheel of cheddar, along with several bowls of soft cheeses sitting next to bowls of apples and pears.

Off to one side was a large covered area where young boys tended three spits, each turning a roasting calf, a sheep, and a pig. Serving tables were filled with platters of stuffed geese, ducks and chickens, steamed trout, and a great haunch of smoked venison, as well as several hams. The crowning glory was a multi-tiered cake. Beverage came from kegs, barrels and bottles from under the shade of the trees.

Alex clapped her hands. She was amazed so much food could be produced without refrigeration and plastic wrap. "How do you do it?" she asked. When she looked up into his eyes, humor sparkled there. He scooped her into his arms and whispered into her ear, "I fall in love with the most incredible woman around."

His breath was warm on her neck, his voice throaty, quivering with emotion. She felt more tears, tears of joy, and wiped them from her eyes. "You make me so happy."

They went to their table and sat just as their goblets were filled with wine. Maguire stood with his mug raised in tribute. "To the Earl and his lovely wife, Alexandra."

"To the Earl and his wife!" shouted the crowd as everyone saluted them. "Slainte!" they cheered.

Maguire still stood. His voice was shaking as he began. "May there always be work for your hands to do." He paused to waved his eyebrows with lewd suggestion, bringing a burst of laughter from the crowd.

"May your purse always hold a coin or two; May the sun always shine on your window pane; May a rainbow be certain to follow each rain." A tear rolled down his cheek, and the crowd leaned to hear the words they knew came next. "May the hand of a friend always be near you."

"Aaahh," the crowd cooed.

"And may God fill your heart with gladness to cheer you," he finished. He raised his mug in honor. "Slainte!"

The toasts continued with joyous abandon. Alex

found she had to take tiny sips or find herself passed out before they cut the cake. Suddenly the music began and she giggled. Jamie flashed her a look of challenge, and took her hand to walk out to the area for dancing.

They paused hand in hand. "Ready?" she asked.

His answering smile was confident. She relaxed into his arms, and let him sweep her away. "You've been practicing," she said.

"Being married to an angel, I wanted to hold you in my arms and float among the clouds," he said. "This dance gives me what I want. Thank you," he added with a wink.

He surprised her when he asked about modern practices. "Is there something special we might do, something from your time?"

Her first thought was of the waltz. "Yes," she said. "The waltz, and it's easier than learning a new kata."

They twirled around and around, gliding across the dance area. Jamie's face spoke of love and happiness, giving Alex a giddy sensation as they spun across the lawn. By the time the music stopped, she gasped, "You will make me dizzy with love, Milord."

"Every day of your life," he answered.

He held her close and Alex saw a kiss was imminent. She lifted her face, one thought clear in her mind.

I have come home.

She opened her lips, felt her heart spin from joy and delight, and knew her life was finally where it was supposed to be.

The day continued with more toasts and more dancing interspersed with non-stop eating. By late afternoon, Alex was ready for a nap with her new husband.

"Can we go upstairs?" she whispered. "Alone?" She

was well aware of local tradition and she did not want a room full on her wedding night.

"I have a plan," he replied. He waved his eyebrows like Groucho Marx, making her laugh. He stood and pulled her to her feet; they marched through the crowd to the great door. By the time they were spotted, they were a step away from being inside.

"Be ready to move," he whispered.

"Are you leaving us already?" came a shout.

"Aye," Jamie replied in a commanding voice.

One by one they turned to see. He reached into his pocket and pulled out a handful of coins. "But ye willna miss us, will you?" He tossed the coins into the air.

The crowd converged on the falling coins with glee. Shouts and scuffles and good-natured laughter ensued. Jamie pulled out more coins and tossed them further out. "There is plenty for all," he cried.

With the crowd diverted, they darted into the hall and closed the door behind them. Jamie dropped the cross bar and said, "There, that should buy us some time."

She grabbed his hand. "Come."

They ran up the stairs, breathless and laughing. They skipped and half-stumbled down the long corridor. At the tower stairs, Jamie stopped.

"Wait," he said. "I have to carry ye from here." He scooped her up and grunted, "Ungh. How much cake did ye eat, woman?"

"Three pieces is all, Milord," she answered, batting her eyelashes.

Despite his complaint, he took the stairs two at a time, racing past her chamber. He stopped at the top outside his chamber door.

"I know exactly how many pieces of cake you ate," he said, his voice suddenly husky. "I watched you eat all three." All joviality was replaced by heated innuendo as he whispered, "And I would watch you eat cake every day of my life."

His lips came down and claimed hers.

Alex felt her heart racing, as if she had carried him up the stairs. His lips were demanding and yet gentle, coaxing her to give all. "Take me," she mumbled. "Molon labe."

He kicked the door open, stepped in and kicked it closed behind him. He set her down, and she began tearing at her too-many clothes.

Her skirt hit the floor. His coat followed.

Next she ripped her sleeves loose and dropped them. He added his shirt to the pile.

She pointed to his pants; he quickly unlaced them. As his pants came down, he jutted his chin at her remaining bodice; she ripped open a seam getting the garment over her head.

After the flurry of disrobing, each stood breathless.

She wore her pink thong; Jamie wore only his passion.

He scooped her up in his arms and carried her to the bed. Gently he set her down, his admiring gaze bringing goose flesh across Alex's body. Her nipples hardened, attracting his attention.

"Ohm," he moaned, closing his lips around one nipple.

Alex scooted farther up in the big bed, dragging Jamie with her. She pulled his head up for a kiss. "Love me, Milord ... love me until I can take no more."

"I am at your command," he answered as he snaked

down her body, kissing her neck, her breasts and ribs, across her belly, and down between her thighs.

His hands followed, massaging, stroking, rubbing her shoulders, her breasts, then across the flat of her belly and down her thighs. He went further and covered the soles of her feet with kisses, whispering what sounded to her like Gaelic.

She was so relaxed, she felt boneless. His ministrations had wiped all tension from her body, leaving the one fire to flicker and burn. "Give me more," she begged.

Jamie's hands moved slowly up from her feet, deep massaging her calves until she felt like a noodle, ready to fall into the fire.

He came to her thighs and massaged the muscles deeply, causing her legs to collapse open. His fingers moved ever closer to her core, building a new tension, fanning the fire—and then his hands moved underneath her and cupped her buttocks, lifting her. Held like this, he kissed her ... gently where her thigh joined her torso.

"Yes," she whispered.

She felt his warm breath before his fingers separated her lips. His lips touched her clit and she jerked at the initial contact, before melting into a single point of focus.

He suckled and licked and stroked like a man enjoying his last meal. Slowly. Gently. Building a fire.

"Please," she whispered. "I need you inside before I—"

He released her buttocks and Alex felt him climb up her body slowly like a man on pilgrimage. He kissed her navel, each nipple, both collarbones, all the while his rigid manhood banged against her body, teasing her as it sought a place of union.

He covered her head to toe, his fierce green eyes laying claim to her heart as his rigid manhood slipped into her body. "Never leave me," he said.

She felt the tears well up, but he wiped them away. "Never leave me," she choked out. He was inside her and around her, yet she could not get enough of him. "More," she begged.

He held his weight on his arms and began a slow and intoxicating plunge and withdrawal. At the bottom of each entry, he gave a little grind, taking her further and further toward ecstasy. When he pulled out, he took his manhood in hand and rubbed the swollen head over her clit.

In he came again, slowly filling the void, the driving grind at the top, and again the withdrawal followed by his wet and swollen length rubbing her down.

She felt drawn to an edge of passion she had never known. Her heart and soul were committed to this man, there were no barriers between them. In the heat of such abandon she was free to go further than ever before. The incredible spiral was starting; she thrashed her head back and forth. "Now." She grabbed him by the hips and pulled him to drive into her deeply.

He grunted, and began the final pace. In he sank, again and again, their bodies slick with passion and heated with desire.

She dug her fingers into his back as her orgasm began coiling deep in her belly. Unlike her usual orgasm, this one rang again and again and again, taking her to multiple climaxes.

"Oh," she groaned and went stiff.

Jamie plunged into her a last time and grunted before collapsing on top of her.

Their breathing was ragged. Alex could not move, nor did she wish to. Jamie was plastered on top of her, his manhood between her thighs, his sweat-soaked body stuck to her, his breath loud in her ear.

She had never been more content. "I love you," she gasped.

Jamie raised his head and gave her a one-eyed look that mirrored her thoughts. "Thank you," he said softly. "Thank you for loving me."

They never rejoined the party, even though they could hear the loud noises of celebration for long hours into the night.

Instead, they stayed in bed and made love again, and again ... and again.

She woke the next morning, early, she judged, by the grey light coming in the window. "Oh," she groaned and rolled over. Jamie slept soundly, one leg thrown across her as if to trap her for all eternity.

He is so at peace.

His face was relaxed of all stress, making him look like a youth in his teens. Her heart swelled with joy and love, and her thoughts turned to Royce. "My love, I found you," she whispered. She stroked the hair from his eyes.

One eye opened to drill her with feigned rebuke. "Woman, ye have drained me. Dinna tell me ye want more."

His brogue was thick, making her giggle. "No Milord, you have served me well."

"Just give me time to eat and I shall—" he began.

"Ssshhh," she quieted him. "I have something to do," she whispered. "Stay here. I will not be long."

She climbed out of bed and washed, knowing he

watched her.

"One night and yer already leaving me," he complained.

She pulled on her clothes. "Nay, Milord. I will return and soon you will wish to be relieved of such manly duties."

"Bah," he answered with a quirk of his lips. He sat up and waved his hand in dismissal of such blasphemy, but his eyes turned inquisitive. He asked in earnest, "Where do you go, Alex?"

She slipped on her riding boots and walked to the edge of the bed. She pulled his face close for a kiss, her lips trembling. Tears filled her eyes with burning emotion.

God, how I love this man.

Her voice came out in the barest whisper. "I must say good-bye to Royce," she said.

He exhaled slowly and reached to hold her face. They touched, forehead to forehead in silence.

Pulling back to look into her eyes, he asked, "How long will you be?"

"Not long. I go to the pond. I feel close to him out there. Something about the water." She shrugged, unable to express herself.

He nodded. "I will call for breakfast and bathwater for your return."

She walked to the door. She looked back, seeing how beautiful he was and was struck by the incredible complexity of her life. She would go quickly and return, for her life was here now, she knew with a certainty. "Make sure the water is hot." She turned quickly and slipped out the door before more tears came and washed away her resolve to complete this difficult task.

As with the aftermath of Megan and Brandon's wedding, the manor was still asleep. She made her way to the barn and saddled Mister Blue.

She let him pick his own pace, a gentle walk, giving her time to sort her thoughts. When she traveled to the past she knew not what to expect. Finding her love for Jamie, the people, this land was in no way what she intended, but life has a way of throwing one off kilter.

"It's not what happens to you that's important, but how you respond," she told Blue. He threw his head, seeming to agree.

They walked through the village and out past the fields. She had the words for Royce all ready in her heart and was about to turn off to the pond when she saw Connor on his new horse. The boy and horse slipped into the woods and out of sight.

"Where is he going?" she wondered. She pulled Blue to a stop, debating on whether to turn for the pond, or follow her curiosity and pursue Connor.

Royce and the past. Connor and the future.

"I'll just peek and see what Connor's up to, then I can circle around and stop at the pond on my way back." She nudged Blue toward the woods.

The morning was still pale and the woods quiet, as though life here was as consumed from yesterday's celebration as were the inhabitants of the manor and village. That Connor was up so early greatly intrigued her. The path broke clear of the woods and a hilltop covered in old stone ruins was before her. When she was about two hundred yards away, Connor rode his horse into the ruins.

She had just turned Blue to follow when Xander came running from the ruins.

"Connor," she whispered.

She maneuvered Blue to cut off Connor's horse, and grabbed the dangling reins. Pulling the animal in, she rode for the ruins.

•

Sir Edward crouched in his well-prepared hiding place near the old stone fort, waiting for the boy to appear. Diligently watching his prey as Raol did in the past had yielded Sir Edward this discovery of the boy's morning habit.

"Every morning he comes. Today he shall not return."

Having brought everything he needed to commit the kidnapping, Edward felt confident he could take the boy alone. He watched. The boy came up the hill as expected. Before he rode into the ruins, Edward walked out and lay on the open ground. When he heard the horse enter, he moaned and weakly called, "Help. Someone help."

The boy dismounted and Edward heard him coming closer. "Help me, please," he cried weakly.

"Sir Edward," Connor called. "Are ye all right?"

Edward felt the early morning sun blotted out as the boy leaned over Edward's prostrate body. Edward carefully gripped the stone he had placed just so. When the boy put both hands on him, opening the collar of his shirt, Edward struck the boy in the head.

Connor dropped silent to the ground. When Edward grabbed hold of the horse's reins, the animal reared and struck out with his front hoofs, grazing Edward's cheek, drawing blood.

He jumped back, loosing his grip on the reins. The animal shied and ran from the ruins.

"Connor!" came the shout of a woman's voice.

Edward stopped. His heart pounded and sweat slicked his hands.

It is she!

"That cursed wench, Alex. What is she doing here?" Edward mumbled. Knowing she had to be within yards, he kneeled over the boy. "Help," he called.

From the corner of his eye he saw her ride into the ruins with the boy's horse in tow. He called over his shoulder. "He has fallen from his horse. I fear he has hit his head."

The woman jumped down. She ran to the boy. Edward backed out of her way.

"Connor, Connor," she cried. "Water," she ordered Edward, pointing. "On my saddle." She looked up, and saw him wipe the blood from his cheek.

"Wait," she said. She stood quickly. "Something's not right here." She glanced around the ruins and her eyes quickly came to rest on Edward. "You. What are you doing here?"

"Setting a trap," he hissed. "And I caught two for the price of one."

"Don't be so sure," she replied. She pulled a knife from her belt.

Before Edward could react, she charged, striking him in the nose with a solid fist.

He cried out and grabbed his nose. Blood spurted through his fingers and he knew the she-devil had broken his nose. The knife was coming. He brought his hands down sharply and knocked the weapon free. She lunged for the knife; Edward grabbed his hidden sword.

By the time she regained the knife, Edward stood with a rapier point at Connor's throat.

"La Diabla," Edward said. He pressed the point of the rapier, nicking the skin next to the pulse in Connor's neck. "Put down your knife."

As instructed, she tossed the knife away. "Not needed. I can kill you with my bare hands," she whispered.

"Not before you tie up this boy." He lightly increased the pressure, and a drop of blood welled up on the tip of his blade.

"Stop," she said. "I will do what you want."

"Behind you is a rope. Come and tie the boy." Edward did not trust her and maneuvered to keep the rapier tip against the boy's throat. "Make the knots tight," he instructed. "Now the feet."

With Connor tied, Edward breathed a silent relief. He said, "Sit here, next to him." When she looked like she would balk, he warned, "Unhh uhh. Sit."

She turned her back to him and sat facing the entry to the ruins. Once she was settled, Edward paused to savor his moment.

Without Raol I have captured two victims.

But she had cost him a broken nose.

We shall see how you like your nose broken.

Time enough for her beneath the stones of Montrose Court, he thought. For now, he had to eliminate her threat. While he was tempted to strike her in the temple as she had Raol, he resisted, needing her to stay alive for a very long time. He tapped the pommel of his sword on the back of her skull. She slumped forward.

He propped her up next to the boy and tied her feet and bound her hands behind her. "There," he announced. He rose and kicked her in the ribs. "Break my nose," he recriminated.

He sat on one of the stones and wet a cloth to place on his nose. Blood stained his suite, ruining the garment.

Another debt she owes me.

However, her arrival was a fortuitous complication.

"One that will require a slight change of plan," he said with a smile.

CHAPTER TWELVE

Galileo Galilei: Measure what can be measured,
and make measureable what cannot be measured.

Jamie stood by the chamber window, gazing out across the entrance to Greyhaven. Last night's loving with Alex had torched a fire of utter completion within his soul, leaving him filled with this incredible joy. But since her departure, a trickle of unease had invaded his peace.

The land was quiet—not even the birds stirred.

Too quiet.

He glanced over his shoulder at the tub of water for Alex's bath and felt the hairs rise on the back of his neck. His internal unease stood and shouted danger.

"The water is cold," he said. His belly tightened with anxiety and he clenched his hands into fists. "She should be home by now."

Motion outside caught his eye, and he watched as Connor's horse came trotting over the rise without Connor on his back. Jamie ran from his chamber.

He reached the barn and caught the warm horse before it reached the water trough. "Easy boy," he said softly as he patted the animal down, searching for injury or sign of what happened to Connor.

"Where did you leave him?" he asked the gelding.

Connor's jacket was tied to the saddle; Jamie shook it out. A scrap of paper fell free.

The moment he saw the paper Jamie knew everything he held dear in this life was in danger. Behind him, Blue's empty paddock reminded him Alex was also out riding.

Alex! Connor!

He picked up the paper, forcing his fingers not to shake with fear and rage as he read the brief script.

Come to the old fort ruins. Bring the Greyhaven land title. Come alone or the boy dies. Take too long and the woman dies slowly. We are waiting.

Jamie's first thought was to raise Maguire and the boys, but in their current state, it would take—

"Too long ... and the woman dies."

Slowly.

He bolted for the manor, running hard, yet silent. No one must be roused.

Come alone ... or the boy dies.

He reached his library and ran for the great desk. He popped a drawer open and grabbed the latest gold crested, multi-ribbon land grant issued from King James. While he did not like being rushed without the time to think things through, that these miscreants wanted his land was clear. He pocketed the McNeill crested signet and a small taper of wax just in case. In a side drawer was a small knife for opening packages. He grabbed it.

In minutes he had Pharaoh saddled. He walked the animal clear of the barn so as not to attract any attention. Once out of earshot of the manor, he mounted and was swiftly on his way. Instead of taking the meandering road through the village, he cut through the backside of the hill, out of sight of anyone who might be up and about. Once he got to the fields, he lashed Pharaoh until the big stallion tore up the earth in a dead run.

When they broke from the woods bordering the old ruins, Jamie slowed the horse. "Easy now and let us see what is here," he said, soothing the excited animal, and himself.

He saw no one, and heard no sounds of horses or men. Slowly he walked Pharaoh through the opening in the stones. Ahead he saw Connor and Alex on the ground, tied up. A first wave of relief at seeing them alive was quickly replaced by alarm skittering down his back. He reached for the small knife. The hairs on the back on his neck rose and he raised his arm defensively in reaction, but—

He never knew what hit him.

Alex watched in misery as Sir Edward swung a tree limb at Jamie. Jamie fell to the ground, and Pharaoh lunged away. Watching Edward with Jamie, Pharaoh pawed the ground, stopped and neighed, but held his position, snorting with agitation.

Sir Edward scrambled down and quickly bound the Earl. He stood back and dusted his hands off, obnoxiously pleased, Alex could see, with his morning's work.

I will kill this little toad before breakfast, Alex swore silently.

"Well now, how about this!" Sir Edward said. He turned to speak directly to Alex. "You killed Raol." He snarled down into her face. "And now I have plans for · you."

Bile was bitter in her mouth and Alex feared she would vomit into her cloth gag. A growing suspicion had nagged her the last two weeks and she wondered—

Am I—?

No time for that, she commanded.

Get out of this trouble first.

She pushed her troubled thoughts aside and closed her eyes, blotting out Sir Edward's taunting, willing her stomach to be still.

I will stay calm and not let him upset me.

"And you, mister Earl." Edward nudged Jamie's foot as he was just coming around. "Not so high and mighty now, Milord, are you?"

Jamie shook his head before glaring back at Edward. He quickly glanced around and made eye contact with Alex.

She gave him a nod that said, "We are all right."

"I see ye ran into my wife," Jamie challenged.

Edward put his hand to his nose; his voice came out soft and muffled. "I will keep her alive for a very long time." He kicked Jamie in the boot, his tone turning hard and vicious. "Where is the title?"

"In a leather pouch tied to my saddle," Jamie said. "If the horse will let you near enough."

Edward's answering smile showed Alex the depth of his depravity. All thoughts for her personal safety receded and a chill settled over her as she considered how to kill him. Beside her, Connor struggled to bring his boots toward her hands. Alex looked sharply, wondering at his intent.

"Lmnn," Connor mumbled around his gag. He pushed his boot closer. "Stmmm," he repeated. He jutted his chin and she looked down. The glittering sharp edge of a throwing star peeked from his boot.

Alex saw the star and knew hope. Her sense of relief came with an adrenaline shot. Seeing Edward focused on Jamie, she angled her hands toward Connor's boot.

A quick move and she grabbed the tip of the star. She pulled the weapon free. With the weapon at her back, she drew the razor edge across her binding. Twice she cut herself, but at last she cut through the rope. She watched Edward carefully, measuring her opportunities.

Edward's smile broadened into a sinister laugh. He waved his hands eloquently as he antagonized Jamie. "I will get your leather pouch from the horse, not to worry." He brandished his sword. Showing he was well schooled in the weapon's use, he flicked the thin sword in the classic move meant to clear blood from the blade. "The question is, who shall taste my steel. Will it be your woman, your boy, or your horse, eh?"

Jamie grimaced, but he called out. "Pharaoh, come, stand," he told the trained animal.

Pharaoh came to stand at Jamie's side. Edward untied the leather pouch and stepped away from the stallion. "Make him stand aside," Edward said.

"Retreat," Jamie told Pharaoh. The big horse quivered and stamped his foot, shaking his head in agitation. "Retreat," Jamie said again, this time a command. Pharaoh backed up and turned, coming to a stop several yards away.

Edward jumped onto a block of stone and opened the pouch. "Oh, bravo," he crowed, pulling out the wax taper and signet ring. He put the items in his pocket and pulled out the official document.

The gold seal glittered in the clear morning light. Edward held the document to his chest, delight bringing a hideous leer to his face. "Ah, I have waited and suffered so long for this moment."

"You will never get away with this," Jamie argued. "Killing all of us. No one will believe I signed my estate to you and just disappeared. They will know foul play is at hand."

"With you gone, there is no one to contradict my story. The sheriff will never find your bodies and I will tell them I gave you a good price. I will tell them how you spoke of joining your uncle Rory in Spain, following the other fleeing lords." He waved his hand at Jamie in dismissal.

"Your son will disappear into the underbelly of London's most depraved elite. Your woman will go into my specially prepared dungeon at Montrose Court and I promise you she will never see the light of day again."

He placed one finger to his chin and paused to consider more horror. "When your Mother comes to me and begs for a home, I will give her the cell next to the red-haired wench." He sneered at Alex and rubbed his wrist. "Oh, do I have plans for you," he said softly.

Alex kept her gaze ice-cold.

And I have plans for you.

Edward turned his attention back to Jamie. "You can watch me falsify your seal. I know you will enjoy that."

When Edward turned his back and jumped down from the stone, Alex brought the star out and sliced through the rope at her ankles. She sat back immediately, resuming her position.

As they watched, Edward started a small fire on the stone block, creating enough blaze to melt the wax.

"Convenient of you to bring this," he goaded. He looked at Jamie and smiled with neighborly good will. "Oh! Can you see? Please stand, you must not miss this part."

With one hand he motioned Jamie to stand. "But nothing foolish," he cautioned. With his sword hand, he picked up the rapier. She saw him firm his grip on the rapier. With Jamie close enough to witness the forgery he was also within range of a sword strike. She carefully pulled off her gag. Quietly, she gripped the star and flexed her muscles in preparation to jump straight up.

Edward held the wax taper over the document as the wax melted. *Drip, drip, drip,* a puddle formed, and Edward pressed the signet ring into the wax. He looked up at Jamie and smiled with evil pleasure.

Alex saw Edward lift his shoulder and knew he was preparing to strike. "Jamie get down!" she shouted and lunged to her feet in a throwing stance. She braced herself to send all her energy into the star.

Jamie must have seen Edward's movement and was already dropping in an evasive move. Alex saw a clear shot and she launched the star.

Edward looked up, startled.

The sharp point on the star embedded in his neck, entering at the carotid artery with a solid thud. He squealed at the sudden onslaught of bright blood and clutched his neck. Feeling the metal biting into him, he pulled, and the star's back barb ripped out the rest of the artery.

When the blood shot out of Edward's neck in an arc, Alex exhaled with relief. She knew he was a standing dead man. Then he pulled the star from his neck and the arc of blood became a pulsing stream ... but not for long. He collapsed to the ground.

"Jamie," she cried and ran toward him.

"Are you hurt?" he asked, climbing to his feet.

"Are you all right?" she gasped. She hugged him close, certain she would never let him go.

"I am fine," he confirmed.

He looked her up and down and ran his hands all over her. Alex could feel him shaking.

Seeing she was unharmed, he called out, "Connor, are ye hurt, son?"

"Oummph," Connor responded, still bound and gagged.

Jamie ran to him and released his son. "What happened? How are you here?"

Connor stood, shaking off the dirt and leaves that clung to him. "I come here every morning at sunrise to work the horse among the stones. He's quite the good jumper," he bragged.

Alex joined them. "You saved us, Connor."

"My sensei taught me 'never travel without a weapon,'" he responded.

"Thank heaven you learned well," Alex said. "Jamie, what do we do now?" She nodded to the bled-out corpse of Sir Edward.

"Connor must go and fetch Maguire and the sheriff. You and I will wait here until they arrive. Are you fit to do that?"

"Aye," she answered weakly, suddenly feeling faint. The lump where Edward knocked her out throbbed, and she shook wildly inside, giving her the urge to hurl again. An ominous cold dampness slicked her palms; her knees went weak and she dropped toward the stone behind her.

"Alex?" Jamie cried as he grabbed her, lowering her gently to sit. "Connor, give me water," he shouted. From the canteen he dampened a cloth and pressed it to her face.

Alex leaned into his arms, willing her body back to order. She took a drink of water and spit to clear her mouth. "Whew," she whistled, before taking the water and splashing her face. She took the damp cloth from Jamie and gingerly dabbed at the lump on the back of her head.

"Do ye want me to send ye back with Connor?" Jamie asked.

"No, I'm all right," she protested. "Just a reaction, I think. I've never killed anyone before. I should stay and wait for the sheriff."

"It seems we McNeills are a hard-headed lot," he said. "Go son, and have Mary tend to your wound first before you say anything," Jamie instructed. "But Connor, tell nothing of what happened here. Just have them get the sheriff and come."

"Aye, Father," he said. Connor mounted his horse and left at a brisk gait.

"Oh, God, I thought I was going to loose you," Alex murmured. She wrapped her arms around Jamie and thanked heaven he was safe, for she knew she had no life without him.

"We are safe now," he soothed. "No harm done, except to the one who got what he deserved." He held her at arm's length. "Milady, that was one hell of an attack," he crowed softly.

She remembered the day Royce gave her throwing stars identical to the one she just used, and how he encouraged her to become adept. Is it possible he knew she would one day save their lives with this skill? "Thank Royce," she said. "Thank Royce."

Having tended their wounds, they waited silently in

the quiet morning.

"Would you have really signed over Greyhaven?"

He squeezed her hand in answer. "You and my son are the most important people in my life. There was never any other consideration."

"He was awful wicked," Alex murmured. "The things he said. Do you believe he spoke truthfully?"

"You mentioned what you saw in him when he first attacked you," Jamie pondered. "While I know such evil exists, I never imagined it was right next door." The sound of hooves pounding came, and Jamie said, "Let me do all the talking."

She shrugged, happy to let him handle this.

The sheriff and Maguire cantered into the stone ruins. In the distance, more lads came driving a cart to claim the body.

Maguire and the sheriff dismounted; Maguire came to Jamie's side, eyes questioning. Jamie lifted one shoulder and jutted his chin to where the sheriff inspected Sir Edward's body.

Sir Edward lie where he fell, the bloody star in his hand, the ragged wound in his neck, blood soaked into his stylish suit.

"Suicide?" the sheriff asked. He squatted over the body and lifted the star from Edward's palm. He grimaced with wary revulsion as he examined the weapon. "Nasty piece of work, eh?" He set it on the stone block. "Where did he find such a thing?"

"Not suicide," Jamie answered. "But kidnapping, extortion and murder." He pointed to the Greyhaven land title on the ground. "He accosted Connor and my wife—"

"Oh, my congratulations on your very recent nuptials," the sheriff interrupted. He motioned Jamie to continue.

"I came out here this morning and found Sir Edward had Connor and Alex tied up. He threatened to kill them unless I signed over the deed to Greyhaven."

The sheriff rocked back on his heels before nodding.

"When I said no one would believe I signed over my estate to him, he claimed he would say he gave me good price and we followed Rory to the continent."

The sheriff cleared his throat. "Aahemm."

"He had plans to jail my wife and my mother at Montrose Court," Jamie continued. "Connor, he was going to sell to the child slavers of London."

At this, the sheriff's eyebrows shot up and his eyes bugged. "So how, pray tell, did he come to have this hole in his neck?"

"Connor had the star hidden in his boot. Alex threw the weapon, impaling Sir Edward. Sir Edward wrenched the thing from his flesh. Death did not take long."

A deep frown came at this announcement, but the sheriff said nothing. He searched Sir Edward's pockets and found a ring of keys before motioning the boys with the wagon to come and load the body. "We shall take Sir Edward home to Montrose Court. Will ye come with us, if you are not in need of care?" he asked.

"We would like to see if his threats were substantive, or just words," Jamie answered. He looked at Alex and she nodded.

"I would like to go," she said.

The signet was located and handed back to Jamie along with the title to Greyhaven. They mounted their horses and led the way to Montrose Court.

As they entered the grand house, Jamie said, "He

mentioned a dungeon with special rooms, and promised Kathleen and Alex would never again see sunlight."

A growl came from the sheriff's throat. "Who works here?" he announced, and rang the bell sitting on a side-table. When no one came, he declared, "In the name of the King and within the law of the land, I name this dwelling suspect to search and seizure." He nodded to Jamie to lead the way. "Let us find the miscreant's dungeon."

Behind a curtain in the library they discovered a metal-grate door. The sheriff unlocked it with the ring of keys, and they proceeded down a deep stairwell.

At the bottom were several doors, each with a viewing grate. Alex peeked into the first room. "Oh," she gasped.

Thought you were going to keep me in here she mused with disgust. A shudder ripped through her head to toe as she understood just what this vile man had planned.

The sheriff came and looked over her shoulder at the ornately appointed room with a lavishly made bed, and manacles attached to the wall on either side. A second set of manacles attached to the bedposts at the foot of the bed.

"I see," he said quietly. He stepped to the second door and looked in, sucked his tongue in disgust and turned away. "And I have seen enough," he declared.

They went upstairs and into the library. The sheriff passed the ring of keys to Jamie. "I will make my report to the king's men. On the matter of Sir Edward's suicide there should be no further investigation." He turned to Alex and handed her the clean throwing star. He seemed to wrestle with his thoughts before saying, "Not to question your abilities, but will ye show me how ye did it, Milady?"

"Certainly," Alex said. She took a few steps with the star and searched for a target. A life-sized painting of Sir Edward hung at ground level in the space between two bookcases. The artist had given him cold, lifeless eyes, and it was as if he was in the room; Alex shivered. She threw the star at the painting. The weapon hit and thudded into the wood behind the canvas, skewering Sir Edward in the neck a second time.

"Ba huh!" the sheriff barked with amazement. Without a word he walked to the painting and examined the weapon. He had to tug to pull it from the wall. He smoothed his fingers over the laceration in the canvas and chuckled. He returned with the weapon and gently handed it to Alex with a nod of respect. To Jamie he said, "A right handy woman ye have taken to wife, Milord."

They walked out the front door. "I will take the body; it will be interred as a commoner. As for the property, ownership of the land and buildings will revert back to the king. 'Tis up to him to decide the property's future."

He walked into the sun and Alex noticed him shiver. He took a step back and looked up at the grand home. "But it will be months or more, I expect, before any one comes out to do an inventory. Plenty of time to bring in a few stone masons ..."

The statement was left open.

"Sheriff, I appreciate your thorough attention to the matter," Jamie said.

The sheriff mounted his horse and motioned to the boys driving the wagon to follow him. "'Tis good riddance to bad baggage, I say. Ireland is a better place without him."

Alex rode silently with Maguire and Jamie. She was exhausted by the time they got home, and once in their chamber, she dipped into the cool bath water, relishing the temperature. She scrubbed her skin pink, pulled leaves from her hair, and rinsed blood from her cut fingers.

Jamie waited with a towel.

"You have saved my life, Milady," he said, enveloping her in the large cloth. He rubbed gently at her wet skin.

She felt his ministrations as if from a distance, distracted by his words. For those very words had filled her mind since the shock of killing Edward rubbed off.

I saved him and saved them all, she thought.

My mission has been fulfilled.

Jamie sensed her quiet mood and pulled her into his lap, sitting in an oversized chair near the fireplace. She was still wrapped in the towel first, and secondly in his arms.

"What is it, Alex?"

"I saved you, that's what I was meant to do, why I came here," she said.

Between them the silent fear of separation pulsed.

Jamie said not a word. He just held her close. Alex could feel his heartbeat thudding against her ribs. She leaned into him, relishing the feel, the smell, the closeness of him, and especially the magic she was feeling.

"But I think there is more for me to do here ... more to the mission." She pulled back so he could see her face. She knew she grinned like a fool, but she couldn't help herself and she wanted him to see.

"I have a secret," she said. She brought one of his hands to her stomach, cradling the new life there.

Jamie frowned at first, but then his expression gradually expanded as he grasped her meaning.

"Yes," she said with a vigorous affirmation. "The mission has been given an extension. Now," she said. "Now nothing could make me leave."

·

Monet's Garden

Tears flowed down Royce's cheeks. He wiped them away with one hand, unable to stop the torrent of emotion that moved through him.

"Why do you cry?" Andros asked.

"Because I am blessed ... and cursed. Because life is heaven." Royce stumbled in his thoughts. "And because life is hell."

Andros passed Royce a cloth and he blew his nose and wiped at his face. "On that day I was scared as hell; more frightened than I ever knew was possible. That I might have lost Connor, and her, was—"

Royce paused and stared at the pond, confessing. "I would have easily died then in their place."

"But you didn't loose them, did you?" Andros said.

"No," Royce cried out, choking and laughing with tears still streaming down. "Can you believe the gift she gave to me?"

"The child?"

"Aye, the child of course," Royce said, loosing himself in the memory of their baby girl. "But the gift I speak of is really beyond words." He shrugged with helplessness, struggling to put the enormity of the topic into verbal form.

"She gave me love and hope, desire and passion,

something to die for, something to live for." He waved his hands, encompassing what couldn't be seen. "You can't put all that in a box. You can't buy it no matter how rich you are. You can't truly get what she gave me."

He stopped, feeling the pieces wanting to fit together, for he knew it was important he figure this out.

"She gave everything of herself. She was the gift."

Royce looked up, feeling again as if he were in free fall, not physically, but emotionally.

Falling with comprehension.

Understanding will set you free.

He clutched at his seat, not wanting to be free; he wanted his Alex. A new fear blossomed in his chest.

Do I deserve her?

Suddenly his throat felt dry and he couldn't force the words from his vocal chords.

Will I get her back?

CHAPTER THIRTEEN

I am hope, great endurance, life embracing, life releasing, life returning. I am life.

Greyhaven, Five Years Later

Alex goosed Jamie in the ribs and tugged at his hair. "Come Milord, wake up. Today is your birthday and our anniversary. You must rise for this glorious day."

Jamie opened his eyes and grabbed her, rolling in the bed to trap her beneath him.

"You've been playing possum," she reprimanded with a kiss.

"And you have been up scurrying about for an hour. How was I to stay asleep?" He nibbled lightly at her ear. Alex relaxed, feeling absolute contentment roll through her body. She could lay here in his arms forever. All he had to do was touch her, and she wanted him. She kissed him, knowing how little time they had.

A small fist banged at their chamber door. "Mommy, let Fallon in," came their daughter's little voice.

Alex's kiss dissolved into shushed laughter.

Jamie groaned, feigning irritation. He rose from the bed and held a hand out for Alex, pulling her up and into his arms. He wrapped her tight and showered her face with kisses. "She takes after you. Always ... wanting attention."

"Da," came the little voice again. "Fallon hears you in there with Mommy."

Alex approached the door. Before opening it, she whispered, "I have planned us an escape."

The door was opened and Fallon bounded in and went straight to Jamie. "Up, Da, up," she asked, raising her arms to be lifted. Once up in his arms, she smacked a rosebud-mouth kiss on Jamie's cheek.

"Fallon loves you," she cooed. "Today is your first day!"

Alex smiled at her daughter's wrangling with language. To Fallon, every birthday was called a 'first day'.

"And do you know who else has a first day today?" Alex asked.

Fallon's smooth forehead puckered in concentration.

She's a thinker, this one.

"No, Mommy. Who?"

"Connor says there is a new foal down at the barn. He is just born last night, so today is his first day."

Fallon instantly squealed with delight and clapped her hands. "Can I see? Will Connor take me?"

Alex pulled a thoughtful face. "Yes, but you must take Kathleen also."

Fallon nodded sagely, and lightning-quick mimicked her mother's face with the same serious expression. "Fallon see Gamma quiet lately. Maybe the baby horse can make her smile."

Alex took her daughter in her arms, acknowledging her child's acute intuitive nature. "Yes, Gamma needs to smile today. Shall we go see her?"

Fallon squirmed to get down. As Alex set her loose, she mouthed to Jamie, "Get dressed, meet me downstairs," and winked.

She caught up with Fallon before the stairs, and took her hand. They walked all the way down to the grand hall, across to the other side, and back up the stairs to Kathleen's solar. Alex asked, "Do you know why Gamma is quiet?"

"No," Fallon answered. "But she has a new—" She stopped and waved her hands imitating Kathleen at the loom. "A new ... tapie."

"Ah, a new tapestry," Alex repeated. "Maybe Gamma's new tapie is for you. Maybe it's a unicorn kissing a dragon."

Fallon took Alex's hand and continued up the stairs. "A unicorn would never kiss a dragon, Mommy."

At Kathleen's solar, they found the door ajar, and knocked. "Gamma," Fallon cried out. Without waiting for an answer, she pushed the door open and ran in.

She saw Kathleen was working at a new tapestry. Oddly, when she rose from her seat at the loom she pulled the curtain to hide the tapestry from view. Kathleen looked up, but before her face lit with joy at the sight of Fallon, Alex saw the stiff shadow of sadness.

Is she well?

She looked closely, but saw no physical change in Kathleen today from the first day Alex arrived. Indeed, she seemed quite eternal, with skin as smooth and unlined as Alex's.

"Come here child," Kathleen cried. When Fallon bounded across the room, love shined in Kathleen's eyes, erasing any signs of ill-ease. Fallon scrambled up into Gamma's arms.

"Baby horse, Gamma. First day. Take Fallon to see?"

Kathleen kissed Fallon on top or her dark red curls. "Of course I will," she said, her words muffled against Fallon's scalp.

Alex thought she heard a catch in Kathleen's voice. "Kathleen?" she said softly.

Kathleen waved off Alex's concern. "I am just in love with this child, 'tis all."

"Connor will join you, while—" Alex let her voice trail off and she caught Kathleen's eyes. Alex gave her the we-are-going-for-a-little-alone-time look.

"Then I must get dressed," Kathleen murmured. She stepped into her dressing chamber and came out quickly. "Shall we go?" she asked brightly, and took Fallon's hand.

They descended the stairs to the great hall, listening to Fallon's chatter all the way. Downstairs, Jamie waited by the door. He gave Alex a questioning lift of eyebrow, and she nodded yes.

Jamie scooped up his daughter and showered kisses on her neck, making her squeal and scrunch her shoulders. "You go to see the foal?"

"Yes, Da," she answered.

"And Fallon will mind Gamma and Connor?"

"Yes, Da," she nodded. "And Fallon will be here when you come back." She threw her arms around his neck and buried her face under his chin. Softly she added, "Worry not, Da, Mommy will take care of everything."

Quick as a squirrel, she wiggled out of his arms and threw him a kiss. "Happy first day, Da!" she crowed before grabbing Kathleen's hand. "Baby horse, Gamma, baby horse, go," she reminded, and tugged Kathleen out the door.

Alex watched them depart and a shiver of déjà vu skittered across her shoulders.

La Casa, on the day I first saw the vision of Jamie, Rosita and the children went down to the barn to see a new foal.

The chill danced down her arms, but she shook it off. The day was too beautiful for dusty memories.

Bringing her thoughts back to Fallon, she whistled, "Whew. She is so precocious. I don't know where she gets everything she says." She took Jamie's hand and imitated her daughter, pulling him out the door into the morning sun.

Jamie greeted the sunshine, lifting his face to the warmth. Eyeing the sky innocently, he offered, "I canna imagine where she gets it."

Alex giggled. "She is smart like her father," she defended.

"So what will you 'take care of' today, Milady?" Jamie asked. He took both her hands and peered into her face.

Five years, and she loved him more and more each day. She lifted her shoulders in joy. "'Tis your birthday, Milord. What would you like to do?"

"But the day is also your anniversary," he countered. "What would you like to do?" His voice went husky, hinting at seduction. "What say you choose 'where', and I choose 'what' we do, fair?"

She felt her body hum at the first moment of his seductive tone. The familiar tingle of desire flared deep; her passion for him never seemed sated. "Let's go to the flower meadow."

"Where you first came?" he asked and bent down to kiss her neck.

A chuckle of knowing rumbled from Alex's throat as

she let her head fall back under the onslaught of his enticing lips. "Yes, and what would you wish to do there, Milord? Might I suggest—"

"Might I suggest we go immediately," Jamie responded.

Alex laughed and took his hand, pulling him in the opposite direction of the barn.

"Shall we walk then?" he asked, confused.

"Ha," she reprimanded. "Just who do you think you're dealing with, anyway?" Tied in the trees were Pharaoh and Mister Blue, both appearing well-packed with supplies.

"So this is what you have been busy with all morning. You always take care of everything," he said, eyeing the picnic basket and blankets strapped to his horse.

They mounted and casually picked their way out to the meadow. Time seemed to have stopped for them, for the day was bright with no cloud overhead. In the far distance, white popcorn clouds jammed the horizon from east to west. The birds were vocal in the trees, and a light breeze kicked up out of the southwest.

They arrived and dismounted on the crest of the hill overlooking the infamous meadow. A blanket and pillows were set out, along with picnic fare. There was cold roasted chicken, fresh bread with butter, cheese and small fried apple pies.

"Wine, Milady?" Jamie inquired as he filled two clay mugs.

Alex sipped her wine and nibbled at the food. She and Jamie rarely had any time alone; she treasured the moments. When the plates were set aside, she leaned back into the pillows braced against a shade tree. Jamie stretched out next to her and took her hand, stroking her palm and kissing her fingers.

"You have made me a happy man, wife," he said. He inched up closer and began kissing along her neck. Soon the laces of her blouse were opened and he placed his head on her chest. "Is that your happy heart I hear beating?" He turned his head and lightly kissed first one breast, then the other.

"Mm," she moaned. "Yes, happy heart." She peeked at him with one eye and saw the bliss on his face. "You," she said with emphasis, "are the most important person in the world to me, you know that?"

"Aye," he answered, his thick brogue turning the single word into a long rumbling purr of passion. He scooted up to take her in his arms and kissed her deeply.

She returned the kiss, her tongue joining with his, their lips touching, tasting and delivering the message of love. Her heart swelled with contentment, knowing her life was just where it should be.

We should go, to make another baby in that great bed.

As the thought entered her mind, a breeze kicked up, stirring the leaves to swirl around them. A fat cloud passed in front of the sun, bringing a chill.

"A good time to go, Milord," she began when a streak of lightning lit the sky from over the hilltop behind them.

One, two, three, four, five she counted off. And then came an earsplitting crack of thunder.

He jumped up. "I have the horses," he said and ran down the hill in pursuit. They were peacefully grazing in the vale before the lightning caused them to skitter to high ground. Alex hastily collected the food and utensils and threw them into the bags with the blanket and pillows.

She backed down the hill from the trees and looked up at the sky. "Oh my, gonna get wet," she muttered. She watched as the leading edge of a dark cloud advanced overhead, overtaking the sun. In the distance more dark clouds marched in a hard line coming in from the north. Illuminating their darkness were streaks of lightning, flashing down, bringing the pungent smell of ozone.

The wind gusted down, bringing cool air, and Alex knew the rain was soon to come. About fifty yards up the hill, lightning cracked into the forest. She turned to motion to Jamie that they were out of time.

On the crest of the hill Jamie held the reins to both horses, one in each hand. The wind blew and a tangle of limb and leaf shot into Blue's hind legs. The horse lunged back, pulling his reins from Jamie's hand. Already frightened, and realizing he was free, the next bolt of lightning sent Blue running.

"Whoa," Jamie soothed Pharaoh.

Pharaoh jerked his head and pulled against the reins, backing up and pulling Jamie down the hill.

She held her breath, watching Jamie and Pharaoh in silhouette, seeing the backdrop of dark clouds, and the boom, boom of thunder in her ears. Her eyes read the track of the lightning as her mind counted off the numbers ...

"Get down," she whispered.

Pharaoh is right. Get down off the crest of the hill.

"Get down," she said louder, panic moving in. "Get down off the hill," she cried, waving at Jamie. "Jamie get down," she shrieked. She wanted to run to him but knew she couldn't get there in time. Her only hope was in catching his eye before—

"Get down," she cried out.

Pharaoh gave one last pull against the reins, jerking Jamie so that he fell to his knees. With the reins free, the stallion backed up and reared. Jamie stumbled to his feet and Pharaoh reared again, seeming to strike at Jamie. Jamie threw his hand up to cover his face.

Alex had her hand over her mouth, watching Pharaoh try to get Jamie to the ground. The lightning was on top of them and the horse reared again.

The lightning struck the ground at Jamie's feet.

Pharaoh was thrown fifteen feet and screamed when he landed hard. Jamie was still in the air when Alex started running. "No, no no, no," she chanted, struggling up the hill with her heart in her throat and her feet tangled in skirts.

"No no no no," she said, crawling over the crest of the hill.

Jamie was on the ground, literally blown out of his boots. Alex ran to him, fell and scrambled the rest of the way on her hands and feet.

"No ... no," Alex cried. She frisked Jamie for injuries and found nothing broken, but he was unconscious and his face was ashen. She groped at his neck for a pulse.

Where is it!

She pulled open his shirt and placed her ear to his chest.

No no no no.

She positioned his head by arching his neck, held his cheeks and blew into his mouth. Pump the chest, fill the lungs. She continued through several cycles and stopped and checked his pulse.

"Yes!" she cried. She rubbed his cheeks and rubbed his hands, doing all she could to help the blood flow.

"Help, we have to have help," she cried. She glanced at Pharaoh and saw he was on his feet, quivering. "Go Pharaoh," she cried. "Go home. Go home and get help."

The animal came to stand over her. He sniffed at Jamie and nudged the body with his nose.

Alex held her husband, crying. "Go Pharaoh. Go home!"

Pharaoh backed up, turned and headed toward Greyhaven.

"Stay with me Jamie, stay with me," Alex crooned as she rubbed his body, checking his pulse and breathing. "Come on, baby, stay with me, stay with me." She choked and broke into tears but she kept touching him and begging him to stay with her. "You promised you wouldn't leave me," she negotiated, and the tears fell even harder.

The sound of a wagon approaching seemed to come really fast, and Alex wondered how poor Pharaoh had run all the way to Greyhaven.

"Help," she cried. "Over here, over here!"

She looked up with immense relief to see Kathleen and Maguire. Maguire's face was pale. Kathleen's as stiff as stone.

"Here, lassie," Maguire offered. "Let me put him up here."

He lifted Jamie, and Alex scrambled in so they could put Jamie's head in her lap. "Lightning," she said in a whisper. "Hit the ground at his feet." She looked up at Kathleen, suddenly suspicious. "Did you know?"

"Not everything," Kathleen murmured as she crawled in beside Jamie. She opened her small medicine kit. "I have Foxglove tincture." She placed several drops under Jamie's tongue.

Alex felt like her head was going to spin right off her

shoulders.

She knew and she didn't warn me?

She pushed the thought aside and turned her focus to Jamie. He was still, very still. She picked up one of his hands and saw the cuticles were pale. She rubbed the hand and blew on it, willing her life force to enter his body and keep him with her.

They arrived at Greyhaven and Connor was there with several lads and they carried Jamie up to the master's chamber. A robust fire already burned in the fireplace and a table nearby was laid out with water and bandages and a full display of Kathleen's medicine store.

Alex glanced at him, desperate to see him revive. She wanted to kill Kathleen for not warning her this was coming, but they needed her medicine knowledge if they were going to keep Jamie alive.

Maguire pulled Jamie's clothes off and they dressed him in one of the nightshirts he never wore. Together they got him into the bed. Alex crawled on top of the covers next to him. She dabbed a cool wet cloth over his face, doing the same at his wrist and his neck.

He squeezed her hand.

"Jamie!" she cried.

He smiled weakly. "Hey," he said.

Alex pulled his hand to her face and kissed his fingers with trembling lips. "Don't scare me like that, Milord."

He attempted to wet his lips and she tipped a cup to his mouth. He sat forward to drink, cleared his throat and whispered, "Did not see that coming." He sat back with an exhausted 'whoosh' exhalation.

"Ssssh," she admonished. "Save your strength. Let Kathleen give you some medicine." She looked at Kathleen standing on the other side of the bed. She held a cup.

"Willow tea," she said. "Drink this Jamie."

He sipped slowly and Alex had to hold the cup for him. Her heart had gone from to racing with fear to frozen with fear.

Foxglove, that's digitalis, and willow tea is aspirin to thin the blood.

A quick glance at his cuticles told her they had not returned to pink. In fact, they looked a little blue.

The lightning damaged his heart.

Outwardly, her face reflected only concern. But inside she shrieked in misery.

No no no no no no no!

She pushed back on her panic and tears, not wanting him to see her break down. "There my love, you have finished your tea," she said.

Kathleen took the cup and Alex caught her eye.

How long? she mouthed.

Soon, Kathleen silently answered and looked away.

Alex felt like an imploding star, collapsing to a fiery ball that was going to blink out into the black of absolute nothing.

Keep it together.

Using the lightest voice she could muster, she asked, "Do you feel any better?"

"I do," he said.

He lied. His breath seemed labored when he said, "Bring Connor and Fallon."

"I will fetch them," Maguire said, rising from the corner of the room.

"Mother," Jamie called, reaching for her hand.

Kathleen kneeled beside the bed. "Save your

strength," she whispered. She placed her hand in his and rested them on his lap.

"How strong you are," he said and lightly shook her hand back and forth. "You will help her with the dragon?"

Alex leaned in, wondering if Kathleen put a narcotic in the tea to sedate Jamie.

Kathleen's eyes filled with tears that ran down her cheeks. "I am here for her as I am for you."

Jamie squeezed her hand. "She could do no better."

He stopped to collect his breath and his face seemed even paler. Alex felt her hold begin to splinter. Her nose burned and the back of her eyes felt the pressure of incoming tears. She dashed at her eyes and willed them to dry up.

A knock came at the door and Maguire stuck his head in. "They are here."

Kathleen nodded and Maguire pushed open the door. Connor walked in holding Fallon's hand. She solemnly looked up at her brother and he released her hand. She walked carefully to the edge of the bed. Kathleen picked her up and set her on the bed beside Jamie.

"My girl," Jamie said.

"Fallon loves you, Da," she said and took his hand.

Alex put her hand to her mouth to choke back a sob. She slid off the bed, unable to watch.

"Mommy fix," Fallon said.

"Yes, Mommy fixed Da," Jamie replied.

Alex hunched her shoulders and squeezed her eyes painfully tight. She pinched the bridge of her nose where a head full of tears threatened to let loose.

"Not fix Da this time," Fallon said. She spoke in her little girl voice, not questioning, but making a declaration with adult matter-of-fact comprehension.

"You help Mommy, understand?" Jamie whispered. Alex turned around to see, wondering at the pact being made between father and daughter.

"And you will kiss the dragon," he said, smiling.

"I know, Da," Fallon answered. She reached up to hug him, pressing her face into his neck. "Fallon loves you."

Kathleen picked up Fallon and held her in her arms. Connor stepped up to the bed.

"Father," he choked out.

"Proud of you, son," Jamie said softly. "You listen to Mam."

"Always," Connor answered. When he nodded to affirm, the tears dripped off his chin. "I will, sir." A sob broke loose, and he bent over to hug his father. "I love you, Da, I love you." He sobbed again before standing quickly. He wiped at his face even though his chin shook and the tears never stopped.

Alex's knees went weak. She glanced at Maguire and his stiffened face was too much to bear. She stepped to the bed and collapsed next to Jamie, huddling beside him.

Jamie called her. "Alex, my love. You gave me life."

She reached for his hand and they held each other close. "S'posed—" Alex choked. "Supposed to—" The words stuck in her throat and she ground them out between stiff jaws, "Supposed to save you."

"Oh," he sighed. "But you did, you did."

Alex brought his hand to her mouth to feel his skin next to her lips. She tucked her head and kissed his hand, not wanting him to see her cry.

"I saw everything, Alex. Everything," he said.

Alex's lips trembled and her heart broke. Deep inside she didn't want to know what he saw.

Ask now or never know ...

"What did you see?" she asked.

"You still have to save them all," he said softly. "You are stronger than you think."

"I have no one else to save," Alex said, shaking her head.

"Save them all, Alex. Then go home and save Royce. The future happens once the past gets out of the way."

"What?"

Those are Master Chan's words.

Alex pulled back to see his face, feeling as though her chest and her life were falling through time again.

"Save Royce, and you save me," he repeated.

"I can't think," she protested. Feeling her face crumble, she waved off his suggestion.

"Save Royce and you save me," he whispered. He reached up to touch her face. "Remember this ... I will love you long after the sun and the moon and stars have faded from the sky."

His voice grew weak, and Alex felt the pulse at his wrist falter. "Don't leave me," she cried.

"We will never be apart," he whispered.

Alex felt him exhale. His chest went still and his hand let loose of hers. "No no no no no no," she cried. She thumped her fist on his chest where the heart no longer beat, and she screamed, "No!" She thumped him again and again and again, crying, "No no no you promised not to leave me."

An arm went around Alex's shoulder and she tried to shrug it off. A cloth smelling of medicine was pressed to her mouth, and she knew darkness.

She dreamed of walking a confusing maze of long hallways with too many exits. It reminded her of her first day at Greyhaven, being lost—

"This way," came a voice.

"Fallon?" Alex asked. Her legs were too heavy to move.

"Come, Mommy, help the unicorn kiss the dragon."

Alex felt her legs dissolve and she suddenly stood on the edge of a great precipice. She looked over her shoulder and there was an empty cocoon hanging by a thread, swaying back and forth.

"Jump, Mommy, you fix, you fix," Fallon cried.

Alex looked forward and saw Jamie holding Fallon, only he was Royce, except he was Jamie.

She shook her head, feeling the winds of time sucking at her feet. In the background she saw the old clock in the library had come to life. She could hear it ticking, ticking, ticking.

She sat up and cried, No!" She was in her old room below the master chamber.

"Easy," Kathleen said. She rose from a bedside chair and moistened a cloth. When she reached to wipe Alex's face, Alex pushed her hand away. "You knew," she said. Her voice came out stiff and wooden, a hoarse whisper of accusation.

Kathleen sat on the bed. "Yes, I knew, and there was nothing I could do."

"You could have warned me," Alex retorted.

"There was nothing you could have done with the knowledge," Kathleen offered. "You think I would not have done everything ... anything possible to save my son?"

Alex knew the sparring words were useless, but anger for her loss filled her heart and she was desperate to unleash her agony before she was consumed. "I could have saved him again," she ground out, feeling the tears come in a torrent. She didn't bother to wipe them away.

Kathleen sighed, a deep sound full of remorse and ... strength. "You have more to do," she said softly.

"Ha!" Alex blew in a snort of disdain. "I am done ... Done with doing and saving and ..." Her throat closed up and she covered her face with her hands as the sobs tore through her.

Kathleen brought a steaming teapot and cup to the bedside. "Drink this, you will feel better." She poured and set the cup on the table. "Drink. I will wake you when it's time."

Alex didn't want to accept Kathleen's help, but the void in her chest was a dark possession eating her alive. She took the cup and gulped the concoction, wishing she were dead.

Sleep came, but it was not peaceful, and the dreams were a nightmare. Once again, Alex walked the long hallways, feeling lost and uncertain of her purpose. A sound came, attracting her, drawing her feet until she stood in Jamie's library. On the wall was a great tapestry. A beautiful creation of color and light showed an angelic unicorn kissing a great dragon that sat docile at the unicorn's feet.

Tick, tick, tick the clock reminded.

Alex woke to the feel of Fallon crawling into bed.

"Love you, Mommy," she said.

Tears flooded the back of Alex's face, but she cursed them to hell, refusing to let them fall. "Mommy loves you, sweetheart." She brought her daughter close to her chest, needing the warmth of her energetic little body.

"Da go bye today," Fallon said. "Will you hold Fallon's hand?"

Fallon's voice came out in a tiny squeak, belying her brave words. The sound was a sword to Alex's heart for she knew her daughter referred to the internment ceremony.

"Will you hold Mommy's hand?" Alex responded. She squeezed her daughter tight. "Mommy needs you," she whispered barely loud enough to hear.

"I promised Da," she answered. She nodded, and Alex could feel the growing wet spot from tears coming off her daughter's face.

Soon Kathleen came with a new pot of tea, and a maid to hustle Fallon off. "Go with Sissy," Kathleen said. "She will help you dress."

Fallon followed Sissy to the door and turned to look back. The forlorn shadows filling her daughter's face brought more tears, blurring Alex's vision.

"Go, now," Kathleen commanded Sissy. Kathleen stepped into Alex's line of sight holding a fresh cup of tea and pressed it into Alex's hand. "Drink," she instructed.

Alex dashed her hand across her eyes and took the cup, gulping it empty. She wiped her mouth on the back of her hand. "What do I wear?" she croaked in a ragged voice.

The dress and veil were black and belonged to someone else.

A young widow from the village?

It was a poor fit and ugly and she was glad, for the garment appropriately reflected the state of her life.

Ugly and ill-fitting.

"Come," Kathleen said. She took Alex by the elbow

and guided her out the door and down the stairs. At the final curve revealing the great room filled with everyone from the village, the sheriff, even an obnoxious overdressed representative from court, Alex felt her knees go weak. She surely would have gone down were it not for Kathleen holding her up.

You are stronger than you think, Jamie said.

"Huh," she snorted with anger.

Bereft of any such strength, she tucked her head, unable to bear the sad eyes of those looking at her. Someone escorted her to a seat at the front, and she was grateful for the chance to sit.

Kathleen has drugged me, but not near enough.

She closed her eyes and shut out the sounds of the ceremony, retreating into her mind, floating in a narcotic haze.

I could have saved him.

Her head moved slowly back and forth with a sadness born of lost opportunity.

You can still save him and save them all.

Alex jerked in her seat.

Save them? Saved him, she protested, *already*.

A vision of Royce speaking with Jamie's voice slipped through Alex's mind.

You are not finished. The future happens when the past gets out of the way. Help me come home.

Her body went stiff. Refuting Jamie's claim she was stronger than she thought, she fainted.

She had a vague sense of being carried and placed in a bed. Her clothes were changed, and cool hands with a damp cloth soothed her brow.

"Drink," came the command, and Alex sipped greedily of the narcotic brew. Down she slipped into the deepest region of brain activity seeking refuge from her pain, refuge from her life.

"Help me, please," she mumbled. She rolled across the bed in her delirium, searching for what she had lost.

"I'm here," she heard.

Her heart expanded, sensing shelter. A face came to mind.

"Royce?"

"I need you. Only you can fix this, Momma Bear."

"Where are you?"

"I am ... without you."

Alex stilled in her pain filled thrashing on the bed. She braced herself against the disembodied sensation rolling through her body. She felt time whistle around her.

"I can't be without you Alex. Without you I don't exist. Please, bring me home," Royce pleaded.

She wanted to resist, for her alarmed heart was speeding up. But she didn't want to miss her chance to know, didn't want to miss another opportunity.

"How?" she asked.

We go together.

Alex retreated to a place of peace.

The night came, the moon rose, the heavens moved.

She woke in the heart of night. She rubbed her eyes, swollen and gritty, and moaned. "Make it stop," she pleaded, but the pain rose fresh and crushing in her chest. "No!" she cried out and threw the covers off. She wore one of the nightgowns that came with her trousseau, a garment she never wore.

Until now.

She put her bare feet on the bedside carpet but didn't reach for her slippers. She walked to the chamber door and out, down the stairs, across the great room, up the stairs and down the hall to Jamie's library.

"There you are," she said, speaking to the great desk that held McNeill secrets. She rummaged across the desktop and in all the drawers and was reminded of when she conducted this same search at La Casa, searching for evidence of James Roy.

She found the book recording the events of the McNeill family and opened to the page about Jamie. There in Kathleen's beautiful cursive handwriting was 'Alexandra Martine' married to James Roy on August 31, 1612.

Suddenly the clock ticked, startling Alex. She jumped.

Tick, tick, tick, just like in her dream.

"No," she said, backing up. "No." She clutched the record book to her chest and ran.

Back in her chamber she dove under the covers. She held the book tight and let the tears come sliding down her cheeks. Silently, she opened the book, tracing the lovely entry of her marriage to Jamie with her finger. Her tears dripped down onto the page, washing away the writing. "No," she moaned, and tore the rest of the page out.

With the crumpled page in her fist, she curled into a fetal position, rocking, seeking relief.

She woke the next morning to a light filled chamber and a tray of food on the bedside stand. Kathleen sat in a chair, watching her.

Alex shifted her position to sit up against the pillows. She sniffed at the tray of warm bread and her stomach rumbled. "How long?"

"Three days."

Alex rubbed her face and took a sip of hot tea. The

liquid warmed her body, which felt like she had been in hibernation for months. She ate a slice of bread with butter and jam, and her mouth watered. She ate another slice, refilled her teacup and finished a third.

"Whew," she moaned. She rubbed her face, scrubbing at her tired eyes.

"I have ordered a bath for you," Kathleen said.

Alex noted the tone in Kathleen's voice.

A touch of steel. Does she know?

"We're leaving," Alex announced. "As soon as we can prepare."

"Where do you go, Alex?"

"Through time, where I belong, to save him." She spoke matter-of-fact knowing Kathleen would understand.

"To save Royce," Kathleen finished.

Alex rose and went to her vanity and began washing her face. "It is what Jamie told me to do." She eyed Kathleen who came to stand behind her. She watched the woman's reflection in the glass.

"And who are 'we'?" Kathleen whispered.

"Fallon is coming with me. Give me back the gold device." Alex gave this request in a no-nonsense tone.

Kathleen retreated to the bed where she spotted the torn page from the family records. She picked it up and spread out the page where Fallon's birth was recorded. "You would remove yourself and your daughter from us as though you never existed?"

Alex walked to her armoire and rummaged deep in a drawer for a pair of pants. "Call us one of the McNeill secrets," Alex quipped over her shoulder. Expecting a contentious response, she waited.

"May I show you something before you go?" Kathleen asked.

"Make it fast," Alex said tucking in her shirt. "We can stop by the solar when we go for the whistle."

Kathleen led the way as though it were Alex's first day at Greyhaven. They made the turn down the hall to Jamie's library.

A chill rushed at Alex from the opened door. Suddenly she didn't want to pass through this portal, didn't want to see what Kathleen had to show.

"Come in." Kathleen held the door.

Alex stepped just over the threshold and hugged the wall. "What?"

Kathleen walked to the wall and pulled the cord on a curtain. A great tapestry Alex had never seen filled the wall. A brilliant rainbow was the background for a dancing white unicorn.

"Kissing the dragon," Alex said. She walked across the room, following Kathleen. "I didn't know this was here," she said. "But I saw it in my dream. What does it mean?"

"I had this hung while you were sleeping. This is the first tapestry I wove when the gift of sight came to me."

She ran her fingers across the tight stitches in bright silk. She stroked the unicorn. "This is Fallon."

"Maybe the unicorn will kiss the dragon," Alex mumbled, remembering speaking those words to Fallon just before—

Alex backed up, no longer interested in what the tapestry meant. "No" she said. "I have had enough." She waved off whatever Kathleen was petitioning.

"She has a life here," Kathleen said. "She belongs here. Her future is here."

"No no no no no," Alex insisted. She turned to leave.

"The dragon will come through time for her," Kathleen persisted. "He is her soul mate."

Alex stopped at the door and placed her forehead against the hardwood frame. "No," she whispered. "Stop telling me this."

"'Tis Fallon who will 'save them all,'" Kathleen continued. "Not you. Her destiny is here, Alex."

"How dare you ask that of me, after everything I've done," Alex snapped. She didn't look up.

Suddenly Kathleen was at her side. "How dare you presume you are the only one grieving."

More tears burned into Alex's eyes. She exhaled and tapped her head on the doorframe, wishing she could stop the world from turning. "I'm sorry," she began. "I know how you must be hurting."

"And Connor," Kathleen reminded.

Alex tapped her head against the hard wood again. How she wished she were somewhere else …

"He will come to the same place you came, in the spring of her seventeenth year. Together they will save—"

"Stop," Alex pleaded.

"Talk to her," Kathleen said. "Ask Fallon what she wants to do."

Kathleen left Alex alone in the library. She remained with her head on the wood doorframe, willing the genie of life to come and make hers whole again.

But no genie came.

She returned to her chamber, unable to bear the sight of the master chamber above. She lay on the bed, rubbing her temples, feeling like a crushed shell of her once happy self.

A tiny tap came at the open door. "Mommy?"

Alex exhaled, fearing what her daughter was coming to say. "Come, Fallon," she called, and patted the bed.

Fallon climbed up and lay beside Alex, face-to-face. She reached out her little hand on Alex's chest above her heart. "Fallon loves Mommy," she whispered. "Will you go to fix Da now?"

Alex touched her daughter's chest and circled her heart. "If I go, will you come hold my hand?"

"Fallon stay here, Mommy." The words were small, but convicted.

"What if Mommy doesn't come back?" Alex asked. She held her breath.

"Fallon stay here, Mommy."

"To kiss the dragon?" Alex whispered, squeezing her eyes tight against the tears.

"Maybe," Fallon offered.

"That's my girl, no push over," Alex said with a strangled laugh, although the sound held no mirth. She refused to break down in front of her daughter who was holding up a good deal better than her mother.

You are stronger than you think.

"Do you want to watch me go?" Alex asked.

Fallon considered this request deeply before asking, "Can Gamma come, and Connor, to hold my hand?"

The bottom of Alex's world finally fell out from under her as the winds of time swept away all ground beneath her. "I am sure they will be there."

With her heart breaking and her life in Ireland coming to an end, Alex couldn't bear to hang around.

Maguire with Connor and Kathleen accompanied her out to the meadow. Fallon rode with her brother; there was little to say on the ride. Alex held the whistle tightly.

"Full circle," she thought when they approached the fateful hill where Jamie had been struck by lightning. She rode Blue across the hill and down into the vale where she first saw Connor and Maguire.

Everyone dismounted and Alex handed Blue's reins to Maguire. "Take care of him, not too much grain," she said with the barest smile. Maguire gave her a chest-crushing hug. Into her neck he mumbled, "Travel with us in yer heart."

"I will," she returned.

She stepped to Connor. "You are sensei now. Practice every day, and teach your sister. And listen to Mam." She choked back a sob, grabbed her stepson, and hugged him tight. "You take care of them. You are the man of the house, now."

Next came Kathleen holding Fallon. Alex sniffed, and tapped into a well of strength she never knew possible.

You are stronger than you think.

"Take care of Gamma," Alex said to her daughter.

"Yes, Mommy." She reached out and Alex took her in her arms. "You go fix Da?" Fallon asked. She put her hand over Alex's heart.

"Yes, I go to fix Da. And you, always remember how much I love you," Alex choked out.

"I will, Mommy. You remember how much I love you," and she pushed on Alex's chest. "I love YOU."

Alex kissed her daughter on both cheeks and the top of her head before handing her back to Kathleen.

"Give my love to Royce," Kathleen said softly. "When you get home look in the secret compartment."

Eyes watering up again, Alex nodded. "I'm sorry I was—"

Kathleen shook her head. "I understand." She hugged Fallon close, and added, "Thank you for this."

Alex wiped away her tears and stepped to her place in the meadow. She took a last look. Fallon grabbed Connor's hand. With her free hand she waved, reminding Alex of Master Chan.

"I love you all," Alex called out.

She closed her eyes and took several deep breaths, calming her mind and heart. An image of Royce came clear to her and she smiled, knowing she was going home. Knowing Royce was Jamie. Knowing they truly were never going to be apart.

Come back my love, come back, she called with her heart.

She counted down to reach a meditative state and fixed the image of Royce in her mind. "Together again," she chanted. "Together again." She blew on the whistle again and again, seeing in her mind Royce opening his arms to her.

"Together again, together again, together ..."

With her heart and soul she filled her cheeks and blew into the gold device.

The timeless vibration overtook her with a sudden swoop of vertigo. The air began to move. Wind buffeted her. A boom filled her ears.

She dropped into free fall.

CHAPTER FOURTEEN

Carl Sagan: Somewhere, something incredible
is waiting to be known.

Monet's Garden

Royce didn't need to strain to hear. The words "together again" echoed clearly across the pond.

Alex is calling! I must go to her.

His relief left him quaking in his chair. He would have jumped straight up but he knew he still had something to workout. A tickling suspicion held him as comprehension wound its way through his heart and mind. He was rooted to his chair. He couldn't leave until he was sure.

"Love," he said, "is more than an emotion for our pleasure." He laughed and added, "And pain, let's not forget."

Andros didn't speak, but motioned Royce to continue.

"Love, other than death, is the most powerful force exerted on a human," Royce murmured, discovering his thoughts as he spoke. "Love is powerful enough to force us to change ... and reach ... our greatest potential."

He jumped up, excited. "But what love really does is

hold us together." He said this last slowly, wondering at the incredible adventure his wife just experienced, all in the name of love.

Staring off into the pond, he said, "We are two parts of the same soul. And love holds us together through out—"

Chan's words danced in Royce's memory. "Love holds us together throughout the refinement of our one soul. Love is the force holding the two halves of a soul together." He reached for a scientific comparison. "Like the weak nuclear force holding together the parts of an atom. Without love, we could not attain our ultimate completion."

Together again, came Alex's voice, bouncing off the water.

Royce looked at Andros. "Is it time?"

Andros stood and offered his hand in parting. "Your visit has been a lesson to me," he said. "Many come here and leave with questions. You, I see, have answers." He released Royce's hand and stepped back. "Remember, together, you are more than you could ever be otherwise."

He passed his hand over the water, and Royce screamed.

•

"Together again," Alex chanted, calling Royce with her heart. "Together again, together."

The free fall was nauseating and horribly frightening. Alex kept her eyes closed and her mind locked on Royce.

Together again, together again, together again …

The sense of free fall stopped instantly. She was suddenly still, the vertigo gone, and hard ground beneath her butt. She opened one eye and screamed.

Master Chan stood exactly as she had last seen him, hand raised in a wave, as if she had just left this instant.

He jumped back and fell against the stone bench. He threw his hand to his chest. "Ooohhh! Alex you startled me."

"What? You are here?" Alex gasped.

"You are here?" Chan retorted. "What happened? Did you go?"

•

Royce screamed in free fall until he realized he was in the cockpit of the Sherpa. "Whoooa ehh … what?" He immediately scanned the controls and looked around.

Seeing Manislu straight in front of him, he said, "Whoa, we are not going there." He banked the Sherpa left in a hard one-eighty turn and headed back to Bimthang. "I'm coming, Alex," he said. "I'm coming back."

•

Alex stood on wobbly legs. "What are you doing here?" she asked Chan.

"Alex," he began, but his voice faded out. He stared at her. "You, your clothes are different, and, your hair is longer than it was two seconds ago. Alex, I haven't left the garden yet. You were just here."

Alex's shoulders slumped.

Royce isn't here!

"No," she cried. But suddenly she paused, head cocked, listening. She looked up just as the Sherpa flew overhead. "Royce!" she shouted. She ran for the landing area.

Across the garden, out the secret gate, and through the maze of corridors that was the academy. She ran down one long hallway, a quick right near the front, and another left before hurtling out the exterior gate to the landing area.

"Royce, Royce," she cried. The plane was just stopped and the engines cut. The cockpit door opened, and Royce stepped out.

"Oh!" she cried and ran to him. She couldn't stop, and smacked into him full force, knocking him to the ground as when they met in the halls of Greyhaven.

"Oh, oh, I love you. Never, never, never leave me again, never leave me again." She held his face in her hands and kissed him.

Royce, Royce, Royce her heart cried in joy.

Her lips met his and tasted their mingled tears. She felt his warm flesh respond. His arms were around her and his bear hug nearly crushed her ribs.

Alex broke the kiss and gazed at his face, touching his cheeks, his eyelid, his nose, his chin.

And he was all Jamie, all Royce. There was no atom of difference between the two.

"Oh God, hold me," she pleaded.

"And never let me go," he bargained.

Alex saw the bottom of Chan's robes as he caught up with them. "Alex, Royce," he cried. He bent and helped them stand.

There were tears, and questions, and hugs, and kisses and everything all at once.

Chan held up his hand. "You two go and be together. We will talk later."

In their room Alex melted into Royce's arms. She had so much to say she didn't know where to start.

"I know," he said to her. "I don't know where to start."

"Where were you?" she asked holding her ear to his chest, listening to the strong heartbeat there.

"I was without you," he answered simply.

Tears flooded Alex's eyes. "I—"

"Sshh," he said, stroking her hair. "I know, I was there."

Alex quieted, realizing how true his words were. "You remember? You know everything?"

"Yes," he whispered. He took her face gently in his hands.

Her heart expanded, filling her chest and her throat with an overload of emotion searching for the right words.

"Molon labe," she said.

"Molon labe," Royce returned.

•

Royce drove the rental car from LAX and turned onto the road to La Casa de la Paz. Alex held his hand, itching with excitement to get home. "Kathleen said look in the secret compartment. What do you think we'll find?"

Royce squeezed her hand. "No telling what mother has left for you."

"My sister will have questions," she said.

"We'll tell her the truth."

Alex made a face, considering how that would go down. She turned her focus to the last curve in the road before La Casa appeared.

Another full circle, she thought.

"There they are," she said. Excitement skittered along her nerves. As glad as she was to see her sister, she couldn't wait to see what Kathleen had left for her in the secret compartment.

Royce brought the car to a stop and the doors were instantly opened on each side.

"Alex," Fallon cried, pulling her sister out of the car.

"Royce," Jake said, grabbing him for a hug.

Before her sister could demand an explanation, Alex held up her hand. "If you'll hold off for just a moment, we have something to do first."

Fallon stepped back with her mouth open in complaint, but she eyed her sister closely and frowned. "What do you have to do first?" she asked.

"Come," Alex said. "Come see."

They entered the house and went straight for the library. Alex paused before the closed doors and couldn't help thinking again, another full circle. She grabbed Royce's hand and they opened the doors together.

The first thing she sought was the portrait.

Fallon!

"Look how beautiful she is," Alex said. They strode straight to the desk, with Jake and her sister silently following.

Alex pushed aside the tumble of papers on top and reached behind the drawer on the far right. The lever action was as smooth as the day Kathleen showed it to her. "There" she said.

A panel popped up and she pried it open; the hidden compartment was full. "Oh," Alex cried. "Look." She reached in and pulled out several packets.

They spread them all out. Each packet was wrapped in plain paper and tied with a string and identified by year, going from 1617 to 1630.

"What is all this?" Fallon asked her sister. She touched a packet and saw the name Fallon written over each year. "Who is Fallon, Alex?"

Alex clutched one of the packets to her heart and looked up at the portrait that had always made her so sad. "She is Fallon, sis. The girl in the portrait is Fallon, and she is my daughter." Alex eyed the many packets and relished the thought of opening them, year-by-year, learning about the woman her little girl had become.

"I went back in time," Alex whispered, "and bore a child. But I had to leave her there."

Fallon sucked in a breath, but nodded, tears filling her eyes. "You named her for me?"

"What? No questions?" Alex returned. "You believe me?"

"Well," Fallon stuttered. "I ... I can find no other explanation ... because ... your hair, your hair is a foot longer than it was two weeks ago." She grabbed Alex in a hug. "Honey, what did you do?"

Tears filled Alex's throat, for the four-hundred-year-old event was still fresh in her heart. "I had to go. She had to stay." A single shoulder shrugged in place of more words.

"Alex," Royce said. "Look at this." He pulled another item from the bottom of the compartment.

"Huuh," Alex inhaled. Even with her experience, what Royce held out stunned her.

"It's a photograph," Royce whispered.

He held a wide-angle photograph six inches long by four inches high pressed between two panes of glass.

"Oh my God, is it—?" Alex took the glass from Royce. "Look, it's Fallon," she cried.

The sepia-tinted photograph was of Fallon and a man surrounded by a dozen children. They stood on a dock that looked someplace tropical, for their sun-kissed hair was tossed in a breeze and their clothing showed tanned arms and legs and bare feet. She looked on the back. In Kathleen's cursive handwriting were the words, *Golden Days* and the date *1632*. Alex closed her eyes as the tears began to fall.

He pressed a letter into her hands. "Maybe you should read this first."

The single sheet was folded once with *Alex* on the front. She opened the page, careful not to let any of her tears fall on the paper. In Kathleen's writing, she read.

The dragon is called Finn and he arrived Fallon's seventeenth year in the meadow where you came. His arrival was as fantastic as was yours! He is a special man who completes her, just as Royce/Jamie did for you. The many children you see were each saved by Fallon and her dragon Finn ~ now they all live golden days where the sun always shines.

I return to Greyhaven long enough to leave directions for the disposition of the estate and to collect any who wish to follow us. I believe Connor and his wife will come. My priority is to make sure you get the packets from Fallon, and the magical picture. Then I return to the island and the children. My love to you always.

Kathleen

Alex searched the photo, examining the faces, especially Fallon's dragon, Finn. "He looks like a good man," she murmured. The realization she did the right thing, however painful at the time, gave her a satisfaction she couldn't express.

And so my daughter lived a life of golden days.

She turned the photo over again and examined it; the picture looked like an old Polaroid. "There," she pointed. In small writing printed at the bottom edge was *Paladin.*

"Paladin's Polaroid." She looked at Royce.

He shrugged and took her into his arms. "I guess we McNeills aren't the only time travelers."

Alex exhaled, reveling in the solid feel of her husband's arms around her, grateful to be home. She thought of her daughter and her adventure with the dragon Finn.

"Paladin's Polaroid," she wondered with curiosity.

"Hmm ... What a tale that must be."

• • •

Dana Lyons

Dana Lyons lives in the mountains of western North Carolina. She loves to work out and live healthy, ever ready to discover new mysteries in life, explore the limitless boundaries of the mind, and find the true power of the heart.

Says Lyons, "Love is not just an emotion in your heart—love is a measurable force that travels the universe like the light of a star. Learn the power of love, and you will create a world you can love."